the GRAVE *with* GREENER GRASS

Finder Series

DL HAVLIN

Relax. Read. Repeat.

The Grave with Greener Grass
(Finder Series, Book 1)
By DL Havlin
Published by TouchPoint Press
Brookland, AR 72417
www.touchpointpress.com

PAPERBACK ISBN: 978-1-946920-95-9

Editor: Kathleen McIntosh
Cover Design: ColbieMyles.com.
Cover Images: grave stone by jayfish (Adobe Stock)

Connect with the author online:
www.dlhavlin.com

ⓕ @ dennis.l.havlin ⓘ@ DLHavlinAuthor ⓦ @ dlhavlin

First Edition

Printed in the United States of America.

To the lady in my life—Jeanelle.

CHAPTER 1

I felt a light tapping on my shoulder.

"Excuse me. Could you spare a few minutes to speak with me when you're finished?"

There were always a few folks who waited to ask their questions until after I had concluded my presentations and prepared to leave. I smiled. "Sure."

The face returning my smile surprised me. She was more my age, late forties, and attractive enough that I should have noticed her when I was speaking. Most of my audience at the libraries, museums, and historical societies that host my programs are in the gray hair brigade, sixties, and. . . .

"How can I help you?" I asked.

"Actually, this might take more than a minute or two? It has to do with my family's history. I think you'd be interested." She extended her hand. "I'm Helen Sumner. The Sumners you were discussing in your talk are my ancestors."

I saw her holding one of my business cards in her hand. "I'm sorry, but my business doesn't include doing genealogical searches. I do know a person who can help you." I reached for my card case and information on Val Foxx.

"No, no, Mr. Harrell. I'm very familiar with what your company does."

I smiled, nodded, and said, "Okay, but Mr. Harrell is my pap."

"Do you prefer Slydell or Jerome?" she asked.

"Neither. Call me Sly or SJ. I answer to both."

"What I'd like to discuss is finding some family property. It's quite valuable. The problem is that it has been missing for over one hundred years, and the most important physical clue we have to locate it is gone. Time erased it."

The woman was dressed more like a junior business executive than the typical retirees or housewives attending one of my historical presentations. I remained silent. Experience had told me that only people serious about using my company's services pressed forward.

The smile disappeared from the lady's face. As if she read my mind, she said, "I am serious." Her tone reflected that.

I nodded. "Since it appears you've checked my business out, you must be aware that what I do is expensive."

"I'm totally aware of that. I can offer. . . ." The woman clamped her mouth shut as one of my hosts from the St. Cloud Historical Society, Hilda, approached us.

"Do you need any help, SJ?" Hilda asked.

"No, I'm fine."

"I see I'm creating a problem here," Helen said. "Could you meet me when you're done? There is a restaurant close. It's on US 192, the main drag. The name is The Catfish Place. They have great Florida Cracker food there."

The woman looked anxious; I wasn't sure why.

"My treat."

"That's not necessary. I know The Catfish Place . . . eat there whenever I get a chance. Meet you in thirty minutes, give or take a few. That okay?" I paused, "Helen, correct?"

She smiled, "Yes. See you in a half hour." Helen bowed her head to Hilda, mumbled, "Goodbye," and left the building as though her feet were resting on hot coals.

"Sorry, Hilda. I'll get outta your hair directly. Fifteen minutes tops," I said.

"I thought she might be a problem. She was here a full hour before you started." Hilda's eyes narrowed. "She drove all the way up here from Bartow to hear you speak. Or that's what she claimed. She knew all about your company. She wasn't wearing a wedding ring, but her finger is white, and there's an indent where one has been worn."

"You know, you're pretty damned good at sleuthing. I might call you up to help me out sometime." Hilda giggled good-naturedly. I added, "I will be careful, but don't worry about the old swamp panther. It isn't my first hunt out in the oaks and cypress."

CHAPTER 2

At two-thirty in the afternoon, only five cars were parked in the restaurant parking lot. Two belonged to the Municipality of St. Cloud. One was a beat-up, dirty pickup that only an out-of-work construction worker would drive. That left two possibilities: a white van and a Cuban gray BMW. As I entered The Catfish Place, I decided it had to be the BMW. The lady wasn't the van type.

As I walked across the floor to her table, I noted that she had selected one tucked in the restaurant's back corner. I took inventory of what possible knowledge I had about her. She looked and acted affluent. Her speech patterns and reactions indicated she was intelligent. She was a multigenerational Floridian, if she wasn't lying about the Sumner connection. The historic Sumner family were cattle barons, wealthy, and part of their empire had been based in Bartow. Bartow wasn't a destination for relocating Northerners.

What was she looking for? A missing deed to property? An antique? That was my best guess. I reached the table. . . . I was about to find out.

"I don't know how to say this without sounding like the stereotypical greedy relative." Helen Sumner's face was grim. "I want you to help my aunt recover a fortune that was promised to the Sumner women 125 years ago. Before you ask, I do stand to profit from its recovery." She hesitated. "But, then, so do you." The woman's features were almost defiant. "What do you know about the Sumner family, beyond what's in the local histories and lore?"

My caution flags went to half-mast. Anyone asking for your help, but was belligerent in their approach, warrants caution. I tapped my fingers on the table. Maybe I *would* let her buy my lunch.

I answered slowly, evaluating the impact of my words on the lady sitting in front of me. "I know about your family's importance in the development of the cattle business for two hundred years." No reaction. "I know that your family was heavily involved in Florida politics from the Civil War to the Second World War." Ditto. "I know that portions of your family had huge property holdings and were involved in some questionable land developments in the early 1900s." A small grimace. "Your family was exceedingly rich and seemingly squandered it." Bingo! Reaction!

"Not the Sumner family, the Sumner men!" Helen's eyes flashed, and her face flushed.

I immediately knew she considered me the enemy based on by my gender alone. My expression must have communicated my thought to her, and she quickly sought to address the hurdle she'd erected. "You're not a Sumner man." Her face softened, and she forced a smile.

"I'm happy I'm not." I didn't vocalize the rest of my thought, *in your presence.* "I'm afraid that exhausts my knowledge of your family, so if that doesn't fit what you were thinking . . . of what I could do for you—" I was looking for a way out; she saw that and cut me off.

"SJ, that's what you prefer?"

"I come to dinner when I hear it," I smiled and stiffened to get up from the table.

"Please, SJ, hear me out," she said.

My general impression . . . she was a bit of an actress. Despite my instinct's rebellion, I said, "I'll listen, but I can't promise I'll do anything."

There was a confident glint in her eyes when she answered, "I believe you will." She took a deep breath, collected and controlled her emotions, and made a noticeable effort to refrain from any show of hostility.

"You mentioned that my family lost a great deal of its wealth. They have *lost the use* of it for generations, that's true, but it is in a safe place. The problem is, we don't know where that place is." Helen paused; I nodded for her to go on.

"This goes back to the 1890s. The Sumner men were like the other men of their time, only more so. Wives did housework, kept the garden, pumped out children, kept their mouths shut, and did what their husbands told them out of and in bed. They were supposed to smile through it all, even when they received a figurative or literal kick. My Aunt Ellen's great-great-grandfather, Samuel Sumner, was a good man for those times but had seven worthless, spoiled sons. The Sumner tradition was to leave the oldest son the land and any other property holdings. Each of the other male children was to receive an equal share of the money accumulated by the father. The oldest was to administer the funds for all. The girls were given ten acres and a dowry of fifty dollars. Great-Great-Grandmother Sally was to be kept in her home and cared for by the eldest son. Her oldest son, Samuel Jr., was the worst of the bad lot."

Helen paused, so I prompted her, "Go on."

"Grandma Sally knew the shortcomings of her boys, and particularly those of Sam Jr., all too well. All seven of her sons gambled, drank, and chased every woman that showed any indication they might . . . bed them. The oldest kept five women in several small towns around the state where he traveled. Her daughters were the opposite. Smart. Responsible. Moral! It wasn't fair for them to receive practically nothing and the undeserving boys a fortune. That fortune was considerable."

I asked, "And . . . you know that how?"

"Sally confided the amount to her daughter, Mildred, long before the events I'll tell you about took place. It has been passed down."

"And that amount was?"

She smiled at me, confidence oozing from her, "Three boxes each containing gold coins that weighed more than sixty pounds each. Maybe more." Her oozing was justified. Her eyebrows lifted, and I responded by nodding for her to continue.

"Grandpa Samuel didn't believe in banks. He'd seen his friends lose everything in crashes in the years after the Civil War. His friend and mentor, Jacob Summerlin, didn't trust banks, bankers, or paper money. Sam Sr. emulated his idol, Jacob, and kept his funds at home, in gold. Sam must have had concerns about his oldest and his other boys, because he only shared the secret of where the money was hidden with Sally. When her husband died, something happened that infuriated her and convinced her to take drastic action."

Helen paused, waiting for me to say something. I obliged, "What caused her to do *something?*"

"Her slime-bag son hauled a bitch into the house the day after his father was buried. She was a real porcupine woman." She paused to see if I understood. I nodded. Helen Sumner was a real Cracker. She continued, "That was too much for her to stomach. Sally had a shouting match with her son, telling him she wanted his girlfriend gone . . . immediately. Sam Jr.'s reaction? He told his mother that if she didn't like it, get out. That's when she did whatever she did. No one knows for sure what that was. We know that Sam Jr. disappeared that night and was never seen again. We know that the treasure disappeared. Sally claimed that Sam Jr. took it and ran off with the girlfriend that night. No one believed that then. No one believes that now. No one could or can prove otherwise."

I smiled and asked, "I assume you want me to find three boxes of gold coins, not two skeletons hid somewhere . . . unless they happen to be resting together?"

"That's it exactly."

"That's not even a starting point, Mrs. Sumner." It was intriguing but a definite mission impossible.

"Two things, Mr. Harrell. First, yes, I'm a Sumner by marriage. That doesn't make my Sumner allegiance any less intense than if Sally's blood ran through my veins. My husband is a nephew of the *person* I hope you'll help. Second, women haven't received fair treatment in Sumner family affairs. When Grandmother Sally died some years after the coins and her son disappeared, she elected to pass on a clue to where the Sumner women might reclaim the money. I want to fulfill her wishes. She wrote her letter on her deathbed, and she handed it to her oldest daughter, Mildred, a few hours before she died. She did so with the instruction that the letter wasn't to be opened until John, her last surviving son, was hanged. Her boys didn't do well."

I started to talk, but Helen's raised eyebrows silenced me. "In that letter were clues to where the treasure is hidden. Aunt Ellen is the fourth person that the letter has been passed down to. Each has tried and failed to find the gold. My reason for being here is to ask you to help find the treasure for my aunt with the help of the clues in that letter. In return, she is willing to give you twenty-five percent of what you find."

I didn't have to do mental calculations. Three boxes, times sixty pounds, times sixteen ounces, times $1700 per ounce . . . that equaled a shit-pot full of money. Was it worth taking it to the next level? What if there wasn't gold at the rainbow's end? I'd discuss that with her after I made a decision on viability. If the treasure existed, I didn't want to discourage her.

I maintained hard eye contact with her as I said, "Okay, it is worth pursuing, but there are some things that need doing before I, we, get started on this. First, I have to meet your aunt. . . . Ellen, wasn't it?"

"Yes. That might be a problem." Her eye contact wilted a tad, so I pressed.

"That's a non-starter. If I don't meet her, I'm out."

Helen stiffened, "I'll arrange it."

"Okay. I need her last name." I wanted to see if she hesitated and possibly made something up.

"O'Neal." Her name was out of Helen's mouth before I'd finished my sentence.

I nodded, "Fine. It might take a few months for me to get on it." I saw discomfort in her eyes. "If the treasure is still wherever, it's been there 125 years. It isn't going anywhere in a couple months."

"That isn't my concern. There is a timing element in this . . . in the clue. My aunt is getting old. If we miss the date, we'll miss a year." She leaned forward. Helen had the look of a person hatching an idea as we spoke. "When could you start?"

The whole idea of a timing element intrigued and challenged me. "When do I have to be available?"

"June 1. You have to be at a place and be ready to interpret the clue at that time."

It was the middle of March. My other projects had lost a lot of importance in the last thirty minutes. "I can do that. Here is the rest of what *we* need to do. You have my card; if you still want to pursue this, contact my assistant, Clareen Simmons. She'll set up a date for us all to meet. It's important that we formalize what we've discussed for both of our protection. Bring a lawyer if you like. I'll have mine there. Bring the clue with you."

"Good. I don't think Ellen would part with it . . . early." Helen seemed relieved.

"Believe me, if you have a lawyer, he isn't going to want me anywhere near that letter until everything we discussed is documented."

"Do you need to talk to Ellen or see her picture prior to the meeting? So you know she's interested?"

The importance of the question escaped me, but I answered anyway, "No, the fact she shows or doesn't at the meeting we set is all I need."

"Good."

We both were satisfied.

CHAPTER 3

O ne of the advantages of living far away from the center of things is that it provides you with precious solitude as you drive the added distance required to get home. And, in that solitude, time to think. Turn off the cell phone, and you transport yourself back in time. It is the essence of who I am, yesterday's man.

The forty-minute drive from St. Cloud to my ranch outside of Kenansville gave me an opportunity to reflect on the flurry of events that had just occurred. Taking Florida 523 meant fewer traffic distractions. I was in rural Florida, more likely to have a collision with a wayward deer or a feral pig than an SUV or a semi. The pastures and prairies passed by with no notice from me. My mind focused on the unexpected meeting with the descendant of a branch of one of the state's true pioneer families. The Sumners. The family was only a notch behind the Summerlins when it came to importance in shaping Florida's early history. It was an opportunity to pull a curtain aside and look into one of the many hidden family histories residing within, I hoped.

If the woman's heritage wasn't a fabrication, getting to delve into her ancestry and the happenings surrounding them would be fascinating. That alone was a delicious tidbit that was too tempting to resist. The thought of recovering the fortune, a huge fortune, and getting my percentage . . . that was more than tempting.

Even if the three boxes turned to one, I did a quick calculation: Sixty times sixteen times $1700 . . . that was over $1,630,000. My share would work out to $408,000. That wasn't bad for something that looked to have no significant danger attached and should not take long to resolve. If she was telling the truth and there were three boxes, great.

With the decision made, I thought about what I could do in advance of the meeting I'm sure the Sumner woman would set up. The obvious things were to authenticate those who were to be my "business partners." I wanted at least basic information on both. Helen Sumner would be easy. I knew what she looked like, her relative age, and I took the opportunity to write her license plate down as I exited The Catfish Place. If she lived in Bartow, we had a great place to start. Ellen O'Neal? There were probably a hundred living in Florida, and there was no guarantee she lived in the state. That was a lot of records to search. I knew just the team for the task.

Russ and Val Foxx are fascinating folks. They travel the country in an RV, true vagabonds who live for the spirit of adventure. When I asked how they could afford to travel continually, Russ grinned and said, "We're computer security consultants . . . and sometimes lack-of-security experts."

They are true masters of the monitor, unexcelled at what they did and do. Valerie has a master's degree in Administrative Services. Her ability to find the most deeply submerged record or the most obscure fact—impressive! Russ is a computer genius. A master of special effects and illusion, he can make computers do unbelievable things. And though it's not spoken of. . . . Russ Foxx is a hacker's hacker!

We became friends. Since then, we have done a few favors for each other, and I procure their services occasionally. I also provide them a concrete pad fitted with a utility pole, located on my ranch, for their use whenever. The last two winters, they've been my guests. It has been a mutually beneficial relationship.

I was reasonably certain I could obtain enough information on the two ladies who were still alive to help me, but I also needed to probe and expand my knowledge of the Sumners. Sumner had been a magic name for a century. I had some knowledge of them because of their importance in Florida's history, so I had a starting place. But the general knowledge had to be supplemented by learning who these family members really were, where they lived, what they owned, what their politics were . . . everything right down to who they were screwing, *if* I could find out.

There were sources that would help on the Net, but a lot of the info that would help would come from visiting where they'd lived, scrounging newspaper morgues, and getting names of "old-timers" from historical societies for oral history or gossip, take your choice. I knew where the family had most of their 1800 holdings. It meant trips to Hernando, Arcadia, Sebring, Lake Wales, Webster, LaBelle, Ortona, and Bartow. I had contacts in four of those cities, and those people could furnish me connections in the towns I lacked. It would keep me busy for a week, but I'd learn a lot in that time.

As I crossed a canal that flowed into Lake Cypress, a black HUMV passed me on a double yellow line. Time to stop thinking about the case and start concentrating on my driving.

The HUMV slowed rapidly, almost coming to a stop in front of me. I couldn't see inside. The rear window had something placed over it to keep anyone from seeing its occupants. My speedometer had dropped to 15 mph. The vehicle made no effort to pull off the highway. Were the occupants having a problem or harassing me?

I decided to pass the HUMV. When I swung into the left lane, the vehicle immediately stayed in front of me. When I returned to the right side of the road, the HUMV cut me off. While the black SUV was still returning to my front, I gunned my engine and tried passing again. This time the HUMV accelerated, racing ahead at high speed. The car quickly disappeared as I slowed to 50 mph. "It takes all kinds," I muttered. I chalked it up to some sort of road rage and dismissed the incident. Freak incidents happen, and that's what I hoped.

As I was figuring the most efficient way to visit the towns where I'd have to seine for information on the Sumners, a motion in my rearview mirror caught my attention. The same black HUMV that had breezed past me at the bridge had entered the road behind me. It had been in a farm lane screened from view by brush on either side, one that could have been picked to conceal its presence.

Having worked in jobs where ignoring unlikely coincidences could cost you your life, I immediately tried to determine if I was being followed. I slowed down. So did the HUMV. I sped up. So did the HUMV. It was obvious he was trying to maintain a constant space between us. I watched the vehicle closely. The driver was matching my speed perfectly. I never slowed down or speeded up so much that it was obvious I was concerned with my tail. The HUMV stayed a thousand feet behind me.

If someone was following me, why? The only plausible reason was to find out where I lived. When I was a few miles from the road leading to my ranch, I decided to cut off my tail. A vast wildlife preserve bordered both sides of the road. I made a high-speed turn onto an access road entering the Three Lakes Wildlife Area. I drove a short distance up the road, parked, removed a twelve-gauge shotgun from the rack behind my head, and waited.

Watching in my rearview mirror, I saw the black vehicle ease into the rectangular glass. Its driver came to a full stop on the highway then slowly pulled away. After waiting for fifteen minutes, I traveled the remaining distance to my home. This time, I was exceedingly aware of vehicles both in front and behind. No black HUMV appeared. I didn't relax until I made a right turn onto Lake Marian Road and reached the familiar gate to my ranch.

CHAPTER 4

"I thought you might like eggs Benedict this morning," Cindy Stallings knew how to start my day off right. She's the do-it-all domestic at my ranch. You can describe Cindy with one word: pleasant. She's pleasant to talk to, pleasant to work with, pleasant to look at; she's just plain pleasant. However, like the lionfish, there are some poisonous spines under an attractive appearance and sedate, friendly behavior. Like a black belt.

"That sounds good." I looked away from the emails on my laptop screen. Her uniform of the day, every day, is white Bermuda's and a white tee . . . no graffiti. No need for attention getters on her clothes, the curves under them are more than enough. Her presence in my household caused local tongues to wag when I first hired the twenty-nine-year-old. But there is absolutely nothing romantic between the lady and me. Something in her demeanor is close to a cold shower. She looks like a movie star and acts like a nun.

"They'll be done in five minutes." She leaned over my desk and filled my half-empty coffee cup. "I relayed the message to the Foxxes that you had something to talk to them about. They asked if nine o'clock would be okay."

I nodded. "I'm going over to the office to talk to Clareen about the lady I met at the St. Cloud Historical Society. She's supposed to call to set up a meeting."

Cindy nodded in a very pronounced manner. "Clareen already called asking about you. The Foxxes will be here in an hour."

As she left, I looked out the windows surrounding half of the house. A great blue heron speared a fish from the pond outside as I watched. Just another day in what I considered paradise. It justified having my office an hour plus away.

Russ and Val Foxx studied the papers I'd handed them seconds ago. Those papers had questions I wanted answered. The other information they contained was all I knew about Helen Sumner and Ellen O'Neal.

I asked, "What do you think?"

Russ smiled, "As long as we have a starting point, it should be a piece of cake." He shook one of the notes I'd given them. "Two days, three at most."

I smiled and looked at Valerie. She was the one that would do most of the work on this project. She hadn't said a thing, and her face remained in its usual neutral mask. "What's your opinion, Val?" I asked.

"It's impossible to tell until I peek at the first threads and see what unravels. If they've lived in Florida all their lives, haven't been married several times, I can do it in a day. If they've lived out of state, had name changes, done time . . . a week." She waved the sheet of paper at me. "This is all you want?"

"For right now," I answered.

She shrugged her shoulders, "He's right." Val nodded at her husband. "Two days, probably. A week at most."

Russ grinned, "Are these two ladies some of the missing members of the Brinks heist? They sound like a desperate duo."

"Would you believe me if I told you that they found the real treasure map mentioned in Robert Louis Stevenson's *Treasure Island*?" I tried to keep a serious face.

Val snorted, and Russ doubled up with laughter.

After a few seconds, Val asked, "If you can tell me why you want this information, I can watch for something that might connect as I go through my searches."

"Sure. I'm helping them find valuables that were lost 125 years ago," I replied.

Russ snickered. "Talk about your wild goose chase. I hope you're getting paid upfront."

Valerie simply nodded.

CHAPTER 5

There are few absolutes in life. Two of them are Kenansville institutions. One is The Barking Dog Bar, and the other is Herman Wilson's General Store and Garage. Everyone within twenty miles knows where you get "*watered*" and where you get "*gassed*." Ten-thirty in the morning is too early for me to bend an elbow, so I passed the Barking Dog's parking lot and pulled under the canopy covering the gas pumps in front of Wilson's.

Henrietta Wilson's grinning face appeared in the driver's window of my CJ5. The weather was good, so I was driving my Jeep, with the top off, always my first driving choice. "Fill 'er up, Mr. Harrell?" her cheery voice inquired. Service was alive and well at Wilson's and in Kenansville.

"Yep. . . . Henrietta, just call me Sly." I knew what would come next.

"Yes, sir, Mr. Harrell." Herman Wilson would tell you very quickly that he raised his "rug rats right." All fifteen of them. The girl who was pumping gas, washing my windshield, and would soon be checking my oil was right out of the middle of Herman's brood. Wilson's kids all had their father's strawberry blonde hair (Herman's was gone), his ruddy complexion, and a physical build perfect for setting fence posts and tossing bales of hay.

"That'll be $29.48, Mr. Harrell." Her smile was genuine, and I asked the fifteen-year-old a question as I placed my credit card in her oily hand, "Aren't you supposed to be in school?"

"This is my day to skip. There are seven of us working here. We take turns missing a day. Old Mr. Parsons, he's my principal, he says, as long as we maintain a high average, he doesn't care. We're about the only ones in school that add a column of figures without a calculator or can make change." A car pulled up at the pump behind me. "Be right back," ended our conversation.

Within a couple of minutes, Henrietta ran up to my Jeep. "Sorry, it took so long. The Internet is loaded up like an Army mule." She returned my card after she wiped it off on her shirt. "Mr. Harrell, my Pa, wants to have a word. He's in the garage. If you wouldn't mind pullin' up there. . . ."

I said, "Sure," and started up my Jeep.

"Sly, you know I don't get meddling into other folks affairs, but I thought you should know about this, leastways." Herman Wilson stretched his 6'4" frame to its full extension.

He folded his arms and leaned against one of his garage door openings. "Yesterday afternoon, two men come in here asking questions about you and such. Irene was pumpin' gas, didn't much care for their look, so she turned them over to me. They was real big guys. First thing they asked was where you lived. You know me. I asked why they needed to know. They said they was friends of yours." Herman lifted one barely visible eyebrow. "You got any friends that drive a black HUMV?"

Herman had my complete attention. "No friends," I said.

"Didn't reckon that. These men didn't look to be your kind. I told them I knew you. I said I wasn't sure where you lived. One of them flashed a badge real quick like and said he knew you from when you worked for his agency. I asked to see the badge, and he wouldn't hand it to me. He just held it up. The man doing the talking had one of them heavy fake southern accents. Anyway, about that time, I leaned over to look at the badge. Couldn't see dick about it, but I sure got a gander at what they had piled on the back seat. They had one of those AK-47s and some handguns. They sure as shit weren't turkey hunters, know what I'm saying?"

I nodded.

"One of them didn't talk much, but I think he was the boss. He said they knew you lived somewhere toward the lake." Herman grinned. "I said I wasn't sure, but I'd give them a guess. I sent them down Peavine Creek Road. Told them to look for two pig skulls mounted on a fence post six miles down. You know that cut off road that runs back to the old, flooded peat mine?"

I smiled and said, "You didn't! You sent them back there? That road looks like it just runs into a flooded field instead of a twenty-foot-deep pit."

Herman shrugged his shoulders. "If they ain't smart enough to not drive into water they don't know, I hope that HUMV has some submarine blood in it." Herman looked happy. "If them folk show around here again, all the boys are lookin' for them. We'll get you word."

"I can tell you three things. They aren't friends. They aren't anybody I've worked with. They aren't the law. As for who they are, you'll be the first I tell when I find out."

When I pulled out of Herman's place, I made a detour before heading to the office. I returned to the ranch. My concealed carry permit and my Springfield Armory 9mm Hellcat accompanied me to Wabasso. It would be my constant companion until the unexplained became explained. Yes, I had a round in the chamber.

CHAPTER 6

Wabasso. Why did I decide to locate my office there? The name has a certain ring. There's plenty of the romantic in me to self-justify that choice. I have a friend that lives in a place called Bokeelia. Names like those make you wonder about them.

But there were practical reasons I decided on the location on Old Dixie Highway. It is just an hour from my ranch. There's minimal traffic for most of the way. As pricing goes on the east coast of Florida, it's a reasonable area. Most importantly, I found the perfect building.

The business of finding things—that's basically what I do—requires some specialized equipment, most of it very expensive or dangerous or both. My lawyer, Riaffort Owens Richards, lives in Vero Beach, a few miles south, and knew of the building. It had been a small local bank . . . with a vault.

Clareen Simmons parked her car in the lot. The lot was huge, and the most vehicles I can remember being there for my business was six. Its primary use now was an overnight stop for semi-drivers and a free one-hour motel for lovers. Clareen complained about both.

The solutions available were to tear up most of the lot and landscape it or put a chain-link fence around the grounds. I'd have preferred the landscape solution, but the fencing was more economical, and it offered another layer of protection for Clareen. I was going to sign the contract with the fencing company that day.

I reached the front door. The door is always locked, so I pushed the buzzer button, one short buzz, followed by two longs and ended by three shorts. It was my identification code. Clareen let me in. I entered the old lobby and saw her sitting at the desk.

When she looked up, she said, "You're late. You said you'd be here forty minutes ago."

"I forgot something and had to go back to the ranch to pick it up."

Some people have an expression frozen on their faces that informs you that you've done something wrong . . . even when you haven't. The expression was there.

"Did you bring a peace offering?"

I shrugged my shoulders.

"No donuts?"

"Sorry."

"Oh, you have a diamond necklace in your pocket. Just for little old me?"

"Little old" did not describe Clareen. If she chose to stand, her five-inch heels would have elevated her head seven inches over my 5'11." Now, at twenty-seven, she could have been a model. Her afro added another six inches to the towering effect.

"The plane's flight from Amsterdam was canceled."

Her dark brown eyes smiled even if her features didn't. "You're going to tell me you're giving me another raise."

"Clareen, you've got to stop puffing on weed." I smiled. She hated drugs of any variety because of the havoc they'd played on her family.

"You are stubborn even for a white man," she concluded.

"I have one good bit of news for you. Today, I'll sign the contract for fencing the parking lot and grounds." The smile and some expression of thanks didn't come.

"That isn't news. There have been contractors measuring everything they could measure around here for three weeks. One even tried to measure my ass, but we'll discuss that another time. You don't have to sign any contract. Mr. Wiess from Indian County Fencing, Barriers, and Walls dropped the contract here two days ago. Told me all about it. I forged your name, and he came back and picked it up yesterday. They will start putting it up Monday." She had a half-smile as she added, "I hope I didn't do anything wrong."

"You know, Clareen, you can take the fun out of the circus," I said and shook my head.

"Somebody beat me to it. There isn't any more circus," she said.

There was no use trying to get the last word. The woman excelled in that. I changed the subject. "Cindy told you about the woman from my talk yesterday?"

"Yes, but I haven't heard from her." Clareen looked down at her desk. "I have eleven letters you need to sign. The mail's on your desk. Most of it is stuff I know you'd turn down. Here is one—"

I interrupted her. "Have you had any strange visitors in the last two days?"

"Strange? No. A couple of contractors following up their bids on the fence, a security system salesman, and a Jehovah's Witness. That's all." She thrust the letters at me. "Look at these and sign them . . . please."

As I took the letters, I asked, "What about strange calls?"

"We get too many of those to count. Probably ten hang-ups a day. There are a few calls each from banks where we don't have accounts, credit companies that want to reduce our interest rate, and fake IRS people telling us that we owe money. Ditto state and fake local agencies, and ditto Apple and Microsoft frauds that have some scam going."

"Do any of the calls stand out?" I asked.

"In the last couple days? No. Last week, or maybe longer, I remember one call that was different. This lady called and asked *not* to talk to you. Said her name was Sue Smith. When I asked why she didn't want to talk to you, there was a pause, and I heard someone else, a man, talking in the background. Then her answer was that she didn't want to waste your time if you couldn't help her. She said she wanted to find out what kind of items you would recover. That's normal. But she asked something different, something no one has asked me before: was it true you had ways to get access to archaeological sites and could get exhumation permits? I told her you had in some circumstances in the past. She asked if you were the professor that did historical seminars all over the state. I told her you weren't a professor, but you did conduct seminars. Then she asked, I remember this because of the call we're expecting, if you were scheduled to do a talk in St. Cloud in a week or so. I said, 'Yes.' She hung up. No goodbye. She just hung up."

"Sounds like our lady," I said. "Did you get a phone number?"

"I remember it was an 863 area code."

"That's interesting, it would—"

The office phone rang.

CHAPTER 7

"The Finder, Inc., this is Clareen Simmons."

There was no response. She repeated, "The Finder, may I help you?" Clareen paused again. The speaker remained silent. "Hello . . . goodbye." She hung up.

"Garbage?" I asked.

"Yes, I guess. It wasn't an 863 area code, and that's what it would be if the call came from Bartow. At least, if it's a landline or a cell issued there." She shrugged her shoulders. "It's hard to tell anymore."

"What area code was it?" I asked.

"813."

"That's the Tampa area." I shook my head. "Probably just a random call."

The phone rang again, and Clareen answered, "The Finder, Inc., this is Clareen Simmons."

There was an immediate response. "I'd like to talk to Mr. Harrell." I recognized the voice as Helen Sumner's.

"I'll take it in my office," I told Clareen.

I pushed the speaker button on my office phone. "Hello, SJ Harrell."

There was a brief pause, and then the voice replied, "Hi, I'm Helen Sumner. We spoke in St. Cloud, remember?"

"Sure. May I have your phone number before I forget to ask for it?"

"My phone is 863-555-1667."

"Mrs. Sumner, we talked about setting up a meeting. Are you ready to do that? If so, when would you be available, and would you like to meet here or at a place you choose?"

There was a pause, longer this time. "I'd prefer to meet in your office. Can we set it for this coming Tuesday?"

"Let me check my schedule." I looked over my calendar as I wrote. I insisted, "Ellen O'Neal must come, and your lawyers should too. What time would you like to be here?"

"Where is your office?"

"It's located in Wabasso; that's near Vero Beach. Would you like me to send you a map? If you'd like, I can email it to you. Or I could send it by mail if you give me your address."

The answer was sharp and instantaneous, "No! I can find it. I'll probably come over the night before. What street is it located on?"

"Old Dixie Highway. It's near the beach road; that's Florida 510."

"Fine."

"Mrs. Sumner, I'd like your lawyer's name so my lawyer can get together with him and take care of any preliminaries necessary."

The pause was long. Finally, the woman spoke, "I was hoping we could avoid that. At least, at this first meeting."

"I want you to understand my lawyer will be at the meeting. If you don't wish to bring yours, that's up to you. *Be sure that Ellen O'Neal will be present at the meeting.* That is a condition."

The disgust was evident in her voice when she answered, "She'll be there if you insist. It's a long trip for an old lady. I was hoping I could bring the note. Ellen won't be able to provide any information past the letter and what she's told me."

"I'm afraid I insist without any exception."

"Okay, Mrs. O'Neal and I will be there Tuesday. How is 10:30 AM?"

"Fine," I said.

Helen Sumner hung up without the courtesy of "Goodbye."

Clareen stood in the door and asked, "Why in the world doesn't she want a lawyer to protect her interests?"

"She's either cheap, or there's a hell of a lot more to this than I was led to believe." My caution flags went from half to three-quarter mast.

CHAPTER 8

I watched him move slowly through the reeds and along the grass line. His dawn patrol was as reliable as Big Ben in London. The big bull gator perused the shoreline by my dock every morning as the sun rose, exposing a minimum of the reptile's top. He was watching for any unwary animal that might happen in his path. A duck, turtle, gar, raccoon, it didn't matter—he's looking for breakfast. His passionless patrol was as impartial and deadly as some humans I knew. They looked for a victim and could care less about anything except their financial digestion.

I tossed the black Johnson Spoon with a yellow "hula skirt" riding on the weedless hook. It was my favorite bass bait. Standing on my dock, fishing rod in hand, and trying to induce a bass to strike was almost as sacrosanct as the "bull gator patrol." The spoon skittered across weeds as it made its way back to the dock. Water exploded, and a large bass attacked the bait as it dropped off a weed into the water.

I fought with the five-pounder until he conceded defeat twenty-feet from the dock. Looking toward the open water of Lake Marian, I saw what I expected. My gator friend had his curiosity stirred. He was slowly swimming toward the fish thrashing on the surface. He stopped when he saw me. We had an unsigned contract to respect each other. It reminded me of the relationship many of my clients and I shared.

I lifted the bass from the water, removed the hook, and tossed him in the opposite direction from where the gator lay motionless in the water. The huge reptile, over eleven feet long, looked into my eyes with his baleful ones. Slowly, he turned and swam away, his long tail swishing a rhythmic motion as he continued his breakfast quest.

My cell phone's buzzer vibrated in my pocket before I could make another cast. I mumbled, "Who in hell is calling me at 5:45 in the morning?" My pants fought me, unwilling to part with its contents without a struggle. When I finally extracted the phone . . . mystery solved. Russ Foxx's name and number lit the white screen. Russ kept very irregular hours, and the clock face meant little to him.

His cheery voice greeted me, "Good morning!"

"Good morning, back to you," I responded.

"I wanted to catch you before you went someplace. Val and I will be ready to talk about the information you wanted on those two women by, say, 2:00 PM. Are you interested in getting together then?"

"Yes." I started walking the dock toward the shore.

"You want to meet at the house?" He asked.

"Yes. You interested in eating some good, fresh shrimp? I stopped by the docks over at Vero yesterday. I'll have Cindy boil them for lunch if you are."

"Count us in! I'll get Val to cook up some cheese grits. See you around two."

I was close to the sand at the pierhead when I stopped to secure the artificial bait to one of the rod's eyes. Before I took the two steps that would put my feet on dry land, my gut insisted that I look at the sand where I would step. An electric current pulsed through me. The coiled body of a large water moccasin lay waiting. Its head faced me, its white mouth open, ready to attack any part of me that came in range of its S-configured coils. The snake was fat and over four feet long. I muttered, "Oh, shit!" I waved my arm at it and yelled, "Get!"

The snake's head reacted to the movement of my arm, but it held its striking position. The moccasin showed no inclination to give up its defensive position in the recess created by the pier's end and the ground a foot below. I berated myself. My .410 shotgun was perched in the Jeep. Carrying a weapon just for such occasions isn't worth much if you don't keep it with you.

The tip of my spinning rod was all I had to convince old scaly to move. I poked at the triangular head and white mouth. The moccasin struck twice in rapid succession. It didn't budge. Poking the snake in the middle got immediate movement . . . and a vicious strike. The clicking noise I heard was the reptile's fangs hitting the graphite rod. The snake grudgingly slithered into the grass and then into the lake.

My adrenalin settled back. The rod tip vibrated as my hands shook. Living in Florida most of my life didn't make me immune from the "sight and fright" a poisonous snake elicited when they weren't expected.

After a few composure-gaining seconds, a last peek to be sure the snake was gone, and a deep breath, I walked to the Jeep. I began thinking. I'm not superstitious, but I wondered if that could have been an omen. Maybe the fates were advising me: be cautious before you step into something unknown.

CHAPTER 9

Russ rubbed his stomach and stared at the bowls of empty shrimp shells. "I sincerely hope my gut doesn't explode."

All the shrimp were eaten. The giant bowl of cheese grits Valerie made, gone. I watched Cindy approach the table carrying a tray of desserts. A collective groan greeted the slices of key lime pie and squares of flan.

"After the meeting?" Cindy asked.

"Yes, let's try that," Russ said enthusiastically. "I'll find a home for some of your key lime pie by then."

Val, always prepared for business, asked, "SJ, are you ready to discuss those women?"

"Sure."

Russ and Val removed their laptops from their cases with the speed and sure hands of a gunfighter in an old Western. The smile that crept on my lips wouldn't go away. I turned and got up from the dining table to get some writing materials and mask my emotions' display. "Where you headed?" Russ inquired.

"To get something to take notes with," I answered.

Russ held up a thumb drive. "You don't need to unless. . . ." He smiled, bounced his head from side to side, and said, "You want to add things."

I found a legal pad and a pen. When I returned to the table, Val drummed her fingers on the wood. It was her "let's get the show on the road" message. I nodded. She started.

"I ended up doing most of the research on this." She looked up from her computer screen with the placid mask she wore twenty-four seven. "The one that we thought would be harder was easy. The one that should have been easy was harder than hell." She punched a few keys on her computer. "I'll do Ellen O'Neal first. She was the easy one." Valerie's eyes remained focused on the screen. "She is eighty-four. Ellen was born Ellen Barnes. She currently lives in Bartow, Florida. She has owned the residence and land for fifty-six years. As far as I can tell, she lives there now, and she's never lived outside the state. Her husband, Stanley O'Neal, died nine years ago." She looked at me for questions. I nodded, and she continued.

"You asked for bloodline. Ellen was born in 1935 to Agnes Mizell and Fredrick Barnes. Yes, she was the oldest daughter. Agnes was the oldest daughter born to Mary Futch and James Treadwell. Mary Futch was the oldest daughter of Mildred Sumner and Moses Barnes. Her birth was in 1892. And Mildred traces back to Sam Sumner and his wife, whose maiden name was Sally Crisp. Ellen O'Neal qualifies as the oldest in the female bloodline. She and her husband were farm and cattle people their whole life. Everything on her fits."

Val stopped to make sure I was paying attention. "You need to know these things: Ellen O'Neal has never held a driver's license or a state identification card. The last time I could find that she voted was before she moved to her current address. As far as I can tell, there are no public pictures of the woman in the last forty years. And these last two items might have some importance." She paused.

"I take it you feel it could have an effect on what I'm going to try to do," I said.

She nodded and continued. "She had a competency hearing three years ago. Mentally, she turned out okay. But the examiners judged she needed assisted living since she had no living relatives they could find. She had three boys, and all were killed in an airplane crash . . . no other kids. She was put into mandated care but refused to sign her house over to the state. Litigation was pending when a long-lost relative shows up. The long-lost relative is Helen Sumner. She gets legal guardianship of the old lady and moves them both back into Ellen's home. At least, that's what court records say."

Russ waved his hand, "This was a real smash-mouth event. The hearing was raucous, and one of the assisted living home nurses took a swing at a man noted as Mark Sumner. That pulled the rug from under the state. It's largely what convinced the referee to turn over Ellen to her grandniece."

Val nodded. "There's more odds and ends in the report on the flash drive. Let's move on to Helen Sumner, okay?"

"Sure," I said. I was more certain than ever I had to visit with Ellen O'Neal before making a final commitment.

"The Sumner woman's history is a jigsaw puzzle. Am I sure I've given you all accurate info? No. Is it the best I can do, with what I have to work with now? Yes." Valerie looked at her laptop screen and threw her hands in the air, a rare show of frustration from her. "As far as I know, the woman moved to Florida three years ago. Her previous residence was Rome, Georgia, for a year. She moved to Rome from Chattanooga. She lived there three months, before that Pittsburgh, a few months . . . Memphis, Tennessee; Corbin, Kentucky; Ocala, Florida; Columbus, Ohio; Valdosta, Georgia—it went on and on. Until . . . until there is a dead spot in her history. There's a four-year break before I could pick up her trail again. That was in Beaufort, South Carolina. She married a Marine named Mark Sumner. Paris Island is right there. They were there eight years before they both disappeared. Prior to that, Helen Sumner lived in Okeechobee City. She was born there as Helen Quarreles. I have a picture of her as an elementary school girl and her high school yearbook picture. If you look at them and then look at her driver's license photo, it's hard telling, but I guess they probably are the same woman. As near as I can tell, she's probably legit, just flakey. And there isn't any arrest record for either of the women."

"How did you get the license photo?" I asked.

Russ grinned and raised his hand.

"There is the fact that the description of her eye color varies from her early licenses to her late ones. It's slight, but . . . the first color is described as light blue, later as light gray. She has had jobs that vary all over the place. Records clerk a couple times, waitress several times, legal assistant, dental hygienist, a couple times as a secretary, disk jockey, and a nurse several times. Sometimes she lived with her husband, sometimes not. His jobs showed up in a couple of places. He appears to have been a metal worker, a mechanic, a security guard, and a sales manager for a chemical distributor. Early on, he was a model citizen. Something must have happened. He was arrested for assault twice, but the charges were dropped both times. I found a note where he got fired for bad relations on one of his jobs. I did check her husband's birth bloodline, and that checks out. He is a direct descendent of Samuel Sumner. He was from Okeechobee, too, so they probably knew each other there. I didn't go past that with him."

"What do you think?" Russ asked.

I shrugged my shoulders.

"Are you going any further with it?" Val asked.

"Yes, but I'm going to treat it as carefully as if I'm trying to pick up a rattlesnake."

CHAPTER 10

They were on time. I watched the Cuban gray BMW pull into the parking lot. The driver stopped as close to the front door as they could. There was a long delay before the driver's side door opened. I recognized the outline of Helen Sumner as she walked to the trunk and opened it. Helen removed a wheelchair and rolled it to the passenger's door. She helped a gray-haired lady from the car. Helen bent over the woman and spoke to her for a full minute. The lady continually nodded her head.

"Your client is being given explicit instructions." My lawyer, Riaffort Owens Richards, watched with keen interest.

Clareen said, "I'm going to turn on the recorders." She disappeared into the back of the building.

Riaffort said, "Do you see that? The woman moved into the wheelchair with hardly any assistance. I doubt she needs it. The woman helping her doesn't have a clue how to help a disabled person out of a car and into a wheelie."

"Thanks, I hadn't noticed that." I watched Helen Sumner as she pushed the chair up the walk to the front door. The facial expressions on the ladies were an interesting contrast. Helen Sumner's face was a storm cloud of suspicion and apprehension. The woman I presumed to be Ellen O'Neal was a portrait of happy expectancy.

Clareen's voice came from the front office just as the two ladies disappeared from my view through the conference room window. "I'll let them in and bring them to you."

"Riaffort, we'll soon find out what we're working with." I sat at the conference table as Riaffort pulled out a chair to do the same.

"It appears she didn't engage a lawyer, as you predicted." He lowered his body into the chair next to me slowly. "You understand, I have to counsel the ladies that they should have a lawyer present to protect their interests."

"Sure."

The voices of Clareen, Helen Sumner, and Ellen O'Neal silenced ours. Clareen ushered them through the conference room door. Riaffort and I stood to receive them.

"Mrs. Sumner and Mrs. O'Neal are here to see you, gentlemen," Clareen announced from the door. She towered over Helen, who looked shocked when she saw Riaffort standing next to me. Her surprise was followed by a look of relief. She made the mistake that most of my lawyer's opponents duplicated. They discounted his legal capabilities because he was black. It always became a horrible mistake they couldn't undo. The sixty-two-year-old looked all the blacker because of his white hair, mustache, and neatly trimmed beard. I gloated inwardly, knowing I had one of the finest legal minds in Florida representing me.

I opened the conversation, saying, "Helen, ma'am, good to see you both. Let me introduce you to Riaffort Richards. He's my lawyer."

Helen half-smiled and nodded. The other lady smiled broadly and said, "It is a pleasure to meet you." Her voice was friendly. The difference in social styles between the two ladies was very clear.

Helen said, "Ellen O'Neal is my friend and relative. She is the one who seeks your help, Mr. Harrell. Ellen, this is Mr. Slydell Harrell, the man I told you about."

"Hi fellows," the old lady said. "I'm a thinking we'll get along real good." Helen scowled at her.

"Please, take a seat," I said and waved to Clareen. "Would you get a pad and take notes?"

Clareen nodded and disappeared before I finished my sentence.

Riaffort asked, "Mrs. Sumner, Mrs. O'Neal, are you waiting for a counselor to arrive?"

"We decided we didn't need one at this time," Helen replied.

"From an ethics standpoint, I have to advise you that your best interests would be served by having representation present." Riaffort was warning them.

"I see this as a collaboration between us all. We are satisfied you'll be fair." Helen Sumner's words said one thing, her face something entirely different.

"It's your decision," I said. Clareen silently re-entered the room, pad and pen in hand. I added, "Ms. Simmons will be taking notes and will provide transcripts for all of us. If you wish to hire a lawyer later, I'm sure he'll want a copy, so I recommend you hang on to them."

Ellen said, "Why, Ms. Simmons, do you take shorthand? I took it in high school. That was so long ago. I thought I'd never use it, but I did. My late husband used to have me make lists of things he wanted for the farm, and I'd take them down in shorthand. I thought people did everything with those electronic gadgets today."

Clareen smiled and said, "I use it all the time. No batteries required."

Helen Sumner frowned at Ellen during the whole exchange. It appeared to me she wanted to minimize any communication between Ellen and us.

"Mrs. Sumner, you wanted to discuss something you and Ellen want to find. Can you tell me about it?" I tried to move the conversation forward and me toward a decision point.

Helen Sumner remained silent.

I asked, "Is there some problem?"

"I'd like to know a little more about your background and capabilities. I know I should have asked this before we met. I want to be diplomatic, but I'm not good at that." Helen's facial expression was more adversarial than collaborative.

"No problem, what do you want to know?"

"Your website states you did this type of work for a private company and the government. Who were they?"

"I worked for a company named Advanced Military Armaments and the US Department of Justice. Between the two, I have twenty-two years' experience. The work I did for them was an exact parallel to the services I offer." There's was no reaction in the Sumner woman's features. However, Ellen O'Neal's face showed she was favorably impressed.

Helen's eyes narrowed, "What were some of the items you recovered?"

"Can't tell you. I signed blanket non-disclosure agreements with both." I waited for a reaction from Helen.

It came from Ellen. "If you tell us, you'll have to kill us, right?" A smile accompanied her words.

"That's it." It was apparent there wasn't anything impaired in the woman's mind. "Can we get to what you want me to do? Then we can decide if the project is a good fit . . . for both of us." My shot across Helen's bow had the desired effect. Belligerence disappeared. I even detected a trace of fear in her features; that told me she probably wasn't the one that was calling the shots.

"How much of the story has Helen told you?" Ellen said.

I looked at Riaffort, and he nodded. "Mrs. Sumner's said that a large sum of money was hidden by an ancestral grandmother. Helen told me the funds were in the form of gold coins with an approximate weight of 180 pounds. She said there was some form of a written clue passed down from generation to generation. There was timing involved. June 1 was mentioned. That's what I remember."

"That's correct, but we can tell—" As Ellen O'Neal spoke, Helen's face clouded, her eyes flashed. . . . she was not a happy camper. Ellen noticed also, and she quickly added, "There I go. I promised to let Helen handle this thing. She did more work on this than me. I'll keep my mouth shut."

"I'll take over from there." Helen began to cool. "Before we go any farther, I want to discuss your fee, Mr. Harrell. Can we review what we talked about at the restaurant?"

"Good. But first, let's get this on a first name basis; call me SJ." I felt Sly was too suggestive to use in a business relationship. "First names all around?"

Nods and "Yeses" came from all.

"When you met at the restaurant," Riaffort interrupted me. "What restaurant, what day, what time?"

"The Catfish Place, St. Cloud, Florida, a week ago today, at three-ish." I filled in the blanks Riaffort wanted.

He spoke, "Put in the correct numbers, Clareen."

She nodded, and I continued. "Helen, correct me if I'm wrong. The figure was twenty-five percent."

Before Helen could respond, Riaffort asked, "Twenty-five percent of what?"

I answered, "Of what I recover."

Helen answered, "Of the gold coins."

"Obviously, they aren't the same. SJ, I would counsel you that you remain firm on recovery versus coins. The funds may have changed form." Riaffort' eyes were as cold as the iceberg that sank the Titanic.

"Good point. It has to be recovery," I said.

Panic invaded Helen Sumner's eyes.

"Recovery is fine," Ellen smiled as she spoke and touched Helen's arm. "That means I don't have to pay *anything* if you don't find *anything*. I only pay for what *you deliver to me*, right, SJ? Just so I understand."

"That's correct." I saw Riaffort frown, but he kept quiet.

There was an exchange of glances between the two women. Then, Helen said, "That's okay. Let's go on." She reached for a portfolio sitting on the desk in front of her. She unzipped it and removed two papers, one old, hand-written, and yellowed, one new, typed, and white. She handed the white copy to me and said, "Please read that. It's a copy you can keep." She watched and waited while I read. It contained the following:

> To my Flesh and Soul daughters.
>
> You are as worthy as any. Let it not be a curse to be one that bears children. I wish a wrong to be set right. I start the count.
>
> Unworthy man gains for he is man. Find the one I bore that lies still who earned nothing yet received all. All that was given was removed. That which was removed will be given.
>
> Let the oldest daughter find what is hers. If she cannot, let her oldest, then the oldest of each generation look for the way. Find the long path to recover what is the Sumner women's due.
>
> Daughters, read this! The first day of June go to the place

where we lie, but not I. The one where the cattle pass. Do as these
words here say. Keep the sun in your front. Stand three paces from
the stone of one of the unworthy ones, the grave with the greener
grass. As the clock's arms reach three o'clock, the son above will
point the way to the son below. Beneath the pointed place is the
plate with many strikes. Start as it says and count the strikes. Goins
lies there, beneath a cloud that covers many points. Beware the
cloud but find all that is yours. Remember as I taught you, one of
a dozen eggs may be bad, check for it to the last.

   Mother Sally.

When I finished, I looked at both women.

"What you have is a copy of the letter Great-Great-Grandmother left to her female heirs." Helen's face softened for the first time. "She wanted us to have our rightful inheritance." She looked embarrassed. "I mean Ellen to have what should be hers."

"And I will be sharing a portion with her," Ellen volunteered.

"That's not important." said Riaffort. "The agreement I write will be between you, Mrs. O'Neal and Mr. Harrell. Your letter is proof of hereditary ownership, and I'll site that in the contract. I will need to see the original, for witnessing purposes."

Helen handed it to Riaffort, who glanced at it quickly and asked, "Is the copy the same as this?"

"Yes," Helen answered.

"May I place my initials on it?" he asked.

Helen scowled, and Ellen looked concerned. "The paper is very fragile." Helen spoke as she thought, "Okay, but be very careful, and not near where Granny Sally's writing is."

Riaffort initialed as though he was handling a thin-shelled egg. I glanced at the handwriting but didn't attempt to read it. Helen carefully placed it back into a file folder as soon as I returned it to her. The room became hushed as I reread the letter. When I finished, I asked, "Can you furnish me a list of all the cemeteries your relatives are buried in? That's the obvious place for me to begin."

The two ladies exchanged eye contact. After a few seconds' hesitation, Helen said, "We can do that, but we think we are sure that we know which graveyard it's in."

That puzzled me. I asked, "If you think you know that, what do you need me for? You go to the cemetery, find the stone, follow the instructions, and zip . . . you have your gold coins."

Helen Sumner looked panicked and confused. After several seconds, Ellen answered my question. "We've tried. It isn't easy because the most important clue, the part about the greener grass, time's wiped that out. We looked and even tried to dig up the spot we thought where it lies. It wasn't there. Well, we got in some trouble over that."

I asked myself if I wanted even a slight involvement in what was likely to be a mess. "Mrs. Sumner, Mrs. O'Neal, the whole business of exhuming graves is a very difficult one. There could be three or more levels of government involved to get approval. The gold coins *might* create a case that they're considered historical artifacts, but that's pretty sl—"

Ellen waved her hand and excitedly began talking, "If going after something historic would help, there could be some very important items buried with the gold. Would something like a crate of Confederate paper money and the sword and uniform General Beauregard wore at the Battle of Chickamauga be important enough?"

The chance of recovering some significant Civil War relics changed my viewpoint. Maybe greed had some impact. Confederate dollars had real value as antiques. I asked, "Do you have reason to believe those items are hidden with the gold?"

"Oh, yes. The gold, and a bunch of other things that belonged to the family, disappeared at the exact same time the coins did." Ellen's eyes glittered. "I'm almost certain we'll find everything together. I believe it has to be in one of the three southern places. Probably at Ft. Ogden. That's where Helen told you about."

I began drafting an idea of how and who to see about exhumation permits.

CHAPTER 11

"What are you doing?" I jerked in my seat, and my knees crashed into my desk. Ken Bass looked over my shoulder, and I was so engrossed in the items in front of me that I didn't sense his approach. His voice pulled me back from thought's parallel world.

I looked over my shoulder at my ranch manager, bodyguard, and fishing and hunting partner. Ken "Trotter" Bass was the best man for the tasks I asked him to perform. At twenty-seven, he was young enough to handle any physical effort and old enough to have the judgment to act independently. We were a team. A team forged with iron bonds in my last two years of service at the DOJ, we both had the potential to be a liability after my final assignment. When I was pastured, I took Trotter with me . . . all 6'4", 235 pounds of muscle and determination. He is completely fearless, with one minor exception: bees and wasps. His analytical mind made him a thinker, not a talker. He is the perfect fit for my business.

"What are you reading?" Four words are a major sentence for Trotter. It's not an intelligence deficiency; he just isn't interested in long communications.

"Client business. It's information for a treasure hunt of sorts." I knew what would come next.

"Am I involved?" he asked.

"I'm sure you will be," I said.

Trotter pointed at the chair next to my desk and lifted his eyebrows.

I answered, "Go ahead."

He studied Sally Sumner's letter with its cryptic clues. Trotter shrugged his shoulders and said, "That's not mine." He turned the list of graveyards around and looked them over. He nodded, got up, and went to the copy machine. When he returned, he put the original in front of me, shook the copy, and said, "MapQuest." He left as quietly as he had arrived.

I returned to the process of picking a starting point. What did I know? The only definite thing I knew was that the starting point was in a cemetery. The reference to a grave was proof enough for me. However, I wasn't ready to make the other assumptions the two women considered certain. They concluded the treasure was buried. They concluded it would be in the same cemetery as the grave. They assumed the burial site was for one of Sally Sumner's dastardly sons. They concluded they had narrowed the total of seven possible cemeteries to one. All their assumptions *could* be correct. However, I believed they were probably wrong about two or more assumptions.

The two pieces of paper were all I had to start investigating. Those papers gave rise to far more questions than they answered. I began writing unknowns down as the unanswered slipped into my mind.

Which of the cemeteries were close to cattle trails used in the late 1800s?

The note referred to the burial of one who "received all"—that was supposed to be the oldest boy, but the oldest son was never found?

Was the "long path" a literal clue or a symbolic reference? What was long?

Why was the date, June 1, critical to locating everything?

Were several or all the Sumner sons buried side by side or in some configuration?

Is their burial arrangement used to provide the "point?" What does point mean?

Was this used to point to the treasure clue?

Is there a sundial built into the gravestone on the grave with greener grass?

How long is a pace? Sally's step length?

What date did Sally die?

How old was she?

What date did Samuel die?

What points to the pointed place?

What is the plate with many strikes?

Strikes are a count but of what?

Is "Goins" simply coins misspelled?

The wording in the note is structured unusually even for that time? Is that a clue?

What is the cloud, and what are the "points" beneath it?

Bad egg???

Trotter walked to the front of my desk. He placed eight sets of directions to the seven different graveyards on the polished wood. He pointed at them and said, "One set of directions from here to each cemetery. One round-robin direction from here to all. What vehicle, and when do you want to go?"

"We'll take my Jeep, and we'll probably start the round-robin day-after-tomorrow. I need to make a few phone calls to set up appointments. The O'Neal woman can probably answer a few of my questions. A couple of answers she should know will reduce our effort considerably. There are some things Russ and Val Foxx will be able to find that can focus our trip and effort better. One, maybe two of the places we can scratch from our itinerary, with a little research from here." I closed my eyes and thought of things we should have on the trip. "I'm not sure where and what we'll find when we visit these places. Take a machete, a grass whip, ax, shovel. We might have to clear an area of brush and weeds. Take a pair of snake boots. And, Trotter, take some varmint control, just in case." I remembered Herman Wilson's telling me of AK-47s in the back of the black HUMV. Were they connected? I told Trotter, "Make sure the varmint controls are automatics."

CHAPTER 12

"Hello, Helen, this is SJ Harrell. I'd like to speak to Ellen for a few minutes." I expected the answer I got.

"Ellen's sleeping. What did you want from her?" Helen's tone wasn't friendly.

"I have a few questions that will help me locate what you're both looking for." From experience, I knew to ask a question in a way that the answer would benefit the person being asked. With a person like Helen Sumner, it was the only way.

There was silence for several seconds. I heard a hand covering what I assumed was the microphone of a landline. Finally, she said, "Ellen's still asleep. I can probably answer most of your questions. If I can't, I'll write them down to ask Ellen, and either she or I will call you back."

"Okay. I have six questions. The first is how old was Sally when she died?"

"I know that. She was seventy-seven years old."

"Good. Do you know what date Sally died?"

Helen remained quiet for a few seconds before saying, "I know the year and month. I'm not sure of the day. She died in March of 1907."

"Which of the seven graveyards was she buried in? That would rule it out as the place to find the coins."

"None of them," Helen was quick to respond. "She is buried in her family's private cemetery in a little town named Bowling Green. Part of her family lived at the trading post near there that was raided and helped start the Third Seminole War. I thought you would have known that *by now*." Her voice had a smart-assed tone that pissed me off. Controlling my tactless side was becoming difficult.

I wrote the information she provided and added a note, *born in 1830—waste of time looking at cemeteries where they lived before 1860*. I asked, "What date did Samuel Sumner, her husband, die?"

She answered immediately, "He died on May 28, 1899."

"Fine." I tried to get some bonus information. Finding out the depth of Helen Sumner's prior involvement in the search would be helpful. "Helen, have you been to the grave that you and Ellen believe is the one mentioned in the letter?"

After a slight delay, she said, "Yes."

"Good. One of the letter's clues refers to the fact there are at least two of the brothers buried in the graveyard. Do you remember where they were located in relation to the grave you think is the key to the riddle?"

"There were other relatives buried close, but I don't remember who was where." That answer was immediate.

I asked, "Were all buried in a family plot?"

"I don't know what you mean."

"During the years when your Great-Grandpa Samuel was buried, families often purchased or reserved a portion of the cemetery for their exclusive use. Do you think that was true there?"

There was a delay of several seconds, followed by, "It definitely is a family plot. I believe there are twenty-four graves in it." Her response's timing and manner confirmed my thought that someone was giving her the answers as we spoke.

"That will help," I responded. "One last question. The list of potential family burial sites your aunt provided all were in towns. At the time, there were often two or more burial places. Many of the towns like Bartow were located near old forts. Ft. Blount was there and had a cemetery associated with it. Did you look at both cemeteries?"

"Let me think about that for a couple of minutes."

The delay allowed me another chance to review the list Ellen O'Neal had given me. Newnansville was in north Florida, close to Gainesville. That wasn't a possibility. The Sumners moved farther south chasing wild cattle herds in the 1830s. Only the earliest pioneering family members would be there. Sumterville was north of Tampa. The family relocated from there in 1842, grabbing land offered by the Armed Occupation Act of that year. I'd crossed it off my list of possibilities.

The five remaining held some promise of housing the treasure, though some were very slim possibilities. The towns listed were Davenport, a short distance southwest of Orlando, and Bartow, south of Lakeland. Frostproof was the next location on the continuing southward migration of the Sumners'. Ft Ogden was a small town south of Arcadia that remains cattle country, as did the last village on the list, LaBelle, located twenty miles east of Ft. Myers. At the time Samuel and Sally lived, all these towns were associated with old Indian control forts. Some had graveyards where locals were buried. They had to be checked.

Sequentially, I'd written the name of each fort next to each corresponding city: Davenport/Ft. Davenport, Bartow/Ft. Blount, Frostproof/Ft. Arbuckle, Ft. Ogden was the fort location, and La Belle/Ft. Thompson and Ft. Denaud.

Helen's voice snapped me back to our conversation. She said, "I had to go get a copy of the list we gave you. Of the seven, the only two I can tell for sure about are the Bartow and Ft. Ogden cemeteries. Ft Ogden is where we think it is buried. All our part of the family is in the Methodist Cemetery in Bartow. I can't help you with the rest."

"Do you think your aunt will know?"

"No."

I couldn't resist the snide tone in my voice. "Okay. Say hi to Ellen *when she wakes up.*"

In the lady-like manner I expected, Helen said goodbye as she hung up. "Up yours."

CHAPTER 13

An hour after I'd completed my conversation with Helen Sumner, her attitude, her lack of civility . . . just plain *her*, bothered me. If I was to be stuck with the woman as the primary liaison between Ellen O'Neal and me, I wanted to know more about her. I had questions, and my gut was telling me I damned well better get them answered. I turned to a new page on my legal pad and recorded them.

What can be done to double-check that Helen is a member of the correct branch of the Sumner family?

What happened in the four years she dropped out of sight?

What information is available on her husband?

Is it possible to get detailed information on Helen and Ellen's lives and their interaction in the last three years?

Can we get pictures of all three at various times?

Since we only have a PO Box as a mailing address, can we get a physical address of where they live?

Was there anything else? I'd leave that to Russ and Val Foxx. They had great instincts for sniffing out morsels of information that generally proved valuable. I added a statement.

Do any data and information mining you think will add to what I might need to know.

What else would help me? One thing! I added a final question.

Did Sally Sumner ever live in western Marion County? If yes, where?

CHAPTER 14

"Let me pull off the road, Russ. It's hard hearing you. Trotter and I are in the Jeep." I drove into a gas station on highway Florida 60. After turning off the ignition, I said, "Okay, I'll be able to hear you, now." I put my cell on the speaker. Trotter would be interested.

"I have your list, Sly. Val has gone over it, too. It's going to take a road trip and some time to do this. To do this right, you're looking at sending us to Beaufort and Paris Island. Who knows where that will send us? The Florida portion won't be bad. We can do them in a couple of one- or two-day trips. That's at the worst. The other stuff. . . . that could get expensive. Don't get me wrong, Val and I would love to do this. It's our thing. I just want to be sure you—"

I cut Russ off. He never used ten words when he had the option of a hundred. "Do it. Give me a guess. How long?"

The speaker was quiet while Russ made a mental itinerary. "It will take seven to nine days," Val answered before Russ completed his calculations. She was also on the speaker. "What are you willing to pay for?"

"Gas, your RV space rentals, and the standard rate you've been charging per day, $200."

"Restaurants?" she asked.

"After last time? I don't know about that. Maybe if you put a muzzle and leash on your husband." A lobster dinner at $170 a pop was too much for me to digest on an expense report.

Val laughed, "You know if you ask Russ to say something, his first words are always, oink, oink." After a pause, she said, "We have to eat regardless. On days we travel in the RV, we'll cook. If we take day trips, how about springing for $40 for the two of us to defer some of our cost?"

"You're picking on me!" Russ grumbled, though I knew it was fake sentiment. He shed insults like an oiled raincoat sheds water.

Trotter leaned toward the cell and called, "Sooey pig! Sooey, sooey!"

"Not you too, Trotter. I thought you were my devoted friend," Russ faked a few sobs.

"I am. I'm honest too." Trotter leaned back.

Val asked, "Do you want to get a report when we've finished all of the questions, or do you want to get stuff as we find it out?"

"Get it to me as you complete a question." After a second thought, I added, "If you think something is important, don't wait. Get it to me right away."

"Where you headed?" Russ asked.

"Bartow," I answered. "If you can get the street address of Ellen's farm, that's where the ladies are living. I'd like to do a drive-by and maybe stop in."

"We can handle that in an hour or two," Russ said.

Val confirmed, "Yep!"

CHAPTER 15

My starting point was the Polk County Historical Society. It would be the hardest stop I'd have to make. The reason was Maureen. Maureen Dieselli was the manager curator. Very personable. Very knowledgeable. Very attractive. And probably very, very, very pissed at me.

The last time we'd seen each other was at the Florida Association of Historical Museums and Societies' annual conference. The association had joined modern world conventions enough to use the acronym FAHMS as its public title. We were both single. Three days of being in almost constant contact found us extending the days into evenings. We exchanged no promises, other than the one that comes from an exceedingly satisfactory liaison.

I hadn't called, emailed, or even texted. She'd made one attempt to reach me by phone.

I sat behind the steering wheel like a clod of dirt after we arrived at the building. I might be there still if it wasn't for Trotter's voice reminding me, "It's ass in gear time."

I nodded grimly and rotated my legs outside the Jeep. My mind searc' resolve to face an unpleasant situation. Someone shooting at me, hearir rattler singing in palmettos, the sight of a shark fin while swimming—

easier to face than someone I felt I hadn't treated fairly. Russ Foxx told me I had a phobia. He called it my "fear of screwing someone over" virus. You hate something when you've had the same experience a few times.

My feet dropped to the pavement. They continued to place themselves in front of the other while the rest of my body and mind protested vehemently.

"What's wrong?" Trotter walked beside me and knew I was troubled.

"You ever do something wrong, or did you ever *not* do something you should have, and get the guilts? Not something bad. Just something you knew you didn't do, even though you should have?" I asked. If my chin hung much lower, it would have touched my shirt.

Trotter shrugged his shoulders and said, "I don't date much."

"You're a lot smarter than I am."

"Not really." He stopped and smiled at me. "Boss, you're looking for love. I'm looking for an evening's entertainment."

"You telling me I'm confusing the two?" I asked.

"Something like that." He started walking toward the front door and said over his shoulder, "It's getting it over time."

A newly hired, teenage face grinned at me from behind the reception desk. At least, newly hired since my last visit. I swapped glances with her. "Welcome to Polk County's learning center for our area's history. My name is Angela. How may I assist you, gentlemen?"

"Yes. Could you tell Maureen that SJ Harrell would like to see her?" I fidgeted as I spoke.

"Yes, sir. Excuse me while I see if she's available."

I looked at Trotter. He was smiling. No, it was more of an evil leer.

I frowned.

He laughed. "You see Ms. Forever. I see tonight's company."

"When I see one that young, I think daughter, not a sheet partner." I tried looking disgusted.

"Fair. But, just saying." The young girl's return ended our discussion.

Angela said, "Mrs. Ford will see you in a few minutes. She has someone in her office right now.

"Maureen Dieselli," I mumbled, not sure if they were the same.

The girl smiled, "She got married four months ago."

Trotter laughed, I blushed, and Angela looked confused.

"It's so good to see you, SJ!" Maureen's smile was warm and genuine. She turned her head toward Trotter. "Who's your friend?"

"This is Ken Bass, Maureen. He wears a lot of hats for me. Ken is a one-person managerial staff. If something needs doing, he gets it done." Her office was awash with wedding pictures. I said, "Congratulations, Maureen. I see you tied the knot since our last time together."

Her smile was warm, happy. "Yes. My husband is Wayne Ford. He is a *wonderful* man. I kept waiting for you, but. . . ." She tilted her head from side to side.

"My loss," I said. That wasn't just a platitude.

"I'm sure you didn't drive here to congratulate me. What brings you up to Bartow, SJ? You here for your business or doing historical research?"

"In this instance, both. I'm looking for information on the Sumner family and, in particular, where they are buried." The strange look on her face surprised me. I asked, "Something wrong?"

Maureen remained silent for several seconds before informing me, "You're the third person that's been in here in the last two months looking for information about the Sumners."

"Really?"

"Yes. You don't have to ask. You're looking for information on Joshua's son, Samuel, and his wife Sally, right?" She spun around in her office chair, removed a file folder from a tray on the table behind her, and swiveled back toward me. She handed me the quarter-inch-thick file. "I think you'll find everything you need in there."

"Yes, you're right. If that material is on Sally and Sam, that's exactly the info I need." Staring at her for a few seconds, I decided what to ask, "Did you know the people that were looking for the same information I am?"

"I know who one was. She's local. The other person wasn't from around here. He signed a name on our visitor's register. Bob Jones. I'd say not." Maureen smiled. "There was something fishy about him. The register says he's from Tampa, but I sent Angela—you met her, right?" I nodded. "I sent her to look at his license plate. . . . First in Flight, he was driving a car from North Carolina. It had a Duke sticker on the rear window."

"Did he say what he wanted the information for?" I asked.

"Yes. The man said he was writing a book about the Sumners. He didn't show much interest in what they did and how they lived. He was very interested in how they died, and as you said, he was particularly interested in their burial information." She took a breath and asked, "Want to know about who else was here checking the Sumners' history out?"

"Sure would."

She smiled, "At least this one had a legitimate reason, or excuse, to be looking. A woman, Helen Sumner, came here looking for all types of information on her ancestors. That's what she claimed. She's lived here for a couple of years. Been in several times over the past three months." She hesitated for several seconds and then said, "I figure her interest is legitimate. She's kin to Ellen O'Neal. You know about the O'Neals?"

"Yes." From what I knew, I didn't need more info on them.

"Most people around here know of the Sumner woman because of the big stink she raised when she first came to town. Helen claims to be kin to Ellen O'Neal. She was incensed by the fact old Mrs. O'Neal was forced into an old-age facility. It made the papers. Sumner claimed the county was trying to steal the old lady's farm and home. It was messy. Eventually, the Sumner woman got Ellen released to her care."

"What can you tell me about Mrs. O'Neal?" I asked.

"Ellen? You can't find a nicer old lady. It's too bad her mind has slipped." Maureen paused and then said, "Maybe it would be easier if I asked what you want to know about her?"

"You know her well?" I asked.

"Yes, she came in here regularly up to three years ago. I've only seen her once or twice since then," Maureen said.

"You mentioned that she had some dementia. I met her recently. She seemed sharp to me for eighty plus." A good opportunity had dropped into my lap.

Maureen squinted and said, "As I said, I haven't seen much of her recently. Her problem comes and goes, so I've been told. When did you see her?" Maureen seemed surprised.

"Several days ago, her and Helen Sumner came over to my office in Wabasso. They have contracted with me to recover something for them."

"Now that really is a shock. Ellen O'Neal is famous for not wanting to leave her home, much less traveling over to the east coast." Maureen pinched her eyebrows together. "The Sumner woman hasn't talked the old lady and you into hunting for Sam's gold, has she?"

I just smiled.

"She has! SJ, that's the equivalent of an urban legend. Everybody in the southern half of the state chased that wild goose a few years back."

My smile continued.

Maureen shook her head and said, "Really?"

"Really."

She leaned back in her office chair and stretched her arms overhead. "You want copies of the stuff in the file? I can have Angela make copies. But . . . I can tell you, if such a treasure does or ever did exist, it would be in the last few places old Sam lived. He and Sally lived here when they first married. His father, Josh, had all the money then. Sam didn't get well-off until after 1882. He had a connection to Hamilton Disston. That's where his money came from."

Nodding, I said, "Thank you, Maureen. That will help a lot."

"Is there anything else I can furnish you?"

"Can you give me directions to the O'Neal ranch? I'd like to ride past and at least eyeball it. Maybe visit the ladies for a few minutes."

Maureen shook her head. "I can tell you how to find the ranch. It's easy to get out there. I'll write directions for you. But, SJ, I don't think the ladies are living out there. I'm not sure, but I thought they moved in together wherever Helen has been living."

"I'd like to take a look," I said.

Trotter and I sat silently while Maureen wrote directions.

Later, as we climbed into the Jeep, Trotter said, "I don't clean geese." He laughed.

CHAPTER 16

"That must be Lake Garfield." I glanced at Maureen's directions as we drove by a large lake surrounded by pasture. "It should be the next road. If the directions are right, the O'Neal place will be two miles on the left after we make the turn."

"What we looking for?" Trotter asked.

"According to what's written here, there should be a gate with a frame around it and a sign with O'Neal printed on it hanging from the cross member." The road I would have to turn right on was in sight. I eased off the accelerator. "This should be Lake Garfield Road."

As we rounded the corner, a pickup truck raced up to the Jeep's rear and stayed uncomfortably close. The truck followed us, and the pickup's driver stayed twenty feet behind. Images of two young men wearing baseball caps filled my rearview mirror. They were laughing, and one raised a bottle of something to his mouth. "We have a couple of drunks behind us," I theorized, waving for them to go around. The man driving the truck obliged. He jerked the pickup to the left and floored it. The tires screeched, and black lines of rubber transferred to the pavement. The truck's movements were violent enough to dislodge one rifle from a gun rack mounted in the pickup's rear window.

I said, "Those boys are in one hell of a hurry."

"Late for lunch," Trotter concluded.

The truck was barely in control. It wandered from the grass on one side of the road to the other as the driver returned to the lane in front of us. Trotter and I watched him speed down the string-straight road. The vehicle raced ahead of us a half-mile, then made an abrupt left turn into a farm lane leading to an old farmhouse far away from the road. It disappeared into a cluster of outbuildings. When we reached the drive they'd turned into, U-shaped timbers framed the lane. Suspended from it, the sign with *O'Neal* printed on it swung in the breeze. *O'Neal* wasn't the only message at the gate. Two "No Trespassing" signs shared fence space, with another cautioning, "Bad Dogs," and another warning, "Active Firing Range, enter at your risk!" Our welcome wasn't a hearty one.

"Not a friendly place," Trotter observed.

I slowed to a stop and took a long look at the house, barns, and those things around them. All the buildings were paint-deficient. Wooden fences around the horse runs were missing boards. Farm equipment sat at random and looked in poor shape. An old car sat on concrete blocks and missed all four wheels and the hood. One of the things I was looking for wasn't visible: the black HUMV.

"Want binoculars?" Trotter asked.

"No. I can see enough. Maureen is probably right. I doubt seriously whether the two ladies are living here. The only things that are in good shape are the Angus and whitefaces in the pastures."

As I finished speaking, someone emerged from the house, got into a car, and drove toward us. The car pulled through the gate and stopped next to my Jeep. A plump, forty-something lady with her hair wrapped in a scarf rolled down the window and asked, "Are you the men here to fix the air conditioner?" She looked bedraggled.

"Nope, sorry."

"I was hoping. Most folks won't drive back because of the signs."

"Are you Mrs. O'Neal?" If she answered yes, I had major problems.

"Heavens, no. I just clean the place," she answered.

I asked, "Do you think Mrs. O'Neal or Mrs. Sumner would mind if we talked with them for a few minutes?"

The lady looked confused. "I don't know Mrs. Sumner and Mrs. O'Neal. . . . she's living somewhere else."

"Thanks for the information. Who owns this place now?"

"Oh, Mrs. Ellen still owns the ranch. It's rented to the MacCord's Farms people. Only the ranch hands are staying here."

I hoped and asked, "I'd like to see her. You know where Mrs. O'Neal lives?"

She stared at me, suspiciously. "I don't know. I had a phone number, but it isn't in service anymore." She paused, looked at me coldly, and said, "Sorry, I can't help you one bit."

CHAPTER 17

"Where are you, Russ?" I asked. The cell reception was poor, and I hoped we'd get in a complete conversation.

"The last town we passed that's worth mentioning was Brunswick. I guess we're an hour out of Savannah. I think we'll probably eat there. I'm not sure—"

I cut him off. "That's good." He happily provided more information than was necessary. "I want to pass along something. The situation I've run into at my first stop makes me think there's an attempt to hide what's really going on. I'm going to call the Sumner woman and try to get this sorted out. Wherever you end up tonight, stay there until I call you back. I may pull the plug on this whole thing."

"It sounds as if you've stepped into some horse hockey."

"It sure looks that way," I said.

"Any problems with the stuff we gave you?" Russ asked.

"The only thing I've checked is where Ellen O'Neal was supposed to be living. That turns out to be bogus. She still owns the property, but someone else is renting it." I heard Val saying something in the background. "According to my wife, she's suspicious of the Sumner woman."

"Yes, I'm concerned she's a fraud." Russ needed to know another bit of information we'd discovered. "My friend, another thing. It looks like there is somebody else competing with us to find the treasure . . . first. Be aware of that and be careful, okay?"

"How do you know?" he asked.

"Somebody has beat us checking on the Sumners."

Russ was quiet for several seconds. Then he asked, "How are you going to determine if you're going to proceed?"

"That's a good question, Russ. The only way I can see to sort it out is to talk to the women and confront them with what's happened so far. When I see what they say, I'll make a gut check decision . . . and stick with it."

After my call to Russ Foxx ended, I asked Trotter, "You got any ideas on how we can get a handle on this?"

"None."

I shook my head.

"What's next?" Trotter asked.

"We find a motel to stay overnight." I closed my eyes. "I'll call Sumner and O'Neal. There's no use going to Frostproof if this thing blows up. This is way too complicated."

"Ever think there's a lot more to this than a few boxes of coins?"

I nodded and said, "Sure, but what?"

CHAPTER 18

"That's funeral music." Trotter wasn't lauding my selection of a music channel. We could agree there wasn't anything on the tube in our motel room worth watching. We perused ESPN, gagged, hit a few movie channels, and gagged again. Trotter's evaluation was succinct and correct, "I see better when the toilet flushes."

"Montavoni, Norrie Paramor, Nat King Cole, that's soothing to the ears, boy," I prodded. Trotter was a rock and roll guy. Country was our compromise; we both liked that . . . he leaned toward Brad Paisley, Lady Antebellum, and Blake Shelton. . . . my taste favored Hank Williams Sr., Dolly Parton, and George Jones. I needed nerve-calming music before the chaotic call I had to make to the Sumner and O'Neal women. Easy listening works for me.

"Sorry, Trotter, I'm not looking forward to calling Sumner and O'Neal. Sumner and my feelings about each other are already a parallel to sulfuric acid and water combining. I need to be as close to catatonic as possible before I call. The music helps."

Trotter lifted an eyebrow. "Say hi. Say good luck. Say goodbye."

"Remember, I signed a contract? I either have to go through with this scavenger hunt or find some way to get them to let me out."

Trotter stood up, shrugged his shoulders, picked up his wallet from the bed he'd been sitting on, and asked, "Is there a bar downstairs?"

"I think so," I said and added, "I can't guarantee the music."

"As long as it ain't burying noise, it will do."

I motioned to a cabinet top where the room keycards resided. "Take one of those with you. Don't wake me if you come back late." As he took a keycard, I advised, "Bartow isn't the pickup capital of Florida."

He said, "You never know," smiled, and left the room.

Trotter had been gone an hour when I decided to make the phone call. It was getting close to 9:00 PM, and rationalizations for not calling were exhausted. The original recording by Dooley Wilson singing "As Time Goes By," my all-time favorite, gave me another three-minute respite before finding Sumner's number on my cell.

When the last piano chord died, I hit the contact line on my phone and waited for her to answer.

The phone rang, five . . . six times, and I was about to hang up when Helen Sumner answered. "Hello," her voice was uncharacteristically timid. It had fear mixed in.

"Hi, Helen, it's SJ Harrell. Do you and Ellen have a few minutes to talk with me?"

There was quiet, absolute quiet.

"Helen? You okay?"

Silence.

"Hey, are you there?" I was becoming concerned. Her previous confident and aggressive manner had fled.

"Mr. Harrell, is that you? Do you have anybody with you?" Helen's voice quivered.

"What's wrong? You sound scared."

"We are. The last few days have been very frightening for me . . . us." I heard her talking to someone in the background for a few seconds before she continued to speak to me.

"Mr. Harrell, do you have any people working for you that are following us?"

"No, why do you ask?"

"We believe someone is trying to find out where we live and to follow us." I knew she couldn't be faking the fear and concern in her voice.

I decided against telling her we were at Ellen O'Neal's ranch earlier in the day. I asked, "Can you tell me what you've been experiencing?"

"The cars following us or the phone calls?"

"You've been getting phone calls, also?" That told me the effort someone was making was far more than someone just trying to gather information. Intimidation was high on their list of objectives.

"Yes. Ellen has received them a lot more than me. We are very, very frightened."

"Tell me about the calls," I instructed.

Helen hesitated for a few seconds, then said, "At first, we thought they were just junk calls. Someone would call, you answer, no one says anything, and they hang up. Then they started to ask for Ellen."

"When did these calls start?"

"The same week I rode up to St. Cloud to see you." I heard someone talk to Helen. She added, "Ellen says she received a few before that. Another week-and-a-half."

"What did they want from her?" I asked, though I had a good idea.

There was a rustling sound, and Ellen's voice replaced Helen's, "Mr. Harrell, they told me we should stop looking for the treasure. They said they were the only ones that could find it. The men told me that something bad would happen to us if we kept trying. It has us all frightened."

"Who is us?" I asked. The word men in her previous statement told me a lot.

"Helen, her husband, and me. And Mr. Harrell, in the last few times they asked for the letter. In the last call, that was just a few hours ago, they told us if we didn't give it to them, they'd come take it, and someone was likely to get hurt or die."

"Do you know who it is or have any idea who it might be?" I asked.

"None!" Ellen's answer was immediate and emphatic.

"Are you in a secure place?"

"Ummm, not really. We are planning to move later tonight." Concern was in the old lady's tone, but not the panic I sensed in Helen's.

"Where are you now?"

I heard the fear more pronounced, "I'm afraid to tell you. We think the phone is bugged. Helen thinks that's how they found out where we are going and how they follow us."

"Ellen, have you identified vehicles that are following you?"

"Yes. There is a silver Toyota with a bent fender and a black SUV." She sounded certain.

"Is the SUV a HUMV?"

I heard them discussing the vehicle with Helen, and I heard a man's voice. Finally, she said, "Yes, it is a HUMV."

"Who is with you?"

"Helen and her husband."

"I know you don't want to tell me where you're going. But when you get there, call me to let me know you're safe. Will you do that?"

Ellen's answer came immediately and with conviction, "I certainly will."

"You have a plan to be sure you aren't followed?"

"Yes. But I can't say. You know why."

I lowered my voice and tried to make my tone reflect the seriousness of my question. "Ellen, have you and Helen been completely honest with me?"

The phone remained silent for thirty seconds. That alone told me something. Finally, she said, "No, Mr. Harrell, we haven't about everything."

"And?" I asked.

"Well, we suspected that someone was watching us, and we thought they might be after the treasure. But we had no idea they might be violent."

I asked, "Anything else?"

The pause was not as long, "Yes. We didn't tell you that . . . well, there may be more hidden . . . stuff to recover than we said. Maybe two or five or ten times more."

CHAPTER 19

I didn't hear Trotter walk through the door. He made sure I heard everything after that. It was his way of waking me without 'waking' me. The green numbers on the alarm clock displayed 2:37. I rolled from my side to my back and said, "Okay, are you wanting to brag, or are you curious about how my phone call went?"

Trotter's grinning face told me things had gone well for him. "Both," he said.

"Which first?" I asked.

"Phone call."

"You want the long version or the short version?" After lifting my body, I leaned on one elbow, shook sleep cobwebs from my brain, and watched him plop down on his bed.

"Short version."

I dropped onto my back. "I'm going to do my damnedest to find the gold, if . . . if there is any. She convinced me."

Trotter smiled, "I have this oceanfront house in Montana to sell." He rolled his hands in front of him, indicating he'd like to hear more.

"She told me someone else is hunting it. Somebody not connected to them. Whoever it is tried to intimidate them with phone calls and threats. That tells me someone else thinks what we're looking for is real. They've been followed. The black

HUMV *isn't* theirs. That tells us something. They claim that's why they have acted strangely."

"Who is *they?*"

"Helen, her husband, and Ellen O'Neal. I spent over half my time speaking to the O'Neal woman. I gotta tell you, if her mind has slipped, I'd have a serious inferiority complex if I dealt with her when she was young."

Trotter asked, "Are they legit?"

"O'Neal is, at least I think so. Sumner, it's fifty-fifty on her," I answered.

"Lots of cloak and dagger," Trotter shook his head, frowned, and said, "Think it's worth it?"

"Yes. By up to ten times what we thought we were going after."

CHAPTER 20

The early morning sky was bright and clear. The very few wisps of clouds gathered the emerging sun rays and lit up in vibrant pinks and oranges. South of Lake Wales, I turned on Florida 17, called the 'scenic highway' by many folks. Staying on super-highway US 27 would have gotten me there quicker, but the two-lane back road furnished so many more diversions.

Citrus groves covered the rolling terrain, some well-cared-for, some clawing to stay alive as their greedy owners milked the last life from their investment. Herons fished in the small ponds I passed. A couple of rabbits nibbled tasty weeds on the road's shoulder. This was a vestige of my Florida, the Florida that I loved.

The corpse seated in the passenger seat of the CJ-5 stayed there by some strange presence of mind Trotter possessed that allowed him to function in his semi-conscious state. That and a fastened seat belt.

I pulled off the road to watch a pair of Sand Hill Cranes stride around a small pasture escorting a pair of big yellow babies. My stop was rewarded. The birds many Crackers call "Iron Heads" issued their mournful, haunting calls.

The lack of motion woke Trotter. But not enough to open his eyes. "Where are we?"

"A little south of Babson Park," I answered.

"Why did we stop?" The corpse was grumpy.

"To hear the Iron Head's call to each other." I pushed his shoulder to stir any bourbon remaining in him and to aggravate his hangover.

"Damn!"

I punched him lightly.

His eyes remained closed. Mumbling lips produced a few words from the corpse, "When are we eating breakfast?"

"When we get to Frostproof. We're going to eat at the Egg Factory."

The eyes opened, and Trotter reclaimed the body from the corpse. With emphasis, he said very clearly, "I like that place!"

That offers proof that the old saying, 'the way to a man's heart is through his stomach,' is true. Well, it is in Trotter's case.

The waitress had her best tip-getting smile in place as she welcomed us to the Egg Factory. She said, "The sign says wait to be seated. That's to make us look like a big city operation, but we are strictly country. Sit any place you'd like."

"Thank you, ma'am," I said and steered Trotter to a table where I could watch people entering the front door. Death, taxes, and the Goodspells eating breakfast at the Egg Factory were three of life's inevitable events. Rhonda and Arnie were regular enough patrons that their favorite breakfast carried their name on the menu. They ran a combination talent booking, travel, and real estate agency. The Goodspells also acted as managers and curators of the Horn and Grove Historical Museum "in town." They owned inherited citrus groves and a 'smallish' ranch—their words—of 2,700 acres. All their businesses had to be profitable; they fully supported the museum they ran. Financially. Administratively. Anything the museum needed, they provided.

Rhonda ran the show. One of the reasons the Goodspells were the sole source of funds was that Rhonda wanted to do things her way. Arnie was happy to allow his wife whatever she wished. He introduced Rhonda as his "trophy wife" gleefully. Sixteen years his junior, she reveled in the title, spent a lot of time and money on maintaining the appearance, and was totally committed to Arnie, who she called

"Sugar D." If someone wanted a brief description of Rhonda, I'd tell them she is a human that could have made Patton shake.

Arnie is intelligent, quiet, but firm. His persona is out of a Tennessee Williams' novel. He looks like Don Knotts—that's Barney from Andy Griffin reruns. He married the former high school homecoming queen, Gator cheerleader, honors graduate in history, and made the decision he'd sit in the back of the bus.

"Do you boys know what you want, or do you need more time?" The waitress placed our silverware, napkins, and glasses of water in front of us.

Trotter was ready. "I want the Papa Hog Sunriser. I want my three eggs scrambled, grits instead of home-fries, pancakes, and get two of the three meats. Give me extra link sausage instead of bacon."

The waitress nodded, "Want any juice with that?"

"Nope," Trotter went back to being economical with words.

"What would you like?" she asked me.

"The three-egg Cracker Special omelet, grits, and link sausage." I anticipated her question, "No juice." Before she could walk away, I told her, "When the Goodspells come in, would you ask them to join us? We're friends."

"Sure. What's your name?"

"Sly Harrell."

She nodded and said, "I expect they'll show up here any moment."

Trotter looked at the front door as a couple pushed their way through. I shook my head and said, "When Rhonda and Arnie show up, I won't have to tell you."

Trotter stated, he didn't ask, "Those are the Goodspells." I looked toward the door, and Rhonda led the way wearing a dress that probably had paraded down a Paris runway.

"Sly! It is so good to see you, *you old son-of-a-bitch!*" I watched Trotter's face as Rhonda examined him like a fillet mignon. I wondered if I could have printed what was in each of their minds. I knew what Trotter's twenty-seven-year-old mind was doing. I could guess what forty-two-year-old Rhonda's mind was thinking.

Rhonda could pass for twenty-seven and thought that way. She extended a hand to Trotter and said, "Sly, quick, introduce me to this beefcake buddy of yours."

I sighed before I did the introductions. "Rhonda Goodspell, meet my friend and business associate, Ken Bass." Arnie appeared from behind her like a destroyer emerging from the shadow of a battleship. "And this is her husband, Arnold." They pumped hands while I continued. "If you call him Ken, he probably won't answer. Everyone uses his nickname, Trotter. And Trotter, same goes for Arnold. He's Arnie to everyone who knows him."

'Pleasures' were exchanged as they sat down to join us. Rhonda waved to the waitress; the woman nodded and put in their order for the usual. "What pried you out of the swamp, Sly? I'd like to think this is purely a social call, but I sincerely doubt that."

CHAPTER 21

"Yes, we know a lot about the Sumners. They were one of the biggest landowners here in the second half of the 1880s. Them, Ben Hill Griffin, and J.K. Stuart ran this county back then. You know what happened to the Sumners, of course." Rhonda's green eyes were speculating: did I know the sordid and complex Sumner family history, would she get a chance to enlighten me, and would she be able to show off some of the exhibits lying in the museum a few blocks away?

"What would you like to know? We have a great deal of information on three of the five brothers, Josh's boys. They lived here when they all became rich. True, some of them got richer later. And a lot of their troubles came about here." She perched like a pond bird ready to spear a fish.

"I'm looking for information on Samuel's part of the family. Anything you have on him, his wife, and his children would interest me. If any of that part of the clan is buried around here, I'd like to visit the graves. You have information on any of that?" I could see by the glow in her eyes that she did.

"You have come to the right place. I have a ton of material on Samuel Sumner's folks. Household goods, farm relics, Samuel's spittoon, the deed to the land that Stuart and Sumner fought over, correspondence, and even a will. . . . Like I said, I have all manner of material on him." Rhonda was bubbling at having an opportunity to show off her collection and knowledge. The word *will* made my eyes widen.

Arnie cleared his throat, "There's an overwhelming amount in the collection we have on the Sumners. If I knew you were looking for something specific, I could probably save you lots of time."

"I'm doing a project for a client. It has to do with what Samuel was likely to have left to his descendants. As I said, I'd like to see where the Sumners are buried. The man's will sounds particularly interesting." I tried not to show a lot of excitement about the document.

"Sorry, Sly, that will was superseded. It was made up when Samuel and J.K. feuded over who owned some property down near Avon Park. Both thought it would come to bloodshed." Arnie leaned forward to make a point. "Jake Summerlin got involved and settled the dispute between his old friends. Still, Samuel and J.K. never had much good to say about each other after that."

"It was about then Samuel hitched his star to Hamilton Disston. That's where he made the fortune he accumulated." Rhonda finished off the last forkful of her particular variant of Eggs Benedict, one especially prepared for her. "I actually have some of the bank records of payments from Disston to Sumner." She suddenly sat up as if a shot of electricity passed through her. "You're going after Samuel Sumner's lost millions. Who is your client?"

It took several seconds for me to decide how I wanted to answer her question. I lied, "I have contractual obligations that prevent me from answering that *fully*. Best that I can tell you is that I'm trying to find something specific that belonged to Samuel. I can't tell you anything about my client."

"You aren't going to hear this from most of our colleagues. I believe a lot of his money disappeared," Arnie said. "My grandfather told stories about the Sumner family and a lot about Josh and Samuel. He said he never met a father and son that were more different. Josh was meaner than a shedding snake, ruthless, and a cheat. Samuel was a good man, fair, and honest. But he said the few things they had in common were all about money. They hated to part with any and didn't trust banks."

"I've heard about Samuel's thoughts on banks."

Rhonda leaned toward me, "Sly, you don't lie very well. There is usually some validity to folklore. We've heard the stories. That means you're working for some descendent of the Sumner clan. Arnie and I can't help you very much on where, but I think we can enlighten you a lot about potentially how much. We need to go to the museum."

CHAPTER 22

Rhonda pulled open a drawer titled, *Sumner, correspondence, business-related, 1875 – 1900*. She carefully removed several albums that further protected the papers contained within. "There are records in here that are critical to what you're looking for," Rhonda said as she carefully found the correct section and book. She opened the volume to the proper location. "I'm showing you these chronologically, the oldest documents first. Read this."

The tan-yellow paper was written on letterhead that read, *Disston Saws & Metals – Philadelphia, PA*.

> *October 27, 1884*
>
> *Dear Samuel,*
>
> *This will confirm our conversations held in Tampa last month. The problems I have with squatters continue to plague my purchase of land from the state. I have received a favorable decision from Governor Bloxham regarding appointing my official agent to evict anyone who is occupying my lands illegally. The surveyors who have custodian duties tell us as much as 1.5 million acres of the 4 plus million I've purchased from the state*

are so occupied. In addition, I have numerous land purchases in process that face the same unpleasant situation.

Therefore, one of the services I request of you is the removal of all those residing on my properties. They may pay me for those lands if they wish to stay at the rate of $1.50 per acre. It is widely known my purchase of lands was for $.25 per acre, but the explanation for this increase is the completion of Plant's and Flagler's railroads, which more than justifies the increase in value. In payment for this service, you will receive $.50 per acre so handled.

Those who you convince to move voluntarily from my lands will earn for you the amount of $.05 per acre so reclaimed.

The remainder of lands occupied must also be reclaimed. Because of legalities arising from the Armed Occupation Act of 1842, there may be conflicting claims on the land. In those cases where forceable eviction is required, I will sell the land to you, and when you have possession, you will resell it back to me. I will pay for the expense you incur, plus I will provide you with lands equal to one-third of the acreage that must be retrieved in this manner.

Questions of legalities will be submitted to my Philadelphia law firm, Horne, Dunne & Horne. Present those problems to my office at the Kissimmee Land Company.

The decommissioning of Ft. Brooke has allowed me to procure a large number of government firearms. These are available for your use. The weapons are still stored in a warehouse near the fort in Tampa. You may find it necessary to use force, though I pray not.

Your faithful partner in this matter,

Hamilton Disston

After finishing, I said, "That translates into a lot of money." My mind guesstimated it was several times more than what Helen and Ellen had admitted.

"There's more here," Arnie carefully turned to the next document mounted in the album. "Clearly, there is more correspondence that is missing, but look at this." The letterhead was from the firm *Horne, Dunne & Horne.*

> *January 1, 1889*
> *Mr. Sumner,*
> *In answer to your inquiry, the sum we hold in escrow for you is in security boxes, not in general bank funds. The amount currently at your command is $272,486.62. As per your instructions, all of the specie is gold coin.*
> *I must advise against the personal withdrawal and transport of such a sum on your person when you visit our city. The danger is obvious. There are excellent services specializing in such transport if it is your desire.*
> *We look forward to your visit in April. It might be wise to delay related actions until that time.*
> *Adrian Horne, Esq.*

I looked up, tried not to smile, and asked, "What else?"

Rhonda turned one page over. The small slip of paper's heading read, *Proof of delivery, Pinkerton – Frawley Secure Transport Services.* It contained two lines of information. Line 1: 17 boxes, gold coin, value $303,988.25. Line 2: 1 chest, deeds to land, worth $58,090. The receiving signature was that of Samuel Sumner. Its date read, May 11, 1889.

Rhonda watched my eyes leave the receipt. She said, "By the time you factor in antique value and such, those figures might double."

I nodded. Sam's treasure had been real enough. The questions left were: Where had it been hidden? Was it still there? There was a very real possibility someone had already found and removed it. The fact others believed it still awaited discovery encouraged me.

Arnie snapped my attention back to the album. "There is one more thing that should interest you. Sam built Disston's sugar mill in St. Cloud." He turned several pages. A barely legible note was scribbled in faded ink on a disintegrating piece of brown paper. The date was not legible, nor did look like part of the original text. What I could read said:

> *Hami----,*
> *In answer to your question, I would be interested in building*
> *a sugar mill on yo-- ----er-- ---- --ke Okeechobee. I would char---*
> *--- th- ---- amount. Thank you for sending my mon-- -- -- here.*
> *Samuel Sumner*

"Sumner was hired to do many projects for Disston. Some of the historians around the state claim Sam Sumner also was a cattle broker for Disston." Rhonda closed the album, returned it to the cabinet, made a stop at the copier, then returned with a small book and a sheet of paper. She handed me the paper first. "This is a copy of where the University people said old Ft. Arbuckle was located."

I examined it eagerly.

"Those two shaded areas are where the archaeologists searched for it. If you want, you get to it by driving to the end of Lake Arbuckle Road. Those shaded areas are on the northeast shore of the lake. They didn't find enough to determine which was old pioneer cabins and which was the fort. The Army used it to assemble some Seminoles for relocation to the West in 1850. It wasn't staffed much after that. There was a military record of nine burials. Nature reclaimed everything out there. The University never found the graves. As I said, you can go down to the lake, but it's a waste of your time." She stood up straight.

"What's in the book?" I asked.

"You asked about Sam Sumner's wife, Sally Crisp. The book is a journal kept by one of her brothers. One of fourteen brothers. She had two sisters. August Crisp was their father. He was an important figure in this part of the state. He and his two brothers were millwrights, carpenters, and undertakers. August taught his sons the skills, and that's what they all did. Sally's brothers moved all around this part of the state. People considered them well-to-do. The journal has some interesting entries about Sally after Samuel died. Her brother complains bitterly about him and his brothers having to chip in to pay for her living expenses when Samuel had a lot of money. The story was that his sons stole it all and left her nothing."

"Can I see them?"

"Sure," Arnie said, "Would you like copies of the pages Rhonda's talking about? There's only a half dozen."

"Sure would." Then I asked, "Are there any cemeteries where I should be looking for possible burial sites for Sumner's sons?"

Rhonda shook her head. "Not any of Sam's brood. There are a few Sumners buried in the old Methodist Churchyard. Not one of them is direct kin to Sam."

"Where is my best chance of finding their graves?" I handed the journal to Arnie, and he left to make page copies.

Rhonda said, "I'd start looking in Ft. Ogden and at the Ortona graveyard. Ft. Franklin, Ft. Denaud, or the LaBelle Baptist Cemetery would be my third choice. By 1890, Samuel had moved his cattle to the Okeechobee, Peace River, and Kissimmee River areas, and that's the area where he lived. I read about five homes he kept strung from the Lake to the Peace River. Someplace down there. That's where they're all likely to be buried."

CHAPTER 23

Trotter's frozen smirk and his silence finally got to me. I pulled the Jeep into a McDonald's for a cup of coffee, took a sip, and wished I hadn't.

"I'll drink it." I had the impulse to pour the coffee over Trotter's head but handed it to him instead.

He sampled the coffee and said, "Not bad." The grin continued.

My cell rang. The screen had Russ Foxx's name and number lit up. I'd forgotten to call him and give him instructions. I said, "Shit!" This wasn't my best day. The first thing I said when I answered was, "I'm sorry, Russ. I forgot to call this morning."

He answered, "No worries. We had a good breakfast, found the docks, and bought shrimp for dinner. Val finished a job for someone else. Life's good. What do we do next?"

"Go on to Beaufort and start investigating," I said.

"They convinced you!" Russ sounded very surprised.

I heard Val in the background say, "You lose. We eat French tonight."

I answered Russ, "Yes, it's complicated. There is a lot higher top end than I was led to believe, originally. Just go ahead as we planned. Get back with me when you think you have something important."

"Ahh, are you concerned it might actually be *lower than you were led to believe?*" Russ was trying to caution me gently.

"I'm not relying on what the ladies told me; I have some very creditable corroboration from excellent historical sources that it was there at one time." I changed the subject by asking, "Where did you end up staying last night?"

"We went back to Brunswick. You know that's in Georgia, right?"

"Yes. How far to Beaufort?"

Russ and Val exchanged a few comments before he said, "To where we want to start, 140 miles; that's three-plus hours driving time. Val and I have done some work on the Net. Val's made phone calls. Seems as though the Sumners had a quiet life before they disappeared. According to what we found, they own a house in the country just west of town. The taxes are current. So . . . we're going to visit that. Val found a contact at the Marine Depot at Paris Island. Sumner's record there was squeaky clean. Helen worked as a waitress for two years and as a dental hygienist for six. The dentist's name is Albertus Sparknagel. He shouldn't be hard to track down with a name like that. Helen's husband was a machinist and metal worker in a local manufacturing plant. That company is still in business. He left after being there eight years. That's when they both disappeared from Beaufort. Those two jobs are great places to start."

"You have a good jump on it," I acknowledged.

Russ asked, "Where are you headed?"

"My next stop is Arcadia. Ft. Ogden doesn't have a place to stay. I have information on how and who to contact at the DeSoto County Historical Society. That's tomorrow's plan, anyway."

"Damn, Sly, you've got plenty of time, don't you?" Russ was never in a hurry.

"I don't know. That's the shitty truth. I have to be standing in front of a grave we haven't located to interpret a clue we don't fully understand on June 1. That's a little more than six weeks from now. You tell me?"

"I get your point, Sly. Just a second—Val is yakking at me." After a few seconds, Russ said, "Val was able to confirm Helen Sumner's genealogical records. The girl that moved to Beaufort from Okeechobee and was married to Mark Sumner. She says she is sure that Mark Sumner is also in the Samuel Sumner branch of the family. He was from Okeechobee also. She, Helen, followed him up to Paris Island. So, Val says we are informationally tight through there."

CHAPTER 24

"I should have never sent you after supper." I looked at fried chicken with its peanut oil coating dripping onto a black Styrofoam plate. The green beans had been overcooked to disintegration. The mashed potatoes' odor made it unnecessary to taste them to find out if they were dehydrated.

Trotter grinned and said, "You don't have to eat."

He reached for the plate. I pushed his hand away. "If you want seconds, go buy your own."

"It's bad stuff." His fake grimace wasn't convincing.

I squinted my eyes at him and said, "You aren't getting this. If you want more, take your ass and your billfold back to the poison parlor where you bought this, and buy your own."

Trotter nodded, grinned, and asked, "Want anything?"

I shook my head, and he left our motel room. The Superior Suites Motel was basic to the point of being anemic. The TV could have been purchased in an antique parlor. It offered a limited menu of programs from a cable service I'd never heard of. I found reruns of the *Blacklist* and settled in to watch.

Trotter had been gone twenty minutes when there was a soft knock on the door. Both the keys to the Jeep and Trotter's room keycard were gone. Why knock?

"The bastard's brought back a bunch of stuff." My words were loud enough to penetrate the door. I laid the remains of my meal on the bed where I'd been sitting. I knew Trotter's fondness for sweets. We'd passed a Dairy Queen and a Dunkin' Donuts on the way to the motel. I was sure he had an armload of goodies from one or both of those places.

Without looking through the peep, I jerked the door open and found no one. Puzzled, I step outside into the candescent light from parking lot lamps. No one was to be seen. The parking lot, the sidewalks, the small swimming pool area . . . all were devoid of people. I took a few steps on either side of my door. The rooms on either side didn't have any lights on, so they were probably vacant. I shook my head and re-entered the motel room.

The rerun episode was a good one, and I lost track of time. When Trotter returned, he had a box of donuts and a bag with more chicken in it. I looked, snorted in disgust, and refocused on Reddington, wiping out a contingent of adversaries with as much conscience as a thief removing valuables from an unlocked jewelry case.

"Want more chicken?" Trotter asked.

"No."

"Want a donut?"

I looked at the box and asked, "What kind?"

"Vanilla crème filled." He opened the box.

My favorite. I tried to show minimal enthusiasm. "I guess so."

Trotter's smile told me I'd failed. He carefully wrapped a napkin around its powdered sugar coating and extended it halfway to me. I shook my head. He wasn't going to bait me up from the bed. He sighed and placed the wrapped donut into my outstretched hand.

I asked, "What took you so long? You were gone long enough to buy out a couple of stores."

He took a piece of paper from his jeans' pocket and handed it to me. Scribbled on it were numbers and letters. I asked, "This a license plate number?"

"Yes."

"For what?"

He tilted his head to one side and asked, "Didn't you say there was a black HUMV that followed you a week or so ago?"

I stiffened, "That's right."

"When I left, one was parked in the motel lot. I drove past. Wrote the numbers just in case."

I read aloud, "KE? – 738? Either an O or a Q. North Carolina plates."

Trotter nodded, "That's the best I could make them out. And Sly," he paused, "When I came out of the donut shop, the same HUMV was parked in its lot."

"Not a coincidence," I said.

"Wouldn't think so."

"Could you see who was inside?" I asked.

"Not well. The two in the front seat were big, and I'd guess they were men. The one in the back was smaller and had long hair. I'm guessing a female." Trotter pointed outside. "I drove around a long time to see if they'd follow me. They didn't. Guess what, when I finally came back here, I saw the HUMV parked across the street."

It was past daybreak when I hollered, "Hey, Trotter, throw the suitcases in the Jeep. I want to get out of here quickly and get to the Historical Society when they open." I waved my cell phone at him. "I want to see how things are at the ranch and the office. As soon as I talk to Clareen and Cindy, I'll meet you in the lot."

Trotter nodded and gathered up what we needed to throw into the Jeep so we could go. I watched him push through the motel room door as Cindy's voice mail responded, "Leave a message, please." My effort to reach Clareen was no more successful. I was leaving a note for her when Trotter reentered the room. He wasn't happy.

"I'm about finished," I said.

"No rush."

I shrugged my shoulders, asking, why?

"Somebody slit all four of the Jeep's tires."

"They're delivering a warning," I growled, "Well, let's answer it."

I removed a black marker and a plain piece of letter paper from my briefcase and printed letters on it. Trotter read it back to me, "I don't get mad. I get even." He asked, "You pissed?"

"Third-degree pissed," I replied.

Trotter became serious. "Those poor bastards!"

CHAPTER 25

"May I speak to Mr. Burrows?" I asked.

A female voice answered from my cell's speaker, "I'm sorry, Mr. Burrows isn't here right now. May I take a message?"

Maybe I wouldn't have to "eat crow." I stated, "My name is Slydell Harrell. I have an appointment with him in an hour."

"Oh! Mr. Harrell! I am so sorry." Pages of a calendar rustled. "I see you had an appointment." She hesitated a few seconds, then said, "An emergency came up, and he had to leave for the day. Can I reschedule you?"

"What is his next available time? I'm not from this area. It's a two- to three-hour drive."

"Oh, I'm so sorry. Let's see." She paused as she looked for a time. "Could you come back tomorrow or the next day?"

"Yes."

"How about tomorrow at one?"

"Put me down for that."

"I promise he'll be here." The lady was embarrassed. Her boss had spared me an identical fate that four flat tires would have caused.

"May I ask your name? You've been very helpful."

"Jenny Dorr," she said.

"I'm looking for information on possible burial sites for some pioneer families. Do you have any knowledge of that?" I asked.

"Yes, I do. I recently did some research for someone on that very thing." Jenny sounded anxious to please, but I was concerned that if I asked if the research was on the Sumner family, a caution flag might arise.

Wording my question carefully, I asked, "Does the research you've done include any knowledge of burials after the civil war up to say 1920?"

"Yes, it does."

How long would it take for Trotter to get the Jeep's tires fixed? Four hours? That was probably a good guess. After a glance at the time, I asked, "Jenny, would you have time to see me this afternoon? I'd like to chat with you for a little while about the research you've done. Would, say, two be okay?"

"One second." The rustling of papers told me she was checking that there would be no interruption of her regular duties. Good, I told myself, she's a detail-oriented, responsible person. I'll get useful information from her. She answered after several seconds, "That would be fine! Is there anything I can have prepared?"

It was my time to prepare an answer. "Maybe. What I'm researching is the cattle ranching families from that period: the Summerlins, the Hendrys, the Sumners, the Stuarts, those folks."

"You are in luck. The work I did included one of those families." Jenny sounded enthused about having the opportunity to share information.

"There's a lot of good information here, Jenny." I turned the pages slowly as I looked at burial records, burial plot layouts, and newspaper obituaries that would have been what I would have requested as info on the Sumner family. "You did a fantastic job."

Jenny beamed, "Thank you!"

"I hope the people you prepared this for were as impressed as I am."

She frowned slightly but didn't say anything. I immediately saw that there might be important information in her expression. I asked, "Don't tell me they didn't appreciate what you did for them? If they didn't, they're real. . . ." I hesitated as I rephrased *asshole*, "rectal apertures."

Jenny giggled but quickly volunteered, "Oh, I never spoke to them. Mr. Burrows talked to the men who asked for the records." Her frown returned at the mention of Burrows' name. That was instructive.

"Well, I'll speak for them when I say you do great work!" I turned the pages. My eyes opened wide as I saw a couple pages on the Crisp family. That was Sally's maiden name. There had to be a connection. Very little information about them. A lot more about a name with which I wasn't familiar. I asked, "So the people requested information on three families, Sumner, Crisp, and Ashton?"

"Yes, at least, that's what Mr. Burrows told me. He's the one that talked to them when they phoned us to ask for the histories. He's also the one that did *all* the discussions when they came in here two days ago." She took a breath and added, "I don't know if he told them about the interesting sidebar tidbits I found."

"I'm curious. Would you mind sharing that with me?" I asked and smiled my friendliest.

"Not at all. There was a connection between two of the families that wasn't genealogical. I didn't make copies of the newspaper articles about one of the Crisp family being arrested and tried for murdering one of the Ashtons."

"That fascinates me, Jenny. Could you tell me more?" I set my brain on memorize.

"Sure. It goes back to something about a burial. Jonah Crisp was the local undertaker, amongst other things. He hired James Ashton to help him from time to time. Jonah Crisp and his brothers buried people all over south Florida. Ashton did work for several of the brothers. What happened was never clear. Jonah hired James to do a burial south of here. Anyway, when they came back, Jonah was driving his hearse. . . . James was a stiff in the rear. Jonah claimed that when he was swinging an ax to cut some roots, he slipped, and he damned near cut James' head in two." Jenny hesitated, then asked, "Are you a Cracker?"

"Sure am," I said proudly.

"Well, then you know Florida people were still fighting the Civil War into the 1960s. So, the local sheriff was a friend of the Hendrys and a Union supporter.

Colonel Hendry had been a rebel but chose to swear allegiance to the US after the war. The sheriff arrested Crisp at Hendry's suggestion. Whidden is an important name here. One of the first families. Those families ran things then. Smith, Mizelle, Tedder, Summerlin, Clark. . . . Some still run things today. The Whiddens were staunch Confederates and friends of the Crisp family. They saw Hendry as a turncoat. Most of the jury were Whiddens or relatives. The trial was a waste of time. What is ironic was that Jonah buried James."

"Thank you, Jenny. I'm a historian of sorts. I love that story."

"Would you like me to make copies of the old newspaper articles on that?" she asked.

"Please do. And Jenny, would it be too much to ask if you could make copies of the files you've shown to me?"

"I'd be happy to!" Jenny was enjoying the recognition. "If you want, I can put a copy of the statute about unwitnessed burials. You'll come across that in the articles."

I lifted my eyebrows. Before I could ask, Jenny answered, "You used to be able to bury folks with no one else present if you were a licensed undertaker. You did have to publish a notice that you did it. I came across that in the Ashton file."

I nodded as she gathered the papers into the file. She said, "I'll be back in a few minutes. It will take me a little time to pull the articles on the murder." She smiled and left me sitting at her desk, wondering if I'd have time to visit the two cemeteries that were reported to be Sumner family resting places.

CHAPTER 26

"Change of plans, Trotter. I want to look at the other cemetery tonight." It didn't take long to disagree with Helen Sumner's and Ellen O'Neal's assessment. The old Baptist Church Graveyard didn't have the right Sumners planted there. The gravel and stone coverings of the graves made it impossible for there ever to have been "greener grass" covering any of them. It hadn't taken long for me to rule it out.

Trotter scowled as we walked back to the Jeep with its newly installed rubber. "I'm hungry," was his verbal way of disagreeing.

"I'm sure you'll live for a couple of more hours before you refill that tank of yours."

Resigned to humoring his boss, Trotter asked, "How far from here?"

"Jenny said they were approximately fourteen miles apart."

"Damn, Sly, that's a long distance from here to bury a loved one if they were supposed to live in Ft. Ogden. Back then, that's almost a day's travel." He looked to be *hungrier*, more than doubting the accuracy of Jenny's info.

"You only have to bury a person once. You don't go there daily."

"We're going tonight."

Trotter settled into the Jeep's passenger seat and for the rest of the evening was quieter than the skeletons buried in the graveyard we were leaving.

Grudgingly, Trotter had to admit, "This sure looks more like the place." We pulled through a gate into a much larger graveyard than the one at the Ft. Ogden Church. Fenced areas within the Joshua Creek Cemetery's expanse verified there were family plots, a key to locating graves from that period.

I wasn't as sure. Many of the stones were old, true. And the oaks the graves were shaded by were many years older than those who rested under them. But! It had too many modern burials, and the graves were maintained by a trust advertised at the entrance. I'd almost convinced myself it was a waste of time until I saw a history-laden maker. The very plain rectangular headstone said, *"Bone," N. Bonaparte Mizelle, 1853 – 1921.* Bone Mizelle was a legendary pioneer on the Florida frontier. I never knew his burial place. What I did know: he was in one of the circles of cattlemen to which Sumner belonged. My mind changed conclusions from low possibility to high probability.

The numbers on my cell reminded me we didn't have much time before light gave out. In a way, we were like the people buried here from that frontier period. Time registered on a clock meant nothing. The position of the sun and the light left before it hid behind the horizon meant everything. I drove down the cemetery lane, glancing at instructions Jenny had prepared for me. Oaks with a unique shape, three monuments that were unusually large and lined in a straight row, and azalea bushes around a fenced area were easy to find. Jenny was indeed a gifted detail person. I pulled as close as possible before pulling off the road on the lane's shoulder. I pointed to the azaleas and told Trotter, "That's supposed to be the Sumner plot."

"What do you want me to take? It looks like it's pretty cleared off." He put his hand on a rake and eyed me.

I shook my head, "Let's just take a look first."

We walked by stones that varied incredibly in age. Birth dates were as early as 1818, death dates to 2019; that's a two-hundred-year span. There were other family plots, fenced and unfenced. The same names repeated over and over. . . . Waters, Mizelle, Hendry, Whidden, and others.

The inner area surrounded by the fence and azaleas were visible as we came close to the Sumner plot. I did a quick count—three rows of eight graves. Twenty-four, just as Ellen and Helen had said. I was surprised how well maintained the plot was. Not even low weeds grew inside, as I'd observed in other family sites.

"What do we look for?" Trotter asked.

"We look for graves with masculine names and write their dates of death. I'll make up a chart and record the individual's name, his death date—year only—and the location." If we could accomplish that before the sun dipped behind the oaks, it would give me something to get us started in the right direction.

Trotter began his chorus, "Patrick Albert Sumner, 1832 – 1868, row 1, grave 3. I'm going left to right, facing away from the gate. Franklin Moses Sumner, 1821 – 1875, row 1, grave 5. Robert Stonewall Sumner 1866 – 1892, row 1, grave 6. Johnathon R. Sumner 1874 – 1884, row 1 grave 7."

Trotter advanced to the next row and started over, "Raffin Benjamin Sumner, 1864 – 1865, row 2, grave 8. William Wilfurt Sumner, 1832 – 1887, row 2 grave 6. Beauregarde Rosston Sumner, 1868 – 1888, row 2, grave 5. Stephen Foster Sumner, 1858 – 1911, row 2, grave 4. William James Sumner, 1868 – 1885, row 2, grave 1."

Trotter took four steps forward and checked the first four stones before saying, "Samuel Joshua Sumner, 1823 – 1899, row 3, grave 4. The date is May 28. Sly, I think we got our man!"

"We have Daddy, but do we have anything else? I'm not sure." I shook my head. "Finish out the row."

Trotter moved to the next grave. "Arthur King Sumner, 1831 – 1906, row 1 . . . Shit!" He dropped to his knees and was eyeballing something with intense scrutiny.

I asked, "What in the hell is it?"

"There are four or five perfectly round holes in the ground on top of the grave." Trotter's pupils went to the plot he'd just had me record. "There are on Samuel's grave too." His gaze wandered from grave to grave. "They're all that way!"

I smiled, "That tells me a lot."

Trotter looked at me like I was crazy.

"Modern technology." I pointed at the remaining three graves. "Let's check them."

Trotter shook his head but moved to the next grave in the row, then the next. At the last one, he said, "All females."

"Trotter, me boy," I said in my best Irish brogue, "we won't have to return here tomorrow."

"Why is that?" he asked.

"Two reasons. First, the letter indicates that at least one of Sally Sumner's sons is buried where the gold is. Father is, but none of his sons are. Second, these graves are laid out northeast to southwest. You cannot stand where the clue in the note says and have the sun in front of you. Besides, someone has been here and gave us a helping hand. Those holes you see are where two pipes, one slid down inside the other, were driven into the ground and into the coffins. It's a trick archaeologists and rescue teams use. You pull the inner pipe out along with the dirt, string a tiny video camera and light down the other pipe and shazam, you can see what's in a void below you."

Trotter laughed, "Damn, that's smart."

"See, coming on out here was a good thing! We don't have to bother tomorrow. Won't you enjoy your greased chicken more knowing that?" I patted him on the shoulder. "There's nothing left of interest for us here, and it's getting dark. Let's go eat."

We'd taken a dozen steps when something tore through the leaf canopy of the oaks surrounding us. The staccato snap of a rifle discharge followed immediately. Trotter dropped to the ground and yelled, "Sly! Hit the deck. Somebody's shooting at us!"

I dropped to one knee and grinned at him. "They aren't shooting at us. They're shooting near us. Big difference. They want to scare us, not kill us. Last thing they want is a bevy of police scouring the area."

We rose together. "That's a good thing, Trotter. Think about it. We now know they haven't found diddly. They'll stay focused on this for a while. Should give us a little time without worrying about those assholes. It tells us something else, know what?"

Trotter shook his head, "The sleuthing is your show."

"Okay. My dear Watson," I faked removing a pipe from my mouth ala Sherlock Holmes, "surely you've deduced that they have not been able to get their hands on a copy of the letter Sally Sumner left. Why, that's elementary, my boy."

CHAPTER 27

"How far is LaBelle from here?" Trotter must have been one of those children who constantly complained about any family trip, "Are we there yet?"

"Two hours, plus a little." We bounced along Florida Highway 70, the heavily traveled two-lane road with washboard pavement that would make the most uncompromising pioneer's teeth chatter.

"When are we going to eat breakfast?" Trotter whined.

"Trotter, remember those bagels and coffee you had before we left the motel? That's breakfast."

"That was a snack." Trotter would eat six meals a day if they were available. If he didn't have something to concentrate on, his mind reverted to food.

I tried a substitution. "I need you to remind me to call that lady at the Historical Society that furnished us the graveyard information."

"That Jenny Dorr woman?" he asked.

"Yes." I didn't remember mentioning her name, so I asked, "How did you know who she is?"

"She wrote her name and phone number on the copies she made for us and on the file folder she put them in." Trotter looked at me with a smart-assed grin he used when he felt he knew something he shouldn't. "Got plans to visit Arcadia again soon?"

"Not for anything you're thinking. You never know where this thing we're working on will take us." I doubt that Trotter heard any of my answer. He looked to the side and mumbled, "They have a hell of a lot of cattle in the one pasture."

I took my eyes off the stream of traffic we were in, which filled the lane traveling the opposite direction. Trotter slumped down in the seat. It was too noisy to hear if he was snoring. I asked in a low voice, "Are you asleep?"

"When are we going to eat?" The train was back on its single track.

"It's time," Trotter reminded me. Of what, I'd forgotten.

Guessing, I said, "There aren't many restaurants along the road we have to travel to get to LaBelle. We probably will have to wait until we get there."

He flashed me his, *you're an idiot*, look. "The call to the Historical Society lady."

"Thanks," I said.

"They do open at nine?" Trotter was pouring salt.

"Yes," my tone was miffed.

"Don't keep Jenny waiting."

I found a spot and pulled the Jeep on the road's shoulder. Pulling my cell phone from my pants pocket became a chore, its corners snagging the clinging material. I mumbled, "Shit."

He laughed while I punched numbers.

I recognized Jenny Dorr's voice. She sounded harried, not the calm and controlled person I had spoken to twice before. After she read her scripted greeting, I said, "Hello, Jenny, it's SJ Harrell."

"Oh, Mr. Harrell. I'm so glad you called before you drove over here. The appointment you had with Mr. Burrows? It won't happen today. He's missing. His wife got a text from him the last day he was at work, saying he was going out to dinner with people he met here. She hasn't heard from him since. His car was found in the parking lot behind an abandoned strip mall in Wauchula this morning. It was burning!"

"What did the police say?" The black HUMV came immediately to my mind.

"They asked so many questions! The thing they were most interested in was the people he gave the information to on the pioneer graves. They were the only people he met with that last day. It means they would be the last people to see him if they were the people he ate with that evening." Jenny was shaken . . . and, I could sense, scared.

"That is horrible. Did they give you any instructions . . . for your safety?"

"No." There was a pause while she thought about my last statement. "Do you think I might be in danger?"

"Probably not, but it wouldn't hurt to be careful. How many people know you are the one who researched those pioneer families?" I believed there was a connection between the two searches—ours and the HUMV owner's. Burrows and Jenny had walked into a kill zone without any knowledge.

"No one except you. Mr. Burrows liked to represent any work we did here. He said it was to shield us, but I've heard he charged for it." She quickly walked that back. "That's a rumor. No one really knows."

"Can I give you some advice, Jenny?"

"Oh, yes, Mr. Harrell!"

"Okay. First, don't let anyone know you did the work on the Sumner family and the rest. Deny it to everybody but the police. Don't volunteer it to them. Second, if you get any strange phone calls or threats, report them to the police or sheriff . . . whoever handles the case. Third, be aware of what's going on around you. Strange people showing up repeatedly where you are. Cars that seem to follow you. Report that to the law also. Fourth, I'd be careful to stay at home or go to places where there are lots of folks you know."

Jenny sobbed softly.

I thought of a plausible alternative. "Does Mr. Burrows have any, I'll say this delicately, close female associates he spends private time with?"

"Yes!"

I said, "That might explain the whole thing. Maybe that isn't good for Mr. Burrows, but it won't affect you."

There was a pause. Jenny asked in an unsure voice, "What if the police ask about you?"

She'd made the possible connection. "Jenny, I don't know Mr. Burrows, I've never even seen him, and I can assure you I had nothing to do with his disappearance. They shouldn't have reason to ask about me. If they do, tell the truth. If they don't, I'd prefer you not get me involved in something I have nothing to do with."

After the call, I started the Jeep on its way to LaBelle. Trotter sat in silence for several minutes before saying, "You've grabbed a tiger by the tail."

I corrected him, "*We've* grabbed a tiger by the tail. *We've!*"

"Yeh, we've."

I drove in silence. So many different possibilities raced through my mind, I feared the mechanism would explode. I'd been complacent, for I'd placed confidence in the fact that I believed those engaged in our scavenger hunt were intelligent and would do intelligent things. Seizing Burrows was stupid. Leaving his car burning in a parking lot was stupid. Possibly brutalizing or killing Burrows was even dumber. My mind was reviewing safety measures for my clients and my people when Trotter interrupted my thoughts.

"Fun and games are over." He shook his head. "Sorry, Sly."

CHAPTER 28

"I hope this place is half as good as you've said," Trotter rubbed his stomach after unbuckling his seatbelt.

"Betty and Billie's Restaurant is a tradition in LaBelle. Prepare that gut of yours for some of the best cooking that's ever been in it." My statement wasn't hyperbole. The food was that good. "I know it's breakfast, but save some space for some of their pies. They are to die for."

I liked LaBelle. It was still old Florida enough to have rough corners. Independent stores, small businesses, and restaurants that weren't part of a chain remained. The growling giant that is big business was placing its blood-shot eye on the community. We slid out of my CJ-5 into a town where corporate money had only tested with a toe. My fear was that it would be followed by a stomping foot that crushed all that didn't suit its whims.

We walked in the morning shade of oaks to a building that would remind most multigenerational Floridians of Grandma's house, not a restaurant. When we climbed the six stairs to the large porch with its collection of swings and rockers, we felt we had returned home.

Inside the door, a fresh-faced country girl stood behind a podium. She smiled as we approached. "Good morning, gents. How many?"

Trotter became talkative, "Two, pretty lady."

"It will be just a minute or two, is that okay?" Her eyes riveted on Trotter.

Trotter smiled, and the girl became "comfortably uncomfortable." She tried to keep from looking at him but couldn't. Her curiosity, or something, overcame reticence. She asked, "Are you two from around here?" She couldn't have cared less if I was from Mars. I remained silent so that Trotter could answer.

"We live up in Kenansville. You know where that is?"

"Sure. My kin are all cow people. I'm a seventh-generation Cracker. I'm darned proud of that." As she spoke, it was evident confidence wasn't her problem.

I smiled, "You have me by two generations."

Trotter asked, "I see your first name is Lily. Mind telling me your last name?"

"My name is Hays. Same as Major William Hays that built Ft. Denaud in 1855. He's my great-great-something."

"Your folks lived here all that time?" I sensed an opportunity.

"Mostly."

I asked, "Do you or does anyone in your family know a lot about old churches and graveyards around here?"

"Yes. My mom is the historian for our church. She knows all the stuff you'd want to know, the stuff you don't want to know, and enough more of what this place's past has been to break a manure wagon."

A waitress waved from the dining room. Lily stepped from behind the podium, said, "Come with me, gents," and led us to our table. Roles reversed. It was Trotter's turn to be in awe.

As she seated us, I asked, "How could I contact your mother? I'm a historian. I'd like to chat with her about this area."

"If you need to talk to her right away, you'll have to go to Ft. Myers. She works Thursday, Friday, and Saturday. Go to The Dancing Dears and ask for Dennia." Lily read my face and offered, "If exotic dancing isn't your thing, come back here other than those three days, and I'll arrange something." She turned, walking away with a smile and a last comment, "Enjoy."

I cautioned Trotter, "Close your mouth. It's wide enough for a vulture to nest in."

The vestiges of our breakfast sat in front of us. The food was as good as I promised. My planning wasn't. When I called the museum, the hours of operation were one to four on Thursdays. Shaking my head wouldn't change the fact we'd have three hours to waste before the LaBelle Heritage Museum's opening. Trotter rolled his eyes when I told him, and he left to find the restroom. Somehow, blaming my cell phone rationalized my screw-up.

"Was everything okay?" Lily stood next to me.

"It was great."

"Your friend stopped by my station on his way to the john. He said you're looking for the graves of some of the pioneers. My mom would be the person to talk to, but I suggest you might want to check out the old Ft. Denaud Cemetery while you wait for the museum to open. The cemetery is across the river from where the old fort was built. Just take the road out front. Go east to the next traffic light, hang a right on Ft. Denaud Road, and go until you reach the bridge over the Caloosahatchee. Go across the river. You'll make a little jog but go straight on Trader Road. The cemetery is on your left up a little-ways."

I was writing her directions on a napkin as fast as I could. "Could you give me your mother's phone number?" I reached in my shirt pocket, fished out a business card, and handed it to her with the promise, "I'm legit."

"It's the same as mine, and Trotter already has it."

CHAPTER 29

My cell phone rang as we crossed Betty and Billie's Restaurant parking lot. The screen told me it was Valerie Foxx. I said, "Hi, Val."

"Where are you?" She is not a gal to waste time on pleasantries.

"LaBelle."

"How quick can you pick up that lawyer you're always bragging about and get up here?" Val sounded stressed.

"Why do you need us?" I asked.

"To get Russ and me out of jail." She was calmer than I would have been, given the same circumstances.

"What is going on?"

"We got arrested for breaking and entering, and we found skeletons there." Her voice broke just a bit.

"Where are you?"

Val took a deep breath, audible over the phone, then spoke, "Beaufort, in the county jail. Sly, they tell me I only have five minutes. How quick can you get your butt here?"

Trotter held his hand up. He was getting the information from MapQuest on his cell.

"Well?" Val asked impatiently.

"Seven-and-a-half hours straight driving time," Trotter advised.

After some quick calculations, I said, "It will take me eight hours, at least. I'll call Riaffort Richards, he's my lawyer, and see if he can get there any earlier. Maybe he can arrange bail if he's there or not. If they have visiting hours, I'll see you this evening. If not, I'll see you tomorrow morning."

"That's good," I heard her sigh of relief. "One detective said suspicion of murder."

"Suspicion of murder? I need some details."

"It's very complicated, and the officer is telling me I have to get off the phone."

"One more thing—should I bring Trotter?" I asked

"Yes." There was a click. I wouldn't find out more until I arrived in Beaufort.

CHAPTER 30

With the stops we had to make, the eight-hour driving time turned into eleven. By the time we arrived, visiting hours were past. There was a Hilton a short distance from the police station and the short-term lockup where my friends spent the night. I tried to do some research but fell asleep on my closed laptop before I started.

Riaffort couldn't leave until the next day and informed me that it was an exercise in futility to get the Foxxes out on bail under the circumstances. Bodies. Suspects from out of town. Out of state lawyer. It was a no-no.

I had Trotter drop me off at the jail before he drove to the Savannah airport to pick up Riaffort. I'd do my best to see Russ and Val and get some idea of what precipitated the whole mess. It only took a few minutes for me to learn it would be a complex problem. Heads turned when I asked to visit the Foxxes. The reception clerk made a call, and a uniformed officer was at my elbow within a minute.

I was ushered into a room that was a box with a table and four chairs shoe-horned into it. They were in no hurry to talk to me. By the time my interviewer arrived, I'd located the TV cameras, three of them, a directional microphone, and even could critique the shoddy drywall repairs made to one of the walls. I theorized some inmate had driven his fist through it.

The "interrogation" team—my terminology, I'm sure not theirs—that arrived wasn't what I expected. The two detectives entered the room confidently. One was a woman who looked more like a motherly "schoolmarm" than a homicide detective. She was average: average height, average weight, neither beautiful nor unattractive. Her smile and first words were consoling. "Mr. Harrell, I'm Nina Dupree, and this is Mark Pell. We're the detectives assigned to look into the incident off Laurel Bay Road." She sat down, and her partner followed. My initial impression was that they were as sharp as marbles.

The man she identified as Mark Pell was built like a fireplug; was a couple inches shorter than me, round-faced, and completely bald; had piercing black eyes; and had a face I guessed hadn't shown an emotion for so long it had forgotten how. He forced what passed for a smile.

I nodded and said, "Hello." Training and experience told me to speak as little as possible.

"I understand you're here to see Mr. and Mrs. Foxx," Detective Dupree said.

"That's correct." I matched Pell's poker face as I spoke and listened.

"I'm sure you won't mind telling me what your relationship is to them?" she asked.

"We're close friends."

"Is that the extent of your relations?" She was fishing for something. I wondered how much information Val and Russ had given her. If she spent much time with Russ, a lot. His tongue defied science: it was a perpetual motion machine.

I answered very carefully, "We have two connections besides friendship. They are occasional subcontractors for my company, and they spend time on my land in Florida during the winter."

"Do you know why they are in Beaufort?"

"Yes."

"Were they conducting business for you? Were you their primary reason for being here?"

"Yes." The marbles were becoming sharper.

"Were they conducting business for you at the Laurel Bay Road site?"

"I don't know." I didn't.

"Then, you're telling me they didn't break into the house per your instructions?" Her smile was still there. I considered it camouflage.

"I don't know."

The smile deepened. She stared at me for thirty seconds, an eternity in such situations, before saying, "Where did you receive your training, Mr. Harrell?"

I let thirty seconds elapse before I answered, "A defense contractor and the Department of Justice."

Her eyes opened a tiny bit wider. That information wasn't within what she envisioned. She tried to fish for a new starting point. "I missed the name of the contractor. What was it?"

"Advanced Armaments."

"What did you do for them?" Her smile had faded some.

"I can't reveal that. I signed a comprehensive non-disclosure agreement with them."

A slight show of frustration flickered through her smile. She changed direction, "Can you tell me what part of the Department of Justice you worked for?"

"Yes."

"They trained you well. What branch did you work for?" She resumed her work unabashed.

"The Attorney General's office." I watched Nina's effort to show no reaction.

"What did you do for them?" She was working like a sculptor, knocking off a piece at a time.

"I was a special investigator for the AG. I'll save you a couple of questions. I can't discuss what I did for him. If you'd like to confirm that. . . ." I deliberately and slowly reached across the table, removed the pen from her hand, and grabbed the legal pad from in front of her. I wrote a name on the top sheet of paper, and I slid the pad and pen back in front of her. "Contact him."

The name achieved the result I hoped for. The smile disappeared for the first time, but no animosity appeared in the expression that replaced it. Just professional interest. She finally said, "I'll do that, Mr. Harrell." She looked into a file. "Your first name is Slydell?"

"Yes." It was my turn to smile. "I'd prefer Sly."

"Fine. I prefer first names," she said, and Mark nodded.

Patton and Lee, two of the finest generals ever to be in command, believed in offense. I started mine. "Nina, Mark, I know you have a job to do. I have my objectives. They won't conflict, and we may even be able to help each other. I had five minutes on the phone with my friends. Other than knowing they were arrested and tossed in jail, I don't know a thing. Yet!" The less they thought I knew, the more they'd reveal any strategy they might have. I asked, "Can you tell me of what my friends are accused? I might be of some assistance."

Nina looked at me, trying to evaluate the level of sincerity in my words. She made a decision, "Things might work out that way, Sly." She grinned when she said my name. "Appropriate. Look, I have to do some rethinking. Can we come back in a few minutes?"

I nodded. "Better make that an hour; he's always busy. Say hi for me."

"I'll do that," Nina said as she and Mark rose to leave.

"Before you go, may I ask why my friends are being held?"

Nina nodded again, "I'll answer that. They're charged with breaking and entering a residence. They were arrested at the scene."

"Is that the reason for the. . . . I don't know . . . let's call it attention we are all getting? It seems extreme." I didn't expect her to answer, and I was surprised when she did.

"Fair observation, Sly. When you discover two dead bodies in the process of making a breaking and entering arrest, questions arise."

She saw the surprise I couldn't hide, and her smile returned. Nina now knew I didn't know about the bodies before my arrival.

I asked, "What can you tell me about the bodies?"

"Nothing before I go."

CHAPTER 31

When the door reopened, the detectives didn't walk through. Riaffort Richards did. He was accompanied by a young-ish gentlemen whose clothes, demeanor, and swagger screamed *lawyer*. I smiled. Riaffort frowned. He asked, "What are you doing in this room?"

"This is where they brought me when I asked to see the Foxxes."

"They haven't charged you with anything?" Riaffort's buddy asked.

"No. I thought they were bringing me in here to meet with Val and Russ."

Riaffort squinted his eyes, "This is an interrogation room."

"I figured that out after I was in here less than a minute." I pointed to the TV cameras and the microphone. "A couple of detectives talked to me a few minutes." I nodded to Riaffort, "You'd have been proud of me." After a few seconds, I asked, "Who is your friend?"

The man introduced himself, "I'm John Quincy Adams. My parents' misguided sense of humor. I've known Riaffort for years; we've attended several legal seminars together. I practice here in South Carolina."

"I understand." After standing up, I asked, "I assume you came to get me so we can get bail posted for the Foxxes."

"That's done. Did you get a room at the Hilton?" Riaffort motioned for me to exit the bugged area.

"Yes," I said as I pushed through the door.

"Good. I have Val and Russ in an Uber car outside. You accompany them back to the hotel. Wait for John and me in your room."

I nodded, "Do I need to check out with the detectives I was speaking to?"

John laughed, "No, you don't. I'll put it to you the way Riaffort put it to them. *You had a free bite of the apple; the next one is sure to have poison in it.*"

"What are you two going to be doing?" I asked.

"Two things." Riaffort nodded toward the front door of the police station. "First, John and I will have to find out if your friends sitting in the car have dug a hole for themselves and, if so, how deep. Second, I'll find out what I have to do to get their RV out of impound."

"He can find his way out?" John looked at me, and I nodded. He added, "We have to go in the opposite direction."

I asked, "What kind of a car are they in?"

John said, "A red BMW."

"Wow! Maybe I should become an Uber driver up here. The room number is 328. See you guys later."

I headed to the exit, and Nina Dupree intercepted me. Riaffort immediately rushed to catch us both. We came together at the same time.

Nina extended her hand with her business card in it. She said, "In case you want to contact me."

"Madam, we've had this discussion," Riaffort admonished.

"No questions, counselor." As she walked away, she added, "Robert says hi."

"What was that about?" Riaffort asked.

"Riaffort, she was delivering a message to us both. She doesn't quit. Her name is Nina Dupree. She's a razor, not a marble."

"What?"

"I'll explain back at the hotel. You shouldn't keep John Quincy Adams waiting." I started to the door.

"Who is Robert?"

"He's proof you don't play chicken with Nina Dupree."

CHAPTER 32

"It was an experience. One I won't brag to my grands about. Movies and TV shows only have part of it right. You can't smell a picture of a jail." Russ was smiling. The man had the most positive attitude of any human I'd ever encountered. "I'll be turning down any request for a return visit. I'll say this. Of all the individuals they could have stuck me in with, I got the least cruddy of the bunch. The two in my cell were a couple of older, drunk Marines that got in a fight over a broad. The only awful part was avoiding the pools of vomit." Russ never has a short explanation.

"How about you?" I asked Val.

"He is right about the smell. At first, I had a cell to myself. I ended up having a roommate. A hooker. The ten-dollar variety. I was happy I didn't need to use the john after she showed." Val looked like she hadn't slept. Russ looked fresh.

"So let's get into the details. You GPS'd the address of their home after you spoke to both of their ex-employers. When you got there, it was isolated . . . how did you put it, Russ, it was back in a jungle? No neighbor homes in sight. You looked around the house. The doors and windows were boarded up. You found one window with plywood three-fourths off, and you pulled off the board. You saw the furniture. It looked like the people had just walked away. Then you noticed something covered on the floor. When you looked close, you could see bones sticking out from a portion of the blanket.

You decided to break in. By the time you got the boards off the door and inside, you think somebody called the cops. You called also. You had just found the second skeleton when the police arrived. They arrested you. Is my summary correct?"

Val nodded. Russ said, "That's pretty much the way it happened."

"I want to wait until Riaffort and John get back before we get into the details."

Russ bubbled, "I have a few friends I'm going to have some fun with over this. Imagine having a president for a lawyer. John Quincy Adams! He seems like such a nice guy!"

"There's no such thing as a nice lawyer." Val tended to live in the real world.

"Did you find anything of interest inside the house?" I asked.

"We weren't inside more than five minutes when three squad cars arrived. We did a walk through and saw the second skeleton. When we first entered, we noticed an old, rusted shotgun leaning against a wall. That was about it," Russ answered.

Val nodded. "Just guessing, I'd say we were the first humans in there since the whoevers were murdered. I'd add two things. We lifted the blankets. There was a marked difference in size. One was a man. One was probably a woman or a kid. The police showed before I could check the smaller one for gender."

"You said two things, Val," I reminded her.

"Neither of them appeared to have a stitch of clothing on them when they died," she said.

I spoke my thoughts out loud, "Some kind of sex thing?"

Val shrugged her shoulders.

"You're probably right. What else would make sense? I wonder if it was a murder-suicide. Maybe it was an armed invasion. Maybe—" supposed Russ.

"Russ, Russ, button it," Val shook her head. "The Pope would kill the Devil if there wasn't a law against murder. So what?"

I couldn't help laughing. The great thing . . . Russ laughed too.

"Anybody know what happened to Trotter?" I asked.

Riaffort said, "When he dropped me at the police station, he said he was going to visit an old friend at the Marine Corps Air Station; that's out the Trask Highway. He said he'd be back by one."

"He has the Jeep. That leaves us without wheels. Riaffort, are we going to need a vehicle before he gets back?" I asked.

"No. John tells me he should have the RV and the SUV you folks pull behind it out of impound by noon."

Both Foxxes looked relieved.

"What's your schedule?" I asked my lawyer.

"It depends on how John does. We confirmed that the emergency call center recorded Valerie's call to 911 twelve minutes before the squad cars arrived at the house. He's trying to get them to drop the charges. Concerned citizens. . . . that kind of thing. He says it's best if we can get our business done in the precinct and not court. The district attorney is one of those hard-asses that tries to fry everyone." Riaffort saw the alarm in Russ and Val's faces. He quickly added, "My man John Quincy Adams is as good as they get. He said the worst you'd see is a stern talking to and a fine. It's the hassle and legal costs. Sly has that." He looked at me. "Right?"

"Right." I sincerely hoped there was something in the pot at the end of this rainbow and that the gold didn't turn out to be a slop pot. "So do you need to ask any questions of Russ and Val before I do my thing? Do I need to wait for your friend?"

"No and no. It will work better if I ask a question or two as you go through your process. I can tell you, if it comes to going to court, he'll want to interview them himself."

"What do you see as our legal exposure?" I asked.

"I see your primary involvement being that of material witnesses. You know that there is a good chance those skeletons are those of the Sumners. If they are, they'll want to know all about why you were hunting them down."

I took a breath. "I agree, but that is just part of my obvious problem. If those two sets of bones are Helen and Mark Sumner, who in the hell is one of the ladies I'm working for?"

CHAPTER 33

"Let's start with what you found out about Helen's husband," I said and looked at Val and Russ.

Val answered, "I have that one." She opened her laptop and brought up a file. "Let's start with the physical description. He's 6'2" tall and 175 pounds. That's on the thin side. I have a picture of him. Long, thin face, deep-set eyes, thick eyebrows, long neck, big nose—he's a kind of Abe Lincoln-looking type of guy. They have dental records, so if it is. . . ." She shrugged her shoulders. "Mark Sumner had been in the Corps for thirty months before he came here. Camp Pendleton was his previous station. He was assigned to the engineers. I had a chance to speak to two administrative people that actually knew him. Honestly, neither could remember much. Both said he was a low-maintenance Marine. Kept to himself. Never got in trouble. One of them thought he'd be a lifer until Helen showed up from his hometown. They got serious, got married, and he got out. He took a job with a local manufacturing company."

"Were you able to visit them?"

Val nodded, "Yes. I got a similar story there. He worked for a Mr. Jacobson. Came to work every day, on time, did a great job, and went home. No problems or hassles. He was an excellent machinist, and Jacobson offered him the foreman's job in their machine shop. Sumner turned it down, said he was happy doing what he did. Then, out-of-the-blue, Sumner called in one morning, left a message with the receptionist that he had a family emergency, said he'd be gone and didn't know if he'd be back. They never saw or heard from him again. That was sixteen years ago."

"Did anyone you talked to remember his wife?" I asked.

"Not well. Jacobson remembered she was good-looking. One of the Marine folks said Helen was very friendly and outgoing. The woman I talked to there also said she was a *head-turner*. Nothing past that."

I turned to Russ, "You do Helen?"

"Yep. I couldn't find much about Helen's first two years up here. One of the restaurants she worked at is gone. No one remembered her at the other one. I did find out that she shared a room with two other girls. I got their names and the apartment address from the dentist. He's a cool guy. I haven't followed up on that lead. Trying to run them down won't be easy. But, but, but, I got a load of information from Dr. Sparknagel. He remembers her well, and he remembers her fondly." It was Russ' turn to get into his computer files. After a few seconds, he said, "Helen Sumner worked for him for five years, plus or minus. He hired her right out of school. Within eighteen months, she was the best hygienist that ever worked for him. We did a Skype conference; he's moved to Columbia. He sent a picture of her." He spun the laptop around so I could see.

Helen Sumner was a stunningly beautiful young lady . . . and *not* the Helen Sumner I was working with! I shook my head and said, "Houston, we have a problem. I'm working with an imposter."

"I thought so," Val added.

"What else do you have, Russ?" I asked.

"Plenty, but I don't believe much of it will mean a lot to you. The most important thing I can say is how she quit. It is a carbon copy of what Val told you about Mark. She emailed the office saying she had a family emergency and didn't think she'd be returning to work. Lots of apologies and such, so Sparknagel didn't question it. He said they sent her last paycheck to her forwarding address, and it came back as undeliverable. The doc did her dental work. I didn't ask if he kept her records, but I would imagine so." He paused, waiting for my signal for more.

"The way both quit . . . that's no coincidence that neither showed in person. Anyone want to make odds on those skeletons not being Helen and Mark Sumner?" Russ was anxiously waiting to unload the rest of his work. I nodded, "Okay, Russ, what else do you have?"

"Personal life stuff. The doc knew her husband, Mark. He called him a mute church-mouse. He met him several times, liked the guy a lot. Sparknagel said Mark coached a little league team, though the couple didn't have children. He mentioned that Helen had a great singing voice. She sang the national anthem at some tournament games. She was a good actress too. Both she and Mark were very active in a little theater group. He couldn't remember which one. She played parts, he made sets—that kind of thing."

"I think that's all I need right now," I said. Riaffort hadn't said anything. "You're quiet. Why no questions?" I asked.

"There aren't any to ask. I see a way forward on the part I'm involved with. We can do some horse-trading with the police department and extract Russ and Val from their problem. As far as your situation with whoever is masquerading as Helen Sumner back in Florida, good luck."

"Thanks, old friend." The sarcasm in my tone was evident. "You plan on trading some information on the imposter for a get out of jail free card for the Foxxes?"

"Absolutely."

"I want to be involved with those discussions, Riaffort. Remember, I have another client who I suspect is a dupe in all this. I want to protect her and her interests. We've verified her bloodlines."

Riaffort leaned backward. "I thought you told me you had done that on Helen Sumner."

"We did. We found a glitch; that's why we're here," I said, then added, "It's a damned good thing we did."

There was a knock at the hotel room door, and Trotter's muffled voice filtered through, "Open the damned door!"

When I pulled it open, Trotter stood with a cup carrier full of coffee in one hand and two large boxes of donuts in the other. I asked, "I thought you were visiting a friend?"

"I was."

"What's all that?" He had enough to feed a Marine platoon.

"*We're* hungry."

We sat waiting for news from John about Russ and Val's vehicles' release, discussing the information the Foxxes had just presented, when Russ mentioned Helen Sumner's participation in the area little theater. Trotter volunteered, "I might be able to get you some information on that. The person I just saw does that kind of thing. She's too young to have known the Sumners, but I bet she would know someone who worked with them. Would you like me to make a call and see if she can make a connection?"

"Yes, I sure would! From what Russ said, they had a good part of their life invested in that. We can pick up some valuable info easier than I expected," I said.

Riaffort asked, "Are you going to follow that lead?"

"Yes, and the little league team also." I took a deep breath. "I'm sure all this has a direct effect on what I'm trying to accomplish."

CHAPTER 34

"Tell me again why we're meeting in an IHOP," I asked.

"It's close to the Laurel Bay Navy Base. My friend doesn't have far to drive." Trotter changed lanes. He was driving the Jeep, and that made me nervous. Trotter was a frustrated NASCAR driver at heart.

"Do better," I insisted.

"It's located close to the murder scene." He added, "Thought you'd want to visit."

"We probably couldn't get inside if we go see it. Do better."

Trotter grinned, "How about, Ann—that's my friend—is introducing us to the lady who manages it."

"Better," I admitted.

"Believe it or not, all my actions aren't a function of my stomach," Trotter's face was covered with a one-up smirk.

I countered, "I agree. The rest is made by the region fifteen to twenty inches lower on your front side." I changed the subject. "Tell me about this Ann. Is she in the Marines?"

"No. She's Navy. Graduated from Annapolis. She runs an office of computer geeks at Laurel Bay. That's a Navy and Marine housing facility."

"Somehow I don't believe you're interested in her knowledge of Microsoft."
Trotter didn't answer.

"Well?" I prodded.

He careened the CJ-5 across two lanes, drawing a chorus of honks from offended drivers. He mumbled, "Don't distract me."

"You are easily distracted. . . . Well?"

He put his signal on and turned into the IHOP. After he parked the Jeep, Trotter told me, "Ann's car is here. You'll see when you meet her." He led me into the restaurant.

The only female naval officer stood up at the table she occupied. She stood up, and up, and up. She wore heels that made her four inches taller than the 6'4" Trotter. He said in a voice just above a whisper, "She has the longest, prettiest legs I've ever seen!"

My eyes asked the question.

He said, "No, never. She's a friend. But I won't say I haven't thought about it."

As we approached, she walked to us and said, "Right on time. That must be due to you, Mr. Harrell. I've never had a date or meeting with Ken when he wasn't a little late." She extended a long, graceful arm tipped by a set of two-octave, slim fingers. "I'm Ann DeVore. Margie asked me to bring you back to her office. We won't be as interrupted there. If there is anything to know about The Port Royal Thespians, she'll know it. She's been active with them for thirty-four years." Ann opened the glass panel to Marjorie M. Spelling's office. It said so on the door.

"What would you like to know?" The pleasantly plump woman sitting behind her desk was in her fifties, with a twinkle in her eyes and a smile on her lips. After introductions, Ann said, "I can't add a thing here, and I'm swamped at the office. Do you mind if I leave?" She was gone before we finished shooing her off. Trotter and I were in what would prove to be Margie's capable hands.

"We're trying to find out about a person we're looking for and her husband." I opened a file folder for effect. "Their names were Helen and Mark Sumner." ·

"I remember them so well. They were lovely people. Helen . . . she was so talented. She could sing, dance, and act. We hated to see them go." She shook her head, and she exhibited a sense of loss. "I'll tell you all I remember."

"Could you tell me where they went after they left Beaufort?" I asked.

"No, Mr. Harrell, I can't. Their departure was so sudden and so unexplained. It was a great mystery. One day they were in here, happy as could be, working on sets and rehearsing. The following day when they came in, it looked like the Sword of Damocles had fallen on them. I asked Helen what was wrong, and she said they had some unexpected, horrible problems. They didn't show for the next rehearsal. We never saw the Sumners again. Several of us tried to contact them. Within a few days, their phone was disconnected. I even tried to find out where they were and if they were okay by asking their *friends*, a couple named Tedder. The Tedders said their house was boarded up. That was strange. Mark was proud of that place. He bought it cheap and fixed it up. Mark said he didn't owe a cent on it and bragged about that. I was surprised he didn't sell it. That's according to the Tedders."

The expression on Margie's face told me all I needed to know about her opinion of the Tedders. She continued, "All I got from them was about how terrible the Sumners' problem was, and they had to go where no one would find them. Gretchen Tedder and Helen were friends. They looked a lot alike; Gretchen was Helen's understudy in several plays. They wore the same size, so it made costumes easy. Harvey Tedder and Mark got on, but that's all. Harvey did save Mark from a beating."

"Tell me about that," I said.

"The Tedders joined our little theater with another couple. Thelma was nice, but Harn . . . that man was the Devil come up to the surface. They, both couples, moved here from Monroe, North Carolina about a year before they all left. Helen, Thelma, and Gretchen were the three Musketeers for a while. I think there was some jealousy there between Gretchen and Helen. Helen was so much better, and Gretchen was permanent second fiddle. Anyway, Harn started hitting on Helen, Mark saw what was happening, and he punched out Harn. Harn picked up a pry bar, came up behind Mark, and would have whacked him on the head. Harvey tackled Harn before he could hit Mark. That was six months before they disappeared. They got back to speaking, but it was strained all around."

"When you say disappeared, did you mean just the Sumners or all of the couples?"

"They didn't disappear at the same time. The Sumners left, and both the other couples said they were going home to Monroe three weeks later."

"What was Thelma and Harn's last name?"

Margie squinted her eyes closed. She said, "If you hadn't asked me, I could have volunteered it. Let me think!" Suddenly, her eyes opened wide. "I remember. Harn always claimed his name was fitting because his daddy was a funeral director and had a crematory. Crisp. Harn's last name was Crisp."

CHAPTER 35

"It should be ahead on the left," Trotter said. He pointed to a green street sign. "That's it. Sandfly Road."

Traffic parted for us as I guided my Jeep down the road into an area that reminded me of coastal Carolina before man left his footprint. Low sandhills covered with oaks, pines, and palmettoes, blended with wetlands . . . swamps and reed marsh. Swaying Spanish moss universally draped the trees. It had been, and is, a remarkably beautiful land in areas where man hadn't left ugly scars.

"According to the GPS, it should be on the left down about seven-tenths of a mile." I took another glance at the Garmin. The indicator was steadily closing on our destination. I asked Trotter, "What did Russ tell you to look for?" Very few houses sat scattered along the road.

"A house on the right side of the road with a wishing well in front. That's a hundred yards before the drive." Trotter added, "The rest is heavy woods."

In less than thirty seconds, the wishing well came into view. I asked, "What's next?"

"Left side, next driveway."

"Damn, Trotter, anything else?"

"Russ said it was dirt, went into a jungle, and you couldn't see any buildings from the road." Long explanations were a waste in Trotter's mind.

We passed the wishing well, and we saw the driveway disappearing into a wall of oaks and underbrush. I slowed the Jeep to a crawl, then pulled onto the shoulder across from the dirt road. Nature was working to reclaim it; small palmettoes, weeds, and a solitary pine sapling encroached.

"Don't think we can go back there," Trotter said and pointed to the bright yellow crime scene tape crisscrossing from fence posts on either side of the drive. Parked a hundred feet down the dirt road was a police car. That sealed the deal—no exploring for us.

I observed, "Russ is right. Unless you knew there is a house back there, you'd think this is a farm lane. That's really thick vegetation."

Trotter nodded, "It's way back in there."

"Russ said there are three acres, and the house is in the middle of it. If the brush is this thick all around it, those bodies could have been there forever. No one would know anything is back there." *No Trespassing* signs were nailed to the fence posts. Though badly faded, they remained deterrents.

"Val said there's a swamp behind the house," Trotter said as he nudged me with his elbow. "We're going to have company." He tilted his head to the rear of the Jeep.

An old lady peddled an adult tricycle down the road. Her eyes focused on us, and she generated some speed for the vehicle she rode. Her white hair was covered with a beaten-up straw hat; she was skinny and had leathery, tanned skin. She didn't look or sound happy when she shouted at us, "What are you two a-doing out here?"

Trotter said to me, "I'm in charge of handling grannies."

"Fine by me."

Trotter said, "Morning, ma'am."

When she stopped behind the Jeep, she hopped off her trike with a spryness that belied what indeed were her eighty years. She strolled to the passenger side of the Jeep, put her hands on her hips, and glared at us. She said, "Well?" through clenched teeth.

"Sorry if we disturbed you, ma'am. We had some friends that came out here and got arrested through a mix-up. We're just curious to see the spot." Trotter smiled, and his tone was apologetically friendly.

"You can thank me for their arrest. You done seen the spot. Move your asses along." I hoped she didn't have a concealed weapon.

"Ma'am, our friends didn't intend any harm. They were trying to help the Sumners." Trotter's smile remained in neon.

The lady's face and attitude changed at the mention of the Sumners' name, but some caution remained. She asked, "You know the Sumners? What are their first names?"

"Helen and Mark." Trotter's mask stayed frozen.

"Well then, I'm truly sorry I got them in trouble." She sounded contrite.

Trotter said, "Our names. He's Slydell, and I'm Ken. We're from Florida, where the Sumners *are* originally from. Ma'am, I'd like to know who is obviously a friend of a friend."

"Emily Busby." She laughed. "The folk around call me Amma Busy-body. Yes, I was a friend. They was good neighbors. Kept to themselves most times. But always brought me strawberries when they picked them, that kind of thing. I loved Helen like a daughter."

I asked, "Have you lived here long?"

"Here on Sandfly Road, forty years. I was born in Charleston. My parents moved here when I was six. I've lived in Beaufort ever since."

"Do you know anything about people that visited them?" I asked.

"You cops or something?"

"We're a private firm that does research to find things," I answered.

"People too?"

I nodded to avoid a verbal lie.

"They're dead, aren't they?" The old lady's eyes moistened.

"We don't know. Not at this point." The look in her eyes told me more than her words. "You've talked to the police, haven't you? Did they tell you anything?"

"Yes. The police said they found something in the house but wouldn't say more than that. It has to be bodies. I'm old, not dumb. There were reporters out here earlier today. They come a knocking on my door. I didn't tell them shit. They told me the policewoman in charge kept telling them 'no comment.' Those reporter people are all vultures anyway."

She wiped an age-withered hand across her face and added, "You asked a question. Helen and Mark didn't have a lot of company. They was four or five couples that visited now and then. I don't know who they was except for two of the men. Reason I know them is they showed up here a couple days after the Sumners left . . . or something. They came to board up the place, leastways, that's what one of them told me. We exchanged names. I remember his because it was the same as one of my favorite pictures, *Harvey.* I always loved Jimmy Stewart. Anyway, his name was Harvey Tedder. He seemed nice enough. The other one. . . . I didn't like that smart-assed bastard one bit. His name was Harn. I remember thinking Harm would have been better. He called me some bad names and tried running me off. You think he had any luck doing that?"

Trotter said, "Ma'am, I'd give ten-to-one odds he didn't."

"You'd be right. Anyway, it was then that the nicer one told me the Sumners had gotten in serious trouble and had to leave the state for a while. He said I'd be doing them a favor if I acted dumb if anyone asked me about them. Dumb me. That's what I did for years. Really, no one has looked for them until now."

I said, "Emily, you did what you thought was right."

"Thank you, but I won't feel less bad." She stood up straight as she could. Her face contorted into one of pure anger. "I know you boys can't tell me, but I just know they are dead. Bless their souls. I want you to find who did it and stick a stake in their hearts for me."

CHAPTER 36

"That's what we found out on our little excursion this morning." My gin and tonic admonished my tongue for drinking early in the day. I sat in the Hilton bar with John Quincy Adams, Riaffort Richards, Trotter, Russ, and Val. "My question to you legal eagles is what is my exposure if I don't pass on the information to the police I've learned today?"

"If you were in Florida, you'd have none past your ethics and conscience," Riaffort said. "You're not a licensed private investigator. No one can extort you using your license as a lever. You're in one of those pleasant cracks that go undetected in our legal system. What you do is unique . . . at least for now. There's nothing in Florida law that forces a private citizen or a business to share information with the state about things you know, legal or illegal." Riaffort looked at John. "South Carolina?"

"I believe the same holds true. In this case, anyway. If a known felony is committed and there is an active search for the suspect, withholding information can be aiding and abetting if the holder of the information is cognizant that there is a crime and that the legal authorities are engaged in ascertaining evidence or apprehension. You have no knowledge of any warrants or other legal documents." John looked at me, his eyes asking if I understood.

I opened my eyes wide and shrugged my shoulders.

"He told you . . . no," Riaffort clarified. He looked at me and asked, "What is your reason for *not* telling them everything? It seems to me to simplify your problems. Let them swoop down on the obstacles for you. How do you benefit by delaying?"

"I don't benefit. I avoid a disaster," I said. "I'm practicing the advice you always give me, remember? Never assume, never presume?"

Riaffort blinked and looked at me quizzically.

"Think. We have two bodies in a house that belonged to the folks we're trying to find. Are they Helen and Mark Sumner? Probably. Are we sure? No. What if some of the things we've discovered here and events back in Florida are coincidences? There is the possibility the lady I've been working with *is* Helen Sumner. I doubt that, but it exists. There's an even stronger possibility that the idiot driving around in the black HUMV taking potshots at me isn't connected to Harn Crisp or Harvey Tedder. Or if they are, and some law enforcement agency starts hunting them, my bet is they'll get more violent. I don't see them giving up on finding what they're looking for. There is another good ethical reason. Ellen O'Neal. If the authorities start hunting whoever is play-acting as Helen and Mark for murder, and they become aware of that, how much would the old lady's life be worth? I don't want that on my conscience."

"Directed verdict for the man with the irrefutable argument." John Quincy Adams held his drink up. "To what makes you smile."

"That all sounds good. Your logic is perfect. Remember, I have to bargain with those detectives. I need to be able to give them something. That is, unless you want the Foxxes sharing cells with Beaufort's societal rejects." Riaffort had the last word; he usually did.

CHAPTER 37

"What's your plan?" Riaffort asked as we entered the Beaufort Police Station. "I'm playing this by ear," I answered.

Riaffort clutched my arm with one of his strong, black claws. "Whoa! We aren't doing that. You said you'd have something ready as bargaining chips."

"Relax. I have a strategy. Nina Dupree is sharp. If we go in to negotiate with her, with one thing in mind, we lose." I stopped and smiled at him. He's a cautious and prudent man, and that makes him such a great lawyer. "I want to give up as little as possible now. I'm going to see if she has something in mind before I offer her anything I don't have to."

Riaffort stood motionless as he evaluated what I'd just communicated. Finally, he said, "I know you well enough to be confident you won't do anything that will get you or your friends in serious trouble. But if I see you heading into water that might have sharks in it, I'm going to call for a conference with you. No arguments, no stalling—we're out of whatever room we meet in. Agreed?"

"Agreed."

When we looked up, Nina Dupree was walking to us. Her greeting was friendly. "Hello, gentlemen. I have the conference room reserved. It's more comfortable than one of our interrogation rooms."

I asked, "Have you two met? Formally?"

"Yes, we have," Nina said, "Counselor Richards, are you having a good day?"

"Thank you for asking. Our meeting will help determine that, won't it, Detective Dupree? Is your day going well?" Riaffort enjoyed the sport of jab and parry he had with any verbal jousters.

The detective ushered us through an open door into a large room with a huge oval oak table in its center. I counted twelve over-stuffed chairs circling it. She closed the door after we entered. Riaffort glanced at me. We were both surprised no one was there from the district attorney's office, even if just as an observer. She said, "Please have a seat."

What happened next rattled me in a subtle way. The opening of the meeting quickly became a test of wills. We sat in silence. No one wanted to start the conversation. I could feel tension building; I knew that was her intent, and I tried to blow off her strategy without success. I succumbed, "Can we discuss what we're here for?"

"And that is?" she said. It wasn't a question as much as a challenge.

"We agreed in our phone conversation to see what could be done to clear up my friends' involvement in something closer to a misunderstanding than a misdemeanor." *Pompous ass*, I called myself as I talked like a lawyer.

"You want me to?" Nina was on the offense, and I was patching my defense without realizing it.

"I want you to drop the charges for breaking and entering for the Foxxes."

Nina didn't say a word. She smiled and waved her hand for me to continue.

"Russ and Val were up here on an assignment from me. I can assure you we had no idea that we'd find corpses."

"What did you expect to find?" she asked.

"Russ and Val were trying to. . . ." the lady detective had me. "You told me I'm good, Mrs. Dupree; you're better."

"It's Ms. Dupree." Nina stopped smiling. "I'm a reasonable person. I'll give if I get. We can shorten this process if we end the game. Why were your people trying to find the Sumners?"

"I have a client that is trying to recover something that is theirs. Helen Sumner could have vital information in recovering it." I told a half-truth.

"What are you trying to recover?" Nina asked.

"An inheritance."

"Consisting of what?"

I smiled, "That's confidential. I can assure you it has nothing directly to do with your case. We are trying to trace the Sumners forward. This is a blank spot."

Nina pounced, "A blank spot—that means you must have done research on Helen Sumner after she left here." She paused. "Or didn't."

Caught! "Look, we are trying to determine the identity of a couple people, all in relation to recovering that inheritance. We hope that will clarify problems in our effort to find the damned thing."

"And those folks may or may not be the same ones that had something to do with what happened out on Sandfly Road? You don't have to answer that. I know that is a possibility." Nina leaned back in her seat and placed her hands behind her head. "You don't want to spook whoever is creating problems for you. You want time; it's yours. I want all the names and information you uncover in, say, three weeks. I'll even confirm who those corpses are and pass it along to you. Our forensic people will have that done inside of two weeks."

"June 1. My project is time-sensitive."

"Those skeletons have been there for years. A little more time won't hurt. Just don't you spook them until I'm in position to sweep them up. You have a deal." Nina stood up and extended her hand.

"And . . . you'll drop the charges against Russ and Valerie Foxx?" I wanted confirmation.

"Why, I dropped them early this morning. We checked, and their call to 911 came in simultaneously with the one from the neighbor. It really wouldn't make sense for them to report a murder they committed. They are as free as a bird dog with a broken leash."

Riaffort laughed loud and said, "Sly, you've been had."

We stood, and I said, "It was a pleasure, I think."

"Mutual," Nina said, then added, "One last thing. Those skeletons did tell us something already . . . . after just a quick look. Those poor devils had a bad end. They were tortured. Most of their fingers were broken, things like that. The woman's neck was broken, and they think she was filleted with a knife from damage to her arms and legs. He was shot in the face with a shotgun. Close range. If the individuals who did this are the people you are facing, I'd be very careful."

CHAPTER 38

The road noise was too loud to hear Clareen's voice through my cell. I pulled the Jeep into a rest area on busy I-95 and called her. Evidently, she was in a hurry. She didn't bother with a greeting. "Where are you now?"

"On the interstate. Just across the Florida line."

"You need to call Jenny Dorr from some historical place in Arcadia. Do you have her number?" Clareen asked.

"Yes, I have it. Do you know what she wants?"

"She wasn't very coherent. The woman said something about a man named Burrows and the sheriff's office. They found Burrows' body." Clareen shuffled her notes. "She said, and this is a quote, 'I told the sheriff about our discussion, and he'll want to talk to Mr. Harrell.' She said she needed to speak to you before the sheriff did. You going to call her?"

"I'll call after I get back," I said.

"You also had a call from some girl named Lily Hays. She says she has you set up with her mother, whatever that means. She also said her mother told her that there were five graveyards in the area that the Sumners were buried in, but she thought the Sumner you would be looking for could only be in one of two." Clareen chuckled. "Lily told me to say *hey* to Trotter. You two double dating now?"

"Funny. I see enough of Trotter's ugly face every day. Besides, Lily's mother is a church historian," I answered.

"*Funny*. When I asked for a phone number where you could reach the church historian, Lily gave me the number and name. The Dancing Dears? An exotic dance club? What's the church? The Chapel of the Bouncing Bed Spring?"

I ignored her quip. "Anything else?"

"Nothing that can't wait."

"Clareen, you can be replaced." I tried to sound serious.

She laughed. "No way! Are you coming to the office or going straight to the ranch?"

"To the ranch."

"You can tell me all about skeletons, president lawyers, and the lady detective who infected you with clown disease. Be ready when you come in here. When will that be?"

"Day after tomorrow, unless one of the calls causes me to do otherwise." I shook my head and asked, "Who did you talk to?"

"Riaffort, Trotter, and Russ . . . all three. Of course, Russ was the most complete."

CHAPTER 39

There's nothing more settling, at least for me, than sleeping in my bed after an absence. The morning sun filtered through my bedroom windows and illuminated tiny dust particles floating in the air. I stretched and yawned. Judging from the amount of sunlight, it was a lot later than my usual time of awakening.

I swung my legs out of bed, stumbled to my clothes chest, and removed underwear and shorts. Cindy would be in with coffee for me, and it wouldn't be good form for me to be bare assed when she knocked. The door to the veranda beckoned, and I stepped onto the eight-foot-wide 'porch' surrounding my home. My coffee and a donut sat on a table next to my favorite chair. That explained why there was no knock from Cindy. I sat down to enjoy coffee, a donut, and the view of nature from my porch.

Two ospreys were encouraging their two offspring to leave the nest for a fishing lesson, one they must learn if they hoped to survive. Various pond birds paraded around the mini lake that circles my house. Great Blue Herons, an egret, and a white crane waded a foot from shore in the shallow water. Every so often, one would spear an unsuspecting fish. Breakfast was served. Turtle heads bobbed in the mirror-placid waters. The persistent tapping noise led my eyes to a pileated woodpecker probing a dead pine for grubs. A vile tempered banded water snake swam through lily-pads and cattails as it decided to change sides of the pond. A chorus of red-winged blackbirds announced the snake's departure, and I was sure another chorus would greet its arrival.

Gentle scratching at my bedroom door reminded me I'd forgotten one of my best friends. As I opened the door, Mandy, my ninety-pound golden retriever, bounced—and that is the proper description—out the door.

"Hi, baby girl! You glad to see me?" Her brown eyes told me she was. Mandy is not a barker. "Want to go for a walk?" I asked.

There was no reason to ask twice. Mandy bounded down the stairs to the yard and stood waiting for me. My bare feet touched the dew-damp grass. The feel of the vegetation and the sand under it confirmed I was home; I was safe.

"Do you want orange juice this morning?" Cindy asked as she placed a breakfast tray on my desk. The three-egg omelet, biscuits, and sausage links were one of seven offerings Cindy prepared on any given morning. I use the time when I eat to check my emails and reply to those that require answers. A fresh pot of coffee was next to the plate containing my omelet. I admit to being a coffeeholic. I'm sure the pathologist will be shocked when my autopsy discovers my kidneys have been replaced by two large coffee beans.

"No, Cindy, what I've got here is fine." I thought for a second and asked, "Has Trotter called or been here this morning?"

"No, Sly, but Clareen called and wants you to call her."

I sighed and removed a pad. Enough different tasks needed handling to require a 'to-do list.' "Okay. Have we heard from the Foxxes?"

"They haven't called or been over, but Willie said their RV is back on the pad, and the lights were on when he came to work this morning. He said to tell you he ran off a couple men who were parked out by the gate on Lake Marian Road."

"Did he say what kind of vehicle they were driving?"

"No, Sly, I'll ask him if you want. He's out moving cows to different pastures. I can get him on the radio," Cindy said.

"That's okay. When he comes back in, ask him for me."

"One more thing. Some man from the DeSoto County Sheriff's office called. He asked if you were in. Since you were walking Mandy, I told him no. When I asked him if he wanted you to call back, the man said no. That surprised me, so I wrote the number the phone call came from, and I checked to see if it was the sheriff's department. As far as I can tell, it isn't. Maybe Russ or Valerie can track it down." Cindy removed a slip of paper from her pocket and placed it on my tray.

"That's great, Cindy," I responded. She loves applause.

She beamed, "Anything else you want?"

"Nope, go do your thing." I slid the pad in front of me and began thinking and writing. There were lots of things that needed doing. Quickly!

Three items were scratched off the to-do list. The fun things on it were gone. I looked at what was left.

Call Jenny Dorr (Call DeSoto County Sheriff's office?)

Call Clareen

Call church historian (Set up visit)

Call Russ and Val

Set up a meeting with Helen Sumner or whoever it is

The rest of the day would be a busy, testing one.

"I'm sorry, Mr. Harrell. I was so shocked when the deputy told me they'd found Mr. Burrows' body, I stopped thinking straight." I could visualize tears in Jenny Dorr's eyes from the sound of her voice. She'd told me she'd given them my name when they asked her if she knew anyone who might know something about the case. "I realized I'd made a mistake before all the words got out. I tried to tell them I was sure you weren't involved in any way. But once you open your big fat mouth, there's no taking it back. I wanted to talk to you before you called them or they called you. Honest, I didn't say anything that would make them think you were part of what happened."

I asked, "Did they tell you anything about Mr. Burrows' murder, other than they found his body?"

"Yes. Enough to upset me and to scare the living shit out of me! Oh, I'm sorry about the language." Jenny paused, gathering courage before she told me the rest. "They said they found his body floating in the Peace River between Arcadia and Wauchula. I made the mistake of asking how he died. The deputy told me his throat was slit. He told me it was cut so deep it wouldn't have taken much more to cut his head off. I'm sure I know why they told me that. Right afterward, Deputy Freeman told me I'd best tell them all I knew so they could catch the killer so that I didn't end up the same way. If he wanted to frighten me, he did. But there's nothing else for me to tell him."

"You told him about the work you did on the pioneer family and graves?" I asked.

"Yes, I did." I heard Jenny take a deep breath. "Mr. Harrell, they asked for your phone number, and I told them I forgot it. They made me promise I'd tell you to call them when you called back here."

"I'll call them. Since I don't have any involvement, there's nothing for me to worry about from the sheriff. You certainly don't."

"Then you're not mad at me?"

"Certainly not!"

"I'm glad. I was worried you'd be upset with me dragging you into this horrid mess."

"You don't give another thought to that." I hesitated. Jenny was in danger if whoever committed Burrows' murder thought she might know who they were . . . or about the graves they hadn't learned of from Burrows. She needed to know. "Jenny, are you married?"

"No. Divorced."

"Do you live with anyone?"

I heard apprehension enter her voice. "No. Why are you asking these questions?"

"I don't want to worry you, but I think you should take a few precautions to be extra safe. You can see how vicious the people behind Burrows' death are."

"Do you think they'll come after me?" There was full-blown panic in her voice.

"No. This is a *just in case* type thing. You need to avoid going places where you're isolated. Try to do things with two or more friends. If you don't have to go out at night, don't. Don't be paranoid about this . . . but look for the same strange people showing up at places over and over. Same is true of vehicles."

There was quiet. Finally, Jenny's shaky voice said, "I thought it was my imagination, but a car keeps showing up everywhere I go."

"What kind of car?"

"I'm not sure of the name. The vehicle is big. I think it's one of those things that replaced the Jeep in the military."

"The HUMV?"

"Yes! That's it."

Her danger just rose! I asked, "What color is it?"

"Black."

I added an item to my to-do list.

CHAPTER 40

Trotter stood in front of my desk. I said, "Whoever is looking for old Sam Sumner's gold is one evil crew. I feel responsible for the safety of Jenny Dorr, even though those killers contacted her before I did. The only reason that they could be keeping tabs on her is that they believe she knows something that will help them. Who knows what Burrows told them when he saw he was going to die? He could have made up something hoping to spare his life."

"When do I go? Do you want me actually to stay with her or shadow her?"

"You go now. Shadow her. I don't want you to play Rambo. Not unless there's no alternative. Keep in the weeds, so to speak. If they show up, stay close enough to protect Jenny if they attempt to abduct her. They'll want her alive to get information. If they do that, put enough lead in them that the authorities will need a crane to pick up the bodies."

Trotter nodded, "I'll need a MAC-10 and three or four clips. My Colt .45 is fine for a secondary. How about lending me one of your equalizers?" Trotter was talking about a weapon of my invention. It is a slicing blade mounted horizontally on brass knuckles. It is worn like a set of knuckles, making it almost impossible to disarm. A five-inch spike extends from the end opposite to the thumb . . . and that functions as a knife. The blade will cut an inch-and-a-half groove in anyone attacking. It's excellent for cutting carotid arteries. A series of ten or so foot-long slices down to bone is very effective in ending aggressiveness in anyone attacking you. Unlike a knife, it leaves the hand available to steady a rifle or hold a grenade.

"Sure," I said.

Trotter smiled, "Don't worry. A shoot 'em up is *the* last alternative." He hesitated, then asked, "What if they don't show?"

"Give them three days. But they will show."

Trotter said, "I hope you're wrong."

"The best possible situation is for you to get in a position to set them up and get the DeSoto County Sheriff's Department to do the heavy lifting."

Trotter looked at me, shook his head, and said, "I don't see how."

"A couple phone calls and you being in the right place at the right time. I'll explain."

CHAPTER 41

"I thought you dumped us in a hole you weren't going to be able to get us out of." Russ shook his head. He smiled and added, "I spent a whole day discussing your parentage with Val. Right?"

"He did. I almost agreed with him for a while. You came through. What's next?" Val was always ready for another adventure.

We sat on my veranda. The midday sun had banished wildlife to the bushes and shade. They were seeking shelter from what they knew *would* happen. My reason for the meeting with Russ and Val was to gather information about what *could* happen. Preparing for the difference between would and could is immense.

"Good question, Val. This thing has made a major turn from a Tom Sawyer style treasure hunt to an Indiana Jones cloak and dagger. I seriously thought of just bowing out. I can't do that. I've involved innocent people, and I still represent at least one innocent person in Ellen O'Neal. I can't completely discount the fact that the person I know as Helen Sumner could be the real one. I doubt it, but until I hear from Detective Dupree up in Beaufort, I can't be sure. So I'm committed. We all need to hope the treasure's size proves the rumors about it are true."

"What's next?" Val asked.

"As I see it, I want to do something to sidetrack or eliminate the competition. Who is the competition? That's a good question. I want to start by determining if the people we knew were associates of the Sumners when they lived in South Carolina are involved. They were extremely violent back then. Whoever we're dealing with now is extremely violent. I don't believe it's coincidence. Plus, there are some 'name' connections."

Russ narrowed his eyes and tilted his head. "Name connections? You've lost me."

I sighed and said, "I need to explain. In some of the research I've done with the historical societies and museums, one name, Crisp, came up several times. The Crisps were undertakers."

"The stories you told us." Russ' eyes lit. "The old ladies told you one of the men in the little theater and the one that boarded up the Sumners' house was named Crisp. His father was a funeral director. That definitely is no frigging coincidence!"

Valerie was already writing notes. She asked, "What was Crisp's first name?"

"Harn. Harn Crisp." I held my hand up and added, "There is one other thing that is not as direct of a connection, but it sure looks promising. When I spoke to the DeSoto Historical Society lady, she mentioned the Tedders as being a long-standing name in the community. There were a lot of gravestones in the cemetery there . . . with Tedder carved into them. The other couple's name was Tedder. They both came from the same community in North Carolina. See where I'm going?"

"Oh, yeah, I sure do," Russ' voice rose an excited octave. "Trailing something for over a hundred years. . . . Wow! That requires a strong belief and *a big pot of gold* at the end of the rainbow."

"Names?" Val asked.

"The Crisp's first names were Thelma and Harn. The other couple's last name was Tedder. Gretchen was the wife's name. Harvey, the husband."

"Do you know their ages?" Russ asked.

"No, I don't. The way the lady from the little theater talked, I got the impression they hung around together. It is a guess, but I'm thinking that should make them close to the same ages." I hesitated for a second, then asked, "Does that give you enough information to launch a search?"

Russ said, "Sure."

Valerie remained quiet before asking, "Can you give us the theater lady's name and contact information? That makes it a hell of a lot easier."

"I don't think it will be a problem, but I'll phone her and get permission for you to call. Val, if you can go after that info, I have something else I'd like you to undertake, Russ."

"Sure. What do you want?"

"I want you to put that imagination of yours in high gear and take a copy of the note Ellen O'Neal gave us. Try to find the maximum number of clues you can and pass the list to me when you finish. This thing is complex, and I don't want to miss something."

"That's not a job; that will be fun." Russ leaned toward me. "You have a copy with you?"

I shook my head, "I'll get Clareen to fax a copy to us later this morning."

"What kind of copy is it? A typed copy of the original? Is it a copy made on a copier? Do you have a copy of the original backside, even if it looks blank?" Russ' sharp mind expanded the parameter where clues might be hidden.

"What Helen gave me is a typed copy of the original. She said it is an exact copy." Russ made an observation I'd completely missed. The words typed on the sheet might only contain part of the keys to the mystery. Once you opened your mind to the possibilities, the potential was enormous. My mind seized upon a few: invisible ink, folds of the paper to read a different message, markings on the back indicating a sequence of words on the front, etc.

I looked at Russ in a way to acknowledge he'd already opened a path to success I hadn't envisioned, and he grinned. He said, "I'll do the best I can, but you'll need to get the original before we'll know all the note can tell you."

"Speaking of telling you," Val opened her laptop, "I have some answers to questions you asked earlier. I can put them on a flash drive?" I reached for a legal pad. She continued, "Or we can go over what I have, and you can exercise your fingers."

I smiled and said, "Enlighten me, oh goddess of the record piles."

Val was already pulling up her files. "First item you wanted to know was if Helen was married to the proper part of the family. A part that directly descended from old Sam Sr. I was able to confirm Mark Sumner is a direct descendent of Samuel Sumner Sr. *If* the Helen living with Ellen O'Neal is the same one that moved from Okeechobee to Beaufort, she's legit. Questions?"

"No." I was seventy-five percent convinced the lady I knew as Helen was an imposter.

"Number two, what happened to Helen Sumner during those four years after she left Beaufort?" Val shook her head. "It is as if the earth opened and swallowed her. No credit cards, no tax records, no licenses, nothing, zippo, nada. . . . There is plenty of information after those four years. *Nothing during them.*"

I shrugged my shoulders. You can't ask questions about nothing. I said, "Go on."

"Three. This will interest you. You asked for info on Mark Sumner. Russ, you did this one. Why don't you explain it to Sly?"

Russ pulled Valerie's laptop in front of him. He motioned for me to come over. Russ said, "You need to see the pictures." After I was standing next to him and could see the computer's screen, he began, "The photo you see there is Mark Sumner #1. That is from the Okeechobee High School yearbook." He advanced to the next shot. "Same guy . . . this a shot from his Marine Corps file." Russ changed the picture on the screen. "This one is from a playbill from the little theater. Same guy, right?"

"Yep." It was apparent; the man hadn't changed since his graduation.

Russ smiled as he pressed a key. A picture of a man who bore minimal resemblance to the one in the first three pictures popped up on the screen. "Meet Mark Sumner #2."

"That is definitely not the same guy," I confirmed.

"So check this out," Russ skipped several pictures ahead. "Meet Mark Sumner # 3."

I whistled. The man on the screen was completely different than the other two. "So we have three Mark Sumners in circulation. Do they all claim to be the Sumner from Okeechobee City?"

"All three claim to be that person. But Sly, Mark Sumners #2 and #3 never appeared while #1 was around. One of them made a first appearance three years after #1 disappeared. The third one didn't show for a couple of more years. The photos I have are from licenses and job files. They had lots of different types of work. Want me to go over them? They're on the flash drive. One even worked as a clerk in the tax office." Russ paused.

"Skip the details for now," I said.

"Guess what?"

I nodded grimly. "Mark Sumner #1 hasn't been seen again."

Russ' hands exploded above his head as he shouted, "Bingo!"

Val said, "I'm giving fifty-to-one odds that the skeletons in the house on Sandfly Road are Mark and Helen Sumner . . . the real ones."

Russ volunteered, "I also was working on your fourth question. I got as far as hacking into the Polk County Court records on the hearings held on custody of Ellen O'Neal. I didn't get far enough in them to learn much. I guess the thing that is a real puzzler is that Ellen O'Neal fully professed complete acceptance of Helen Sumner as her niece. At least, that was true to the point I got through."

"I had five. You asked for pictures of Helen, Mark, and Ellen." Val switched files, and she rotated picture after picture going backward in time. "Look, and you tell me."

The first picture I looked at was one taken within the last six months. She was definitely the lady with which I had been dealing. As each photo slipped back into time, the aging process reversed, but not so much that her identity remained in any doubt. True, she wasn't the same dewy-eyed girl in the period right after her 'disappearance.' I didn't have any questions until I looked at pictures before she vanished. I had to really look at them. The one that sold me was a picture of her in the playbill for *Macbeth*. I concluded the differences I saw could have been time. I said, "It could be the same woman."

Val, serious as usual, offered, "I'll still give fifty-to-one."

"I've seen all I need to on Mark . . . whichever he is. What about Ellen?" I asked.

"I haven't got a lot to show you," Val said. She grumbled as a new set of photos appeared on the laptop screen. "Talk about camera shy. She's eighty-four, and I doubt she's ever had forty photos taken of her. Most of them were before she was thirty. That's her high school graduation picture." She tapped a key a few times. "This is the best one. It's her wedding picture. She was a cute country girl. Problem is, that picture is sixty-four years old. Does she look anything like that today?"

I studied the photo. The set of the eyes, nose, and general shape of the face were the same as the woman I knew as Ellen. She tilted her head in a distinctive way. It probably was her. . . . I wanted to see more. "Show me what else you have." I needed reassurance for the doubts circling. 'Helen Sumner' made me cautious; a nagging doubt remained.

"Here is a picture with one of her three boys. They were all killed in a plane crash." Val brought up a different image.

"How old is that one?" I asked. The boy in the picture was probably ten at most.

Val looked at a note on the screen, "It says, 'taken in 1968.' There is only one more recent photo."

I scrutinized the picture. The woman in the photo wore her hair in the same style as the Ellen I knew. The features looked right. The woman was standing in the picture. . . . I'd never seen the lady I knew out of the wheelchair. After vacillating from yes to no and back, I made a decision.

Val prompted an answer, "Is that her?"

"Nobody looks the same at eighty as they do at thirty. Yes, that's her." I hoped I was correct and added, "Were you able to get a street address in addition to the PO Box?"

"No. The box and the farm address are it." Val shook her head. "You have to make a strong effort to be as secretive as they've been about where they live. I thought that I could get it from the hearing transcripts. No luck. There is a reference to a sidebar with the judge to have all reference to street addresses of 'temporary' living quarters removed from the record. Why. . . . I don't know. They've been very careful not to let a street address get published."

"Anything else?" I asked.

"Both Mark Sumner #2 and #3 have had some contact with our legal system. Particularly Mark #3. He has been arrested for domestic violence four times, assault and battery three times, suspected arson, petty theft, leaving the scene of an accident . . . he's not Mr. Clean Jeans." Russ sighed. "Mark #2, not so much. He has an arrest for being drunk and disorderly, and he spent eighteen months in prison for embezzlement."

"Forewarned is forearmed." I was not surprised by the way this thing was developing.

"Oh, one more thing," Val hit another key on her laptop. "I don't know why this is important, but . . . Sally Crisp spent some of her young years in a place called Rock Springs in Marion County. That's near Dunnellon. She went to school there for a few years. I found a picture of her with her brothers and a sister working in the family garden."

At the mention of Marion County, I smiled. It broadened exponentially when Val added the word garden.

CHAPTER 42

I figured I might as well get it over. Sooner or later, I'd have to call Officer Freeman at the Desoto County Sheriff's Office. I looked up the number on my computer and dialed it.

A cheery voice answered, "DeSoto County Sheriff's Office, Deputy Irene Stagg, how may I help you?"

"Do you have a deputy named Freeman that is part of your department?" I asked.

"We have a Homicide Detective named Horace Freeman."

"Could you put me through to him?" I braced myself for a long ordeal . . . questions and possibly a trip to Arcadia.

"May I tell him who's calling?"

"Slydell Harrell."

"Oh, yes. I'll put you right through."

Hair on my arms and neck reacted as if electrified. It was clear I'd been a topic of discussion in their office. I waited apprehensively. Finally, a deep, bass voice growled, "Freeman here."

I felt like a deer in the headlights, but I did my best not to sound like one. "Detective Freeman, I'm SJ Harrell. A lady from the DeSoto Historical Society told me you'd like to speak with me. How can I help you?"

"Don't think you can. That Jenny Dorr is a sweet little thing. I can't understand why her husband divorced her." My first thought was that he was using some strategy to lower my defense.

I tried starting over, "Jenny said you wanted to speak to me about some research I'm doing on pioneer families."

"I doubt that has a damned thing to do with the Burrows murder. I called Maureen Dieselli, shit, I mean Ford, up in Polk County. It will take some getting used to, her being remarried and all. Anyway, she told me she knew you well. She said you'd kill quail, turkeys, ducks, deer, and hogs, but she doubted you were into killing two-legged pricks."

"Oh," I was speechless.

"The Burrows thing . . . he was bound to finally find a husband that wasn't into sharing his wife with *him*. Doc Briggs did the autopsy. Crime of passion—Burrows was tortured some before he killed him. Jenny tell you he damned near had his head cut off?"

"Yes."

Freeman cleared his throat. "Lots of hate, lots of hate. Broken fingers. Had his tender parts mangled. Crime of passion. We don't have no psychopaths here that would do that. That's what it would take." He took a breath. "I been here since two days after God made this county. That's so to speak. Been in the sheriff's department 'bout as long. I know most everyone around here. There are some husbands who'd like to do it to him. We're checking them out." He paused again, then said, "Now, if you come across something to help us, I'd welcome you calling."

"I'll do that, Detective Freeman. Have you any concerns about Ms. Dorr's safety? Someone might think she saw something."

"No. There isn't a person in the county that would pluck a hair out of her head. She'll be just fine, other than worrying herself into a tizzy. Jenny is scared of the shadow that goes wherever she does." Freeman laughed. "Thank you for calling."

After I hung the phone up, two thoughts hit me. First, it was frightening that law enforcement could so quickly focus on what they thought they knew to the exclusion of all other possibilities. Second, how futile it was to dread the unknown. The dreaded call turned into a non-important blip in my day instead of a significantly complicated debacle. And it provided me another detail. Broken fingers.

CHAPTER 43

"There are things we need to discuss." Clareen was upset; I could tell from the pitch in her voice.

"What's wrong? What did I do?" I knew to get her problem taken care of first if I wanted mine to disappear.

"You didn't do a damn thing! That's the problem. The contractor you hired to put up the fencing! He's a world champion asshole. I need you to come over here and get his ass in gear and. . . ." Clareen was so mad she was speechless. That happened only biannually.

"What's the problem?"

"The problem is he is a worthless piece of shit!" Her screaming at the phone caused the speaker to buzz. "Get over here. Get this idiot straightened out."

"What else?"

"Let me get my list." There was a pause before Clareen's calm voice returned to her cell. She said, "You've got five requests to do historical presentations. Two are from libraries, two from museums, and one from Melbourne's Rotary Club."

"When?"

"The first one is three days before Memorial Day. It's for a military museum in Punta Gorda. The rest's after June 20. They're scattered through June and all of July."

"Go ahead and schedule them. Next."

"There are a dozen-plus requests for your services. About half weren't anything you'd be interested in. The rest I sent fee schedules and our form letters. I did customize three of them. Those are the ones I thought had some potential. There was one I kept for you to look at. It's from a veteran who had his military citations disappear, stolen—"

"What difference does that make?"

"He doesn't have them. He earned them. He needs to get them back. Sly, one is a Medal of Honor."

"Clareen, tell him I'll do my best, no charge. Send a note out to Russ and Val. Ask them to check for anyone trying to sell US military decorations since the medals showed up missing. Tell them to use their imaginations to dig up info that will help. Anything else?"

I heard paper rustle. Clareen said, "Last item. Nina Dupree called from the Beaufort Police Department. She wants you to call her. I asked what it was about. She just laughed. I tried, but she is as closed-mouthed as an oyster."

"I should have warned you about her," I said.

"That Nina woman sure tried pumping me. She asked the same question in more ways than the number of pimples on a teenager's cheeks." Clareen chuckled. "She found out we have oysters in Florida too."

"What did she want to know?"

"Why you were searching for the Sumners. What you'd found out about them that could have made them murder targets. I'm sure Detective Dupree got tired of hearing, 'I don't know' and 'Ask Mr. Harrell.' You have her number?"

"Yes," I said as I added an item back on my to-do list.

"Do you have anything for me?"

"If you're holding any checks that need to go out, use your judgment. Unless you have a problem with any of them, forge my name, and send them out. Hold any that you don't agree with or bother you."

"In other words, business as usual." Clareen laughed. "The other day, you said I could be replaced. Won't happen. No one can forge your name as good as I do."

CHAPTER 44

My phone rang before I could make the call. When I answered, I was greeted with, "Detective Nina Dupree, how are you, SJ?" A bit of Beaufort sunshine came from my cell's speaker. The sweet, melodic tones of her coastal South Carolina drawl sweetened the area around my desk.

"I'm doing fine, and you, Nina?"

"Good. Do you have a minute or two?" The pleasantries were over.

"Yes. What can I do for you?" I asked.

"Let's start with what I can do for you. We've positively identified one of the skeletons. The male is Mark Sumner. The coroner was able to positively match the forensics to Marine Corps medical records. The dental records weren't a perfect match, since work was done after he left the Marines. The shotgun blast to the face did a lot of damage. But he had a training accident and broke one bone in his lower leg and cracked the other. A screw was used to hold the complete brake stable. The x-rays of it and the skeleton were identical. The skeleton your people found was Mark Sumner." She paused, waiting for me to say something. When I didn't, she continued, "The other skeleton. . . . We're going to have to wait for DNA to come back. Most of the teeth in the woman's mouth had been pulled out. Our technician said she couldn't be sure, but there was some evidence somebody extracted them right before or after she was killed. My guess . . . that was part of the torture she endured. Of course, the flesh was gone. We hope to extract enough DNA from the hair, and we'll crush up a bone if necessary."

"Then she was tortured?" I asked.

"Yes, definitely. If you don't mind, I don't want to discuss the details. Let's leave it at what that couple went through was horrific. Marie, that's our coroner, served in Bosnia, exhuming mass graves. That was torture city. She said it was as bad as anything she saw there."

"Do you think it was the work of a psychopath? Maybe a serial killer?"

Nina's sigh was audible through the cell speaker. "Yes and no. I think the person who did what was done to those two had to be a psycho. But there is plenty of evidence we found at the crime scene to convince me they knew who killed them."

"What evidence?"

"Past the identification of who the bodies are, what's your interest?"

I debated how much I should share at the point I was in my effort to recover the gold coins and whatever else might be buried in a grave. After several seconds of consideration, I asked, "A few hundred thousand dollars. The interest I have in determining who those skeletons are and who killed them is incidental to that. However, it might work for both our interests to share some information. My office manager said you were very interested in learning about our project."

I waited for a response. There wasn't any. I said, "Nina, you got me on the silence of the lambs once. Sorry, it won't work twice."

"Can't blame a girl for trying. I was hoping your people found a knife with prints on it you hadn't told us about."

"Nope, I can't blame you. Sorry, no knife."

Nina chuckled, "Okay, what are your concerns about sharing information with me?"

"Honest?" I asked.

"Honest," she affirmed.

"I might have info that will give you some leads. But I'm afraid that, if I do, you'll want to try to catch the fish and spook them. If the people are the same ones you're looking for, I don't have to explain how violent they can be. Let's say the death of those two in Beaufort *are* connected to the people I believe are chasing the same money I am. I don't know if they are for sure. They've been looking for years. They'll do whatever to get their hands on it. Body count doesn't matter. Problem is, I can't prove they are the same folks. You can't either unless you know a lot more than I think you do. Puts me in a spot. You understand my position?"

"You don't want me stirring the pot before you have recovered the money," she answered.

"That, and I want my client and myself alive to enjoy it." My tone was as serious as my expression she couldn't see.

"That's understandable." The phone went silent for several seconds. I heard a sigh. "I won't be able to spook the fish. I'm going to have to hope you're able to send them my way. SJ, I've been scrapping up scum for a long time. Normally, I can find some crumbs left behind. Not this time. The people who did this did the best job of cleaning a murder scene in the fourteen years I've been on the homicide squad. It's damned hard to find evidence after all the intervening years. If we'd have learned about the murder in a week, we'd be in the same place as we are now. Our lab techs say they doused the whole place with a chlorine-based agent; they're guessing Clorox. We were excited when we first got in there. Your people didn't have much time in the house before our squad cars arrived, and I don't know their training level. It looked like an evidence bonanza to us. Oh, contraire! There were six place settings on the dining room table. Unused. A meal was still in the kitchen oven. No sign of forced entry, other than what your folks did. There is evidence both victims were tied into chairs; you can see where varnish was worn off by their struggles. The perps took the rope with them. Not a smudged print, no fibers. The place had to be a bloody mess. The only blood we found was under the corpse locations. No blood showed up with luminal anywhere else. They left the place as sterile as an operating room. It's frustrating! We talked to the same people you did. The Sumners' employers, the Paris Island people, the neighbor lady. . . . I'm ninety percent sure we know it was done by one or more of the *group of four*. We can't extradite a person for questioning. That would be our straw to grasp. You can't bring murder charges with what we have. Our DA would laugh. It's all circumstantial, and it's all challengeable. Proving anything leaves reasonable doubt. Hell, overwhelming doubt."

"Is there anything I can do?" A couple things came to mind, but I've learned to avoid volunteering.

"I don't think so. Of course, if you see any way to connect them to a direct piece of evidence, let me know. That's as likely to happen as Harvey Weinstein being nominated as the next Pope. If you find out they're headed our way, let us know. They seem a lot smarter than to set foot in South Carolina again." Nina hesitated, then added, "If you get into a discussion with them, turn on your cell phone recorder. Who knows? I would appreciate you keeping me informed on what is happening down there and what you learn. I'll do what I can. You'll get an identity when we verify the other skeleton is Helen Sumner. The real one."

"You have the same feeling I have? These folks aren't amateurs."

"No, they aren't. I think if we go back far enough, we'll find they've had some kind of training. Unfortunately, I have three current cases. My resources are stretched, so my captain is telling me the Sumner case goes to the end of the line." Nina hesitated before delivering bad news. "The DNA results on who we believe is the Sumner woman will slide, probably a couple weeks."

"Oh shit." I apologized, "Sorry about that. I was hoping I wouldn't be in limbo that long." That left me another problem: how to work around a person who was almost surely an imposter. It would require a strategy in addition to the plan I had for the search.

CHAPTER 45

I looked at the next to last item on my to-do list, *Call church historian*. Written next to it was the phone number of The Dancing Dears. As I punched the numbers on my phone, I had a wager with myself: would the lady I called be more church historian or professional stripper?

A seductive voice answered, "The Dancing Dears. You've reached us while we are busy. For a table reservation at Lee County's only quality erotic dancing nightclub, press one now. . . . For a menu of our most popular dishes, press two. . . . If you wish to schedule a private room, press three. . . . Press four to leave a message and include your phone number for a response." I was strongly leaning toward dealing with the professional stripper type.

After pressing four, the tone sounded, and I started, "My name is Slydell Har—"

A soft alto voice interrupted me, "I've been expecting your call, Mr. Harrell. I'm Dennia Hays. My daughter tells me you're a historian, and you have an interest in locating pioneer graves in and around our community. I may have the information you need. I would be happy to assist in any way I can. Excuse me for being abrupt. We are busy."

"No problem. . . . Thank you for your offer, ahhhh, that's very nice of you."

"My daughter told you I spend four days a week in Fort Myers. Monday and

Tuesday are the best days for me to meet with you. I suggest that because, based on what Lily's told me, I can save you a great deal of time by taking you to the graves you're seeking. I believe I know the only two places they could be located." She paused. When I didn't answer quickly, she said, "If you can't work your schedule to meet those days, I can draw—"

It was my turn to interrupt. "No, no. I'd love to meet you. You're right; it would save me considerable time. If I sounded . . . strange. . . . I wasn't expecting you to be so helpful. I'm used to having to twist arms to get help at times."

"I researched you on the internet. As my daughter told you, I'm interested in history, and that interest extends past church and genealogical issues. Your speaking engagements sound interesting. I'll be picking one of your topics of interest to me when you're scheduled within a reasonable distance."

"What would you consider a reasonable distance?" I asked.

"Inside four hundred miles."

"That's a pretty long trip. I can get you a list of something closer than a six-hour drive," I started to pull my schedule up on my computer.

"Thank you, but I have a Cessna 172. That's three hours for me."

"Oh . . . that's great." I didn't know what to say.

"Let's get back to your project. What day is best for you? I don't have anything scheduled for the next two weeks." Dennia was extending a get-out-of-jail-free card. She recognized I was surprised and off balance.

"This coming Tuesday would be good," I stammered.

"Lily told me you live in Kenansville. What's that, three hours? How does eleven sound?"

I recovered. "Eleven sounds terrific. Can we meet at Betty and Billie's?"

"Perfect."

The only thing I was sure of after the call: I was fascinated by the lady to whom I'd just talked.

CHAPTER 46

The phone rang once, twice, and then a click preceded the message, "The number you have called is not in service at this time. Please check your number and dial again."

I redialed Helen Sumner's number. The same thing happened. I summed up my feelings, "Oh, shit!"

I placed the handset back on the cradle, shook my head, and assessed the situation. Where was I? I was now fully committed to a project that benefited at least one person I believed to be an imposter. An imposter who I couldn't contact. An imposter or imposters who may or may not be connected in some way to three murders. Who may have enemies who were after the same treasure we were. And probably was connected to an entity that was both following us and trying to scare us away at the same time. In addition, I had already spent significant funds on the project.

Even if I was willing to walk away from the money I had sunk in recovering Sam's gold, there was one thing I couldn't abandon: Ellen O'Neal. She needed help and wasn't aware of the danger she was in. No doubt, the Invisibles behind the violence would kill her when the treasure was found. I reiterated, "Oh, shit!"

CHAPTER 47

Fishing is my refuge. I've faced and solved most of the problems that have entered my life in a boat with a fishing rod in my hand. This problem would be no different. I laid my fishing rods and tackle box on the dock. Before I stepped in the boat, I let my eyes slowly traverse the expanse of Lake Marian. The pinks and grays of predawn blended with the mists rising from the waters. I decided to wait for a friend. The big bull gator would soon make its morning shore patrol.

I watched the shoreline on the left. Somewhere along that stretch of thick bull rushes and cattails, a two-foot-wide path was cut through the heavy vegetation. It led to the lair of the gator. The gator used this opening to give him access to the apron of lake waters made of lily pads, flags, and peppergrass. Each morning, he followed the same predictive behavior. An apex predator, the bull gator, would cruise the shoreline until his breakfast was served. The only variable was of what that breakfast would consist.

The analogy was too perfect for me to ignore. Like the bull gator, one or more of the persons pursuing the treasure was an apex predator. Their behavior would be consistent. When faced with an obstacle in human form, they destroyed it. Killing was their nature. There was no avoiding this truth. I must do one of the two options available to me: flight or fight.

Flight was an impossible option for me. My value system wouldn't allow a vulnerable like Ellen O'Neal to be abandoned . . . with the probable loss of her life as a result. That gave me cover for the decision I'd made even if the old lady wasn't involved. Scum like the sub-humans who killed Mark Sumner and probably his wife needed filtering from society. The preferable answer was a jail cell. If that wasn't possible, there are rare selective cases I allow vigilantism as an option. The first answer was clear. I must be prepared to kill to defend myself or for those around me.

I stepped into my boat and placed my fishing tackle inside. Using my outboard motor wouldn't be necessary. Untying the boat, I used a single paddle to move the boat along the shore silently. This process, called skulling, is hundreds of years old. Like the method I'd use to find the fish, it would not rely on technology.

My nose and the consistency nature often creates would point me to what I was searching. In Florida's southern swamp lakes, beginning in late April, many panfish spawn. I would smell them. Not the fish—I'd find them by the process they use to make their nests. Bluegills, shellcrackers, and other bream make round holes in the lake's bottom to lay their eggs in and raise their young for a short period. These nests are called "beds" by fishermen. That process disturbs decayed vegetation on a lake's floor and releases methane gas. I travel the shore until I find the gas' odor and use the wind to point me at the place where I know hungry fish wait.

The musty-green odor entered my nostrils a hundred yards from the dock. I pointed the boat's nose into the gentle breeze and moved silently toward the methane's source. Skulling is accomplished by using a figure-eight motion to push water. Since the paddle never leaves the water, no sound is made, not even dripping. The boat moved slowly forward, a hundred, then two hundred feet, until light colors from the exposed sand on the bottom marked the spot. Nestled in the peppergrass fifty feet from the shoreline, the fish had uprooted much of the vegetation where the beds were located. This created an open spot in the weed bed. I allowed the boat to glide to a halt.

Fly rodding is my favorite way to fish. Fooling the fish with an artificial fly gives me more satisfaction than drowning some form of live bait. The rhythmic motion of the fly rod has a calming effect I can't explain. I know its impact on my psyche; that's all that's important to me. It releases my mind from tension. The calm allows logic to prosper. It may or may not act that way for others. Fishing is the 'oil' that helps me solve my problems. The tiny rubber spider tied to the end of my leader was soon fluttering over the expanse of water and landing on the surface above the beds.

The black bit of sponge with white rubber-band legs lay motionless in the water, its impact hardly disturbing it. I twitched it once, moving the spider a few inches. A large bluegill immediately popped it from the surface. My light action rod bent far over as the fish fought. It was soon in my hand and back in the water. As the process repeated, my mind cleared the jumbled mess surrounding my search for Sumner's gold. The repetitive function of catch and release freed it.

By the time I pointed my boat back to the dock, my thoughts reordered. I could put aside any worries about my inability to contact Helen, or whoever, and Ellen. They would find a way to contact me to learn if I'd made progress. The first priority I had was to find the correct cemetery. I wasn't close to solving that yet. The next was to find the grave with greener grass. I was confident I would be able to do that, and others wouldn't. It was my ace in dealing with the mystery. The next step was to be sure all the clues from the letter were interpreted. Russ and Val were busy with that. Retrieving the gold came next. I concluded that, until I'd located the treasure, there was little danger to my people or me. Once the gold was found . . . this is where I had to face the fact; my competitors would be willing to kill me and those associated with our effort.

"Yoo-hoo, Sly!" Cindy was standing at the end of the dock, waving and shouting.

I waved and yelled, "I'm headed back."

She stood patiently while I skulled the boat the remaining fifty yards. When I was twenty feet from the dock, she said, "You said you wanted to know if we saw that black HUMV. I went to Wilson's Store to get milk and bread this morning, and when I was driving up Lake Marian Road, I passed one parked on the farm lane at the old Friedman Place. It was still there when I returned. You said you wanted to know right away."

"Thanks, Cindy. I'll go check it out." I tied the boat to the dock.

"Do you want me to call Trotter?"

"No. I don't believe they'll want to bother us just yet. Did you lock the gate when you came back?"

"I sure did. Is there anything you want me to do?" she asked.

"No. You can go back to the house." I stepped out of the boat as I spoke. A splashing and disturbance along the shoreline to my left caused my head to swivel. Several ducks were taking flight . . . less one of their brethren. The old gator took one more chomp before swallowing the mallard. I took it as an omen and reminder. I was dealing with a predator, a dangerous one!

CHAPTER 48

My cell phone rang as I approached the ranch's gate. I braked my CJ-5 to a stop. The cell screen told me that Trotter was calling. "Hello, how did it go last night?" I asked.

"I could have stayed in bed. Sorry, I fell asleep twice last night, but I'm sure I didn't miss a thing. I didn't see anything suspicious. No HUMV. No silver Toyota with a bent fender. No other car lurking in the bushes. No shadowy figures skulking the neighborhood. The only activity was a large number of male cats hanging outside of a neighbor's house. I imagine, from the screeching and fighting there was, for an object of their affection inside."

As I unlocked the gate, I said, "Being that the black HUMV is, or was, parked up the street this morning, it doesn't surprise me."

"Damn, where did you see it? Was it on the shoulder of the main road or parked on one of the side roads?" Trotter asked.

"I didn't see it yet. Cindy saw it when she went to the store. It was sitting on the Friedman place's access road. I'm driving up there now to take a look for myself." The gate swung open, banging against the post used as a stop.

"You want me to come back to the ranch? I think staying here is a waste of time."

"No. Let's give it one more night. I'm ready to get on the road. Anything else?"

Trotter cautioned, "Watch your ass, Sly."

The HUMV hadn't moved from the spot Cindy had described when we discussed it. Its dark tinted windshield and windows made its interior impossible to see. I drove past at thirty miles per hour so that its occupants were sure to see me. I had traveled less than a quarter-mile when I saw the black vehicle pull out of the side road and follow my Jeep. One question I'd asked myself was answered. They zeroed in on my CJ-5 as my vehicle of choice. That meant I was probably their only interest at my ranch.

The HUMV did not attempt to close the distance to my vehicle. When I accelerated to forty-five, they maintained the 1,500-foot space between us. A confrontation wasn't to my interest. Nor did I want the people following me to be sure I was aware I was under surveillance.

Getting gas would be a perfectly natural reason for my trip. The Jeep headed for Herman Wilson's General Store, its left turn on to Canoe Creek Road hardly requiring any conscious effort at the steering wheel. I maintained highway speeds until I pulled under the large canopy over Wilson's gas pumps. The image of the HUMV flitted across my rearview mirror.

"Fill 'er up?" Henrietta Wilson's red curls, freckled face, and broad smile appeared next to the Jeep.

"Sure," I smiled back. "Your father around?"

She nodded, "He's in the garage back by the tire display."

"I'll leave the keys in the ignition in case you need to move my Jeep."

Henrietta laughed, "We ain't ever that busy. But I love driving your Jeep. I'll pull it up to the garage doors when she's finished."

I found Herman assembling a large cardboard display that proclaimed the virtue of Firestone tires. He was talking to himself, and his face was ruddier than usual. His frustration was only a few degrees short of boil.

"Hey, Herman," I said and added, "You working on some kind of puzzle?"

"These confounded things. The folks that make them must do it to see how damned mad they can make a soul." He put the gaily printed display on the ground. "You need to talk to me for a few minutes, so's my blood pressure gets right. What you be needing?"

"I need a favor. You remember that black HUMV that was trailing me some time ago?"

Herman nodded, "Yep, sure do."

I pointed toward Canoe Creek Road. "Whoever it is showed up parked on Lake Marian Road this morning. They followed me here to the gas station. I'd like to confirm the license number and a description of who is in it. Can you do that?"

He smiled, "I reckon I can do a bunch better. Irene talked me into getting some of those hi-tech snooping cameras because of the drive-offs we have from time to time. What if I were to copy off a couple times when that there HUMV got gas here? I got some flash drive things. I could do it tonight if'n you want."

"I'd love that!"

"Consider it done!" Herman's smile was wider than the Cheshire Cat's.

"What can I—"

"Nothing. Just tell me when those Shellcrackers hit the beds at your end of the lake."

"Well, I can put you in the know," I said, "with information from this morning. The big Copperhead Bluegills are on the beds right now. I can't imagine the Shellcrackers aren't."

"Lordy, I'll be down to see you!" Herman was not a catch and release fisherman. An invisible neon sign screamed 'fish fry' on his forehead.

Grinning, I said, "You don't need to haul your boat down. I won't be needing mine for a few days. Use it."

"Now, you won't have to tell me that twice."

I was sitting on the veranda when Herman's smiling face appeared from around the corner of my house. "Hey, Sly. I'm gonna give them Shellcrackers trouble, but I brought that flash drive I promised you. They's three times that car was in. License is bell-clear to see. Two different people got out while gas was being pumped, and you'll get a quick gander at them."

"Thanks, Herman." I took the tiny drive from Herman's colossal hand. "Leave a few for seed," I said, knowing his response.

"Hell, no!"

I slipped the drive into my shirt pocket. Soon I'd get my first chance to see who my adversaries were.

CHAPTER 49

Cindy and I stared at the computer screen. I could read the North Carolina license plate number very clearly: KEQ 7358. Herman was right. The images were clear and sharp. Recording the license number was quickly done. One pass through the file accomplished that. Absorbing the size, shape, and facial features of the two men who stood outside the car while Henrietta pumped gas was something else.

Cindy whistled softly. "Those men are huge. Particularly the one in the polo shirt. It's too bad that they are turned away from the camera most of the time. I never got a good look at their faces."

I reran the file. It was the fourth time since we concentrated on viewing the men. For the first time since I moved to Kenansville, I regretted the service attendants who pumped gas at Wilson's gas station. The three sequences captured two men getting out of the HUMV to stretch their legs while the attendant pumped gas. Most of the videos showed the men's backs.

Cindy commented, "The one wearing the red tee shirt is good looking. Black hair with loose curls like those is rare. He looks like someone I've seen, but I can't remember where. How big is he? About the same size as Trotter?"

"That's about right. Maybe a shade shorter and a little wider. He looks like Jeff Chandler with dyed hair."

Cindy looked at me for several seconds before asking, "Who is that?"

"A movie star." I saw the blank look on her face. "That's a poor reference for you. He died in 1961. That's damned near thirty years before you were born."

"I don't have a thousand DVDs of old films like you." Cindy always thought she should know about anything we discussed and was miffed when she didn't.

"You can borrow as many as you want as often as you want," I said.

I started playing the flash drive file again. The other man *was* huge. He was a minimum of six inches taller than his car-mate. That would make him close to seven feet. I guessed his weight as right at three hundred pounds. I froze the motion midway through the second sequence. It was the only time his face was exposed to the camera lens. His eyes were deeply sunk in a face with a receding hairline, very prominent cheekbones. His nose and ears were large, and his chin was pointed and tipped with a goatee. Altogether, he was a brutish looking fellow with hands and feet outsized even for his big body. His size was unique, a mark the Foxxes could use to identify him. Before I shut my computer down, I forwarded a note to Russ and Val, along with the file containing the video sequences from Wilson's gas pumps.

Cindy asked, "Who does he look like?"

"No one. The closest image I can think of would be a cartoon character I saw in a horror magazine."

"Sly, I think you need to be sure you always carry a gun. A big one." She was very serious.

CHAPTER 50

The multitude of times I've driven the sand ruts that connect my ranch house to Lake Marian Road doesn't lessen the experience. That's particularly true when I knock down the CJ-5's windshield, and the last barrier between me and the rural wilds I love is removed. It's a personal fetish of mine that rejuvenates me. Most of us have a place where we find the fuel to live our life. Those that don't should search out their restorative fountain. Art museums, libraries, cathedrals—there is an infinity of choices. . . . My place is the natural world. The half-mile drive passes through pine tree flats with palmettoes covering large areas, improved pastures of lush Bahia grass, stands of oaks that escaped the early 1900s lumberman's ax. Twin grooves circle swampy cypress heads.

Spring brings drought to the central Florida plains. The parched foliage is thankful for any moisture, including the heavy morning dew that glazed the grounds I drove past. Sandhill cranes looked for breakfast in the fields and cried their haunting call. Swamp rabbits nibbled at this and that as they hopped along the ditches on the roadside. A red-tailed hawk swooped down on an unsuspecting field mouse. Three raccoons disappeared from my view as they sought shelter in a cypress swamp the road closely skirted. They fill my body with energy, optimism, and hope, just like Henrietta Wilson fills my Jeep's tank with gas.

The long-abandoned cattle pens, used by the former owners of the ranch, remain a landmark that stands near the front gate. It is a connection with the past I refuse to destroy. Its presence makes history come alive every time I see it. Deep inside, something tells me that the jumble of old wooden planks and posts will be important to me in the future. I've learned to trust such feelings.

Was the black HUMV still parked somewhere along Lake Marion Road? Determining if we were being surveilled was the purpose for my trip. I slowed the Jeep to thirty miles per hour. A glance down the Friedman farm road confirmed what I knew I'd see, the black HUMV. It also confirmed another of my thoughts: the people inside that vehicle believed I was their best chance of finding the gold. Until I located the treasure, I was safe, as were those associated with me. Afterward, I needed to be sure my life insurance was paid up.

"Want more coffee?" Cindy asked. I was so engrossed in an email from Russ Foxx that her words didn't register the first time she spoke.

"Want more coffee?" Cindy repeated.

"Yes." I came out of my fog and looked up at her. Her knitted eyebrows told me something was bothering her.

"What?" I asked.

"Are you alright? You never miss the opportunity for another cup." She was the person who had first called me a 'coffeeholic.'

"I'm fine. This email from Russ is intriguing. I must have shut everything else out." I turned the screen so Cindy could see what I was viewing. "What do you think?"

"My God! I can't believe that!" She had the same reaction I'd had when I opened Russ' info. A playbill from the Beaufort Little Theater that featured the play *Frankenstein*.

Russ had written a note above the playbill, *'I had a hunch and followed it up. It's hard to believe we got this lucky. This is dated eight months before the Sumners' disappearance.'*

The playbill featured a large picture of the Monster, Dr. Frankenstein, and Elizabeth. Despite the makeup, the Monster was readily identifiable as the man videoed in the gas station.

So were the other two characters. The printing below the heading confirmed, "Starring as Elizabeth Lavenza—Helen Sumner . . . as Dr. Victor Frankenstein—Harn Crisp." Most importantly, the playbill identified the Monster as, "Frankenstein's Monster—Edward Kraggen."

Cindy poured a cup of coffee as I replied to the Foxxes, asking them to proceed with investigating Edward Kraggen. I was sure they had started without my request. They were two smart people.

It was past noon, and I hadn't heard from Trotter. That wasn't like him. Did he run into trouble? I called to find out. He answered, sounding like he'd just been awakened. He had.

"I was up all night. Got side-tracked. Just went to bed. This damned motel is noisy." He wasn't fully awake.

"You okay?" I asked.

"I was 'til you called." Trotter is grouchy when he doesn't get his beauty sleep.

"Wake up. I need you sharp." I raised my voice, "You awake now?"

"Yes. Stop being a shithead."

"Did anything happen last night?"

"Not one damned thing. The cats returned. That's it."

I told him, "The black HUMV is still here, spying on me. I figured you'd draw a blank."

"But this morning was different. Something happened."

I asked, "Did somebody show up at Jenny Dorr's home this morning?"

"No, but something damned important happened. Last night, the sheriff caught three men digging up graves in the cemetery where we looked, the Joshua Creek one. They claimed someone hired them. The waitress in the restaurant where I ate breakfast told me about it. I decided to drive out there. Remember the graves we found where Sumner family members were buried? They dug down to the coffins on two of them." I heard Trotter exhale. "Sly, you aren't gonna make me stay another night? I can't imagine anything else I'd need to stay here for."

"No. Go ahead and get some sleep. Come back this afternoon." I now was sure of a couple of things. Helen, Ellen, and whoever else had taken a shot at recovering the gold. And I'd soon be receiving a call from them.

CHAPTER 51

Space Coast Fence. That name was plastered on pickup trucks and box trucks scattered around my office parking lot. Clareen hadn't wasted time in reissuing the contract for enclosing the property. A man testing the electric gate opener frowned as I pulled up to enter. I said, "I'm the owner." His frown turned upside down.

Clareen was waiting at the front office door. "Hi, Sly. Look behind you." She nodded toward the street.

I didn't bother to look, "The black HUMV. He followed me from the ranch. I'm surprised he got this close."

Clareen held the door open and followed me inside. She asked, "What do you think?"

"I assume you mean the parking lot. Everything looks great from the little I saw."

"I guarantee it is all to specification. You'll find a case of bourbon on your desk. That's less one bottle I took for services rendered. Dan Chan said it was great stuff. It's to die for. It's a brand I never heard of . . . Noah's Mill. Dan gets it shipped to him from Louisville. The case is a present from him."

My fondness for high-quality bourbon was well known. Nevertheless, it meant that Dan Chan was a man that took the time to take care of details. That alone increased my confidence in the quality of the fencing job in progress. "Say thank you to Mr. Chan for me. If we don't meet today."

Clareen reached out and grabbed my arm before I could sit behind my desk. "I had a call a little while ago. I wish I had recorded it."

"Who from?"

"Ellen O'Neal. . . . I think."

"Tell me about it," I said.

Clareen blinked a few times and said, "You might as well sit. This will take a few minutes." She waited for me to drop into my office chair. "I answered the phone the way I always do. I did notice the area code wasn't from around here. It was 828. Anyway, when I finished talking, this lady's voice says, 'Who is this?' I gave her my name, and she asked, 'Do I know you?' I said, 'I'm sorry, I don't recognize your voice. Who are you?' She answered, 'Ellen O'Neal.' I asked, 'Don't you remember? I'm from Mr. Harrell's office.' She replied, 'Oh, I remember that. Dearie, is Helen there?' I answered, 'No.' Then she asked, 'If she calls or comes there, will you tell her to come home? I'm not having a good day. The doctor had to leave, and I'm here by myself.' I started to ask where she was, but she hung up. It was weird."

"Did you get her phone number?" I asked.

"No! I have the settings on my phone set up so that it only records a number if I punch a code to instruct it. The 828 area code is from western North Carolina." Clareen shook her head. "Sorry, Sly."

Clareen placed a box in front of me. The label's return address stated it had been shipped from "HTG Collectables, New York, New York." She prompted me to open it.

The shipping carton was a ten-inch cube and was light. I slit the tape with a letter opener and pulled back the flaps. Inside, several plastic Ziplock baggies contained items I immediately recognized. Two Purple Hearts. A dozen battle ribbons. A Silver Star. And a Congressional Medal of Honor. "Russ found them!" I exclaimed. "That was fast."

"He said he had an idea they'd end up one of four places. The third place he checked was a charm. I paid what the outfit that had them asked. I'd already talked to Riaffort. He said he'd get our money returned, plus his fee, plus, plus." Clareen nodded at me. "Sly, this isn't routine correspondence. You do this kind of thing special. You write it."

I nodded. "Be sure you send a $200 check to the Foxxes and get Riaffort to collect for it, too. Do you have anything else that I need to look at?"

"Nothing pressing. Do you expect to be in next week?"

"No. I want to find that grave location, and it may take the whole five days."

She snorted, "Since when have you worked five days?"

"I do what I—" The phone rang, ending our conversation. Clareen raced to her desk, and I gathered items I wanted to take with me.

Clareen stuck her head in my office. "You'll want to take this call, Sly. It's Helen Sumner. I have her on hold. Just pick it up. I've got her on your line."

"Definitely." I held my hand on the phone for several seconds while I composed my thoughts. Before lifting the handset, I called out to Clareen, "I want you to listen in and take notes. Tell me when you're ready."

Within seconds, I heard, "Ready."

"Pick up on my count to three . . . one . . . two . . . three." I lifted the handset and did my best to sound completely normal. "Hello, SJ Harrell. Is this Helen Sumner?"

"Yes, Mr. Harrell."

"I've tried to contact you, Helen, but the number I have is out of service. Last time we talked, you were about to move. Did you?"

"Yes."

"You changed phone numbers also, I take it?"

"Yes, my new num—"

I interrupted her. "If you're speaking from your new phone, I have it on my screen and already have written it down." After a second's hesitation, I added, "I had decided that you had abandoned your search."

"Oh, no! Nothing like that. We wanted to be sure we had relocated into a safe place and changed everything to be sure no one could locate us before contacting you. We are committed to you and finding the gold. Totally. Have you got any good news for us?" Helen was fishing.

"Yes, I'm made progress." I decided to fish a bit myself. "May I speak to Ellen?"

There was a pause. "I'm not with her right now. I'm making the call from another location other than where we are living. I don't know how sophisticated our enemies' technology might be. She's at home resting."

"She's not resting well. Ellen, or someone using her name, called my office. My assistant said she sounded upset and confused. She told Clareen the doctor had left, she was alone, and she wanted you to call her or go to her."

"Oh, my! She must be having one of her bad days. Tell me anything you know about finding the graves; then, I'll have to go to her right away."

"I won't tell you where over the phone for security reasons. You just confirmed my concerns. I will tell you I think I've reduced the possible places to three. I expect to make a great deal of progress next week. They aren't in the cemetery you believed they were located. By the way, one of my people tells me that cemetery had grave robbers last night. You hear about that?"

After a couple of seconds' pause, Helen said, "Yes, it's been on the news. Three Mexicans, I understand. Probably looking for something to sell for drugs." I immediately thought, *Blame the stereotype*. It confirmed my suspicions that Helen and company were behind the midnight exhumations.

"When can we meet again?" I asked.

"I don't know, Mr. Harrell. I am sorry, but I have to get back to Ellen right away. I'll call in the middle of next week." She hung up before I could ask another question.

Clareen stood in my office door, cocked her head to one side, and said, "I got it all, but I'm not sure what I got. You get anything out of that?"

"Yes. She and her buddies are in the Arcadia area. A grave robbery isn't state-wide news. Her crew was the one that orchestrated it. They've run out of ideas to try and find it themselves, so they have to put all their eggs in my basket."

I thought the chess set was set up and was ready for play. The problem was, there were three players. That makes for a complicated game.

CHAPTER 52

"Is the reason you were so willing to go with me today your interest in this hunt or your interest in the girl we'll see at the restaurant?" I asked as we pulled up to the ranch's gate. Trotter was driving his pickup so that, if the black HUMV sat in its usual position, we wouldn't be followed.

Trotter mumbled, "Some of both."

I exited his F-150 to let us out. He added as I unlocked the gate, "And I work for you." As I climbed back into the truck, he asked, "What did her mother sound like when you set this meeting up?"

"Not anywhere close to what I expected. She didn't talk like a stripper or a church historian, at least, not the ones I've come in contact with. Her speech patterns are closer to an English professor. I'd give her a ten rating for mental acuity. She has her own plane. Dennia Hays gave me the impression she was a high-powered business executive type." I shifted in the seat. "There was a quality in her speech. . . . I wouldn't call it sexy . . . not exactly sexy . . . more magnetic."

Trotter grinned. "That's dangerous."

"What's dangerous?"

"Falling for a voice." He looked at me for a couple of seconds before adding, "Ever see some of those phone sex women?"

I just shook my head.

"Three hundred pounds. . . . Faces to scare roaches. . . . Last bath two years ago. . . . Eat Limburger cheese and garlic." Trotter shook his head and made a face. "Nasty!"

He nodded toward the approaching Friedman dirt road. The roof of the HUMV was barely visible. "Our friend is still parked in the same spot. He's quite a creature of habit."

As previously planned, I dropped below the level of the window. After a few seconds, Trotter said, "Okay for you to come up. We're past far enough that no one can see you from where they're parked." We'd soon find out if they'd follow.

I turned my body and neck around so I could watch the road behind us. No black HUMV emerged. When we reached the stop sign at Canoe Creek Road, Trotter asked, "We good to go?"

I made one last check. There wasn't anything on the road we'd just driven. "Good to go!" We were on the way to LaBelle, and I hoped to take a big step to solve the location of what we were looking for . . . with some fringe benefits.

Lily Hays' smile greeted us as we approached the hostess station at Betty and Billie's Restaurant. "Hey, guys. You have a good trip down?" Her words were for both of us; her eyes were for Trotter alone.

I let Trotter answer. "Very good. It's not a bad trip at all. Hardly any traffic."

Lily's smile widened. It was precisely what she wished to hear. "My mother asked me to apologize for her. She'll be a few minutes late. I'll go ahead and seat you."

We followed her. I couldn't tell if her walk was intended to be sexier than usual. Intended or not, it carried the promise of hidden delights for Trotter. Lily garnered attention. She could have led us to our table covered with a sheet and gotten the same result. Lily didn't have to try to be something she already was.

"It's the table that provides you with the most privacy. True, it's a long way to the can, but you can't have everything. See you later." We watched Lily glide across the floor. The sway of her hips had a magnetic impact on all men's eyes, not just ours. A glance at my friend and associate informed me I had ceased to exist. His eyes didn't have the lust that was often present when a feminine form passed by. Admiration? Almost a reverence. I brought him back from the fantasy world to which he'd traveled. "You're going to be putting a lot of miles on your truck."

Trotter didn't reply for a full minute, staring at where she'd disappeared from our view. When he did, he turned, facing me with a deadly serious expression. "I'm going to marry that girl."

Ten minutes past, fifteen, then thirty. Trotter and I had discussed the trip down, the black HUMV, and the panfish bedding until it was threadbare. We were both fidgeting, and I was beginning to have some doubts. I focused on seeing a woman dressed in a Dior dress stroll across the restaurant floor in high heels, clutching a Gucci purse. My guess was blonde hair halfway to her waist. Blue eyes, a confident smile, and carrying a New York model's charisma. I'd gotten to the point of predicting if her dress would be a plain colored . . . blue or maroon . . . or a striking floral print.

"Sorry I'm so late. I had a mare foal early on me. She was stubborn, and it took some extra time." I looked at where the voice was coming from. The face I looked into didn't disappoint. It was more beautiful than I could have imagined. The rest . . . it was a shock. Green eyes, dark auburn hair shoved into a Stetson, a plaid shirt with a bloodstain on one sleeve, and tight-fitting jeans encasing legs and hips that made me swallow. Hard. "I hope you don't mind women with a little perspiration around their edges. I figured it was better for me to be some late than terribly late." She pulled a chair out from the table and sat without fanfare. The woman extended her hand to Trotter and said, "You must be Ken Bass. Lily says you go by Trotter. I'm Gardenia Hays, but everyone calls me Dennia."

"Pleased to meet you."

She turned to me. "Mr. Harrell, I'm pleased to meet you." Her smile was warm and authentic.

"We have two things in common, Dennia, right from the start. We both are fascinated by history, and we both shorten our first names. My birth certificate says I'm Slydell Harrell. I prefer Sly or SJ. The J is for Jerome, but I don't talk about that." We simultaneously extended hands for a firm handshake. My eyes checked her left hand. No ring. I hoped Dennia felt the same electricity I did.

"Was everything satisfactory?" Lily bent over slightly and smiled. Her mother looked a little miffed. I followed Dennia's line of sight. Her eyes focused on the two buttons that had slipped through the holes designed to hold them. I doubt Trotter noticed. He was already mesmerized. Lily looked at her mother for a split second with a message that said, 'My business.' Miffed turned to resigned. "Are you boys staying over tonight?" Lily asked.

"If the graveyards we're going to visit are close, probably not," I said. "We'll know quickly if the places your mom shows us are what we're looking for. However, if they are, I. . . . we'll be spending time down here." Lily's eyes sparkled brighter at the latter possibility.

Trotter looked at me with an expression that was a combination of a threat and a prayer. "We'll probably eat here before we leave for Kenansville." I dropped my chin as a single nod.

"My shift ends at three-thirty." Her disappointment was evident.

I saw an opportunity. "I'm sure there are other nice places to eat. We'd love to have you and your mother join us for dinner this afternoon." There were smiles all around, but Dennia said, "I'm going to have to pass. Tomorrow is a travel day for me. And honestly, I want to visit with my mare and her colt. Lily would be happy to keep you company if the invitation still stands?"

"Absolutely," I said, hoping my disappointment didn't echo in my voice.

Dennia turned to me and maintained eye contact, being sure I realized she intended to do that. "If you'll be so kind, I'm sure I'd like a rain check in the future."

CHAPTER 53

I could feel the warmth from her body on my left arm. All three of us sat in Trotter's pickup's front seat.

"That's a summer sky," she commented. "We won't have a day it doesn't make 90° until November."

"It's been very dry up our way," I said.

"Here too. We have plenty of ponds scattered around my acreage for the livestock. I have some neighbors who farm, and they're having a big problem keeping their beans and tomatoes green."

"What's their irrigation source?" I asked.

"It varies. Wells. Ponds. Canals. Some are close enough to the river to pump from it. The problem is water consumption regulations." She waved her hand and pointed her finger at something in front of the pickup. "That historical marker on the left side of the road is for Fort Denaud. That's where the first fort was built in 1838. The Army abandoned it until the third Seminole war. It was repaired in 1855 and burnt down in 1856. They rebuilt it in 1857 and '58 but moved it north of the river where the cattle trails were. There's nothing left of either. Right past that is the bridge over the Caloosahatchee River. The pioneer families lived north of the river, and that's where they built their cemetery and church. The town they called Denaud grew up there. I'm betting that we find the graves you're looking for in a portion of the cemetery that was separated from the rest of the church graveyard. That was a later development." She held her hands six inches apart. "The space between my palms represents the road built in the early 1900s. North of the road is the current cemetery. South of it is what old-timers call the cow hunter's ground. There are forty to fifty graves, a few unmarked. Most folks that lived in a thirty-mile radius in the 1880s, '90s, and early 1900s were buried there. The burial dates in that portion are before 1915. At one time, there was a wooden fence around it. Rot and termites destroyed it. It hasn't been maintained for thirty years. You have to look close to see the stones; it's so grown over. Most people don't even know it exists."

We were across the bridge, and Trotter was slowing for a stop sign. Oaks and heavy brush covered the lands hiding small houses on three corners. An open field occupied the fourth. Dennia volunteered, "We're almost there. We make a jog to keep going straight for a half-mile. Turn left, and it's another half-mile on the left."

"There's barbed wire around it," Trotter found it as he cleared a path to explore the cemetery.

"The land surrounding it is private property. It keeps cows off the graves." Dennia looked at Trotter's tennis shoes. "You have boots with you?" she asked.

"Yes."

She pointed to a clump of palmettos thirty feet to the side. A four-foot diamondback rattlesnake lay on a sandy patch, sunning itself. Trotter nodded and backed up.

"I'll take the lead. My continentals are snake-proof." I replaced Trotter while he returned to the truck to get his boots. I took a few swipes with my machete and found a spot where the wire was completely missing. It was my first look at the graveyard.

No saplings of heavy brush grew inside the confines on the fence line. This told me it was spasmodically cleared. I imagined cemetery maintenance was a lot like any other. Those that screamed received service; others did not. Only the very tops of a few monuments were visible from the road. Once inside the screening vegetation, the matrix of graves was clearly delineated. There were twelve graves in a row and six rows. Many vacancies interrupted the lines of headstones. Weeds reached the top of many of the forlorn slabs of rock. Two low iron fences surrounded blocks of graves that I assumed were reserved for family burials.

Trotter tapped me on the shoulder and waved me out of his way. He carried a weed-trimmer in one hand and a gas can in the other. "It will be easier if we clear the whole thing." As I stood watching, there was another tap on my shoulder. Dennia extended a rake to me and held one in her other hand. "We might as well do this right." Soon neat piles were setting at the head of each row.

"Damn, isn't somebody going to be upset with us doing this?" It occurred to me the sheriff might be on the way.

"No. We're invited guests," Dennia said. "I told Oscar, the caretaker, we were coming and would probably clean areas around some of the graves. He was happy. One less thing for him to do." Within an hour, the graves were all cleared of high weeds. We were close to finished. I looked at dates and names. My excitement rose. The name Sumner on many stones and the burial dates corresponded to what we searched for. I needed the names of Sam's sons and Sally Sumner's clue letter to see if this was the right cemetery.

Trotter finished the last few swipes with the trimmer and shut it down. Sweat flowed down our shirts, dripped off our chins, and stung our eyes. I said, "You two rest. I've got to get a file out of the truck. Give me the trimmer, gas can, and rakes. I'll take them back." I gathered them up and walked through the path.

When I emerged from the other side, a pickup truck was pulling up behind Trotter's. A thin older man opened the door and slid down to the ground. He smiled and said, "Hey, friend. Would you be with Mrs. Hays?"

"Yes, sir. Are you Oscar?"

"Reckon I am guilty of that. I heard you a-working back there. Clearing the ground is fine. Be sure you don't damage any stones. If you happen to, please tell me, okay?"

"We have the whole area inside the barbed wire fence cut down and raked into piles. No problem with any of the stones." I motioned to our truck. "If you see my pickup here again, we'll be doing research on the burial sites for a client. That okay?"

"Sure. I reckon it is on the Sumners or their kinfolk. They have over half the grave lots in there." He tilted his head to one side, "You don't believe in ghosts, do you?"

I answered carefully, "I haven't seen one yet, but I try keeping an open mind about such things."

Oscar's face turned serious, "I'm of the same mind. I ain't sayin' I ever saw a ghost here. There's plenty that say they have. Most of us locals stay away from here at night."

I nodded solemnly, "Thanks for the warning." I placed the tools in the truck bed. Oscar watched me as I removed my file folder from the pickup's front seat.

"You know, it is strange. I been-a workin' here, full- and part-time for thirty-six years. I ain't never hear tell of one single soul tryin' to find those Sumner graves. In the last six weeks, you are the second set of folks that came a-lookin' for a Sumner. Two big old fellows was here a-tryin' to find Samuel Sumner. The cattle baron. He ain't buried here. So they moved along."

I asked, "Big guys? I might know them. Was one close to seven feet tall?"

"Yes!" His eyes widened. "I ain't never saw such a big man before." His cell phone buzzed, and he said, "I got to get a-movin'. Say hey to Mrs. Hays for me."

He was in his truck and gone before I could ask any more about his previous guests.

"Here's another one," Trotter said as he bent over a gravestone. "'Mathew Ryman Sumner, Born June 18, 1851, Died November 3, 1903.' Is he on the list?"

I looked at my notes. Samuel Sumner Senior had eleven children, eight boys and three girls. We had accounted for three already. "Yes, he's one." I ran my finger down the list, put a check in front of the name, and confirmed the death date. "That's four."

"This might be one," Dennia knelt in front of a large, square stone with a four-foot-high obelisk centered on top. "This is for sure. 'Johnathan Doggette Sumner, Son of Samuel Sumner and Sally Sumner (nee Crisp), Born on December 16, 1846, Died on July 9, 1896, Rest in Peace.'"

I marked off the name off and confirmed the date. "Number five."

"Here is a Lillian Sparks Sumner." Dennia paused and said, "I don't think this one would be of interest. This is Mathew's wife. She wasn't buried until 1909."

"Here's another Hendry. That's four of them so far." Trotter was close to the end of the row he was checking. "We have two more to do. Which one do you want, Dennia?"

"I'll take the last row."

As Trotter and Dennia looked for graves with the name Sumner on their markings, I drew a cemetery map showing each of Sam Sumner's children's burial locations.

They quickly moved past four stones. Then Dennia stopped and read, "'Judith Anne Sumner, born April 26, 1876, Died June 2, 1885, Taken too soon.'"

I looked at the list. Her name was on it with a notation, 'Yellow Fever,' next to it. So did the next name. The dates of death were only weeks apart. I marked the list, said, "Six." Then I told Dennia, "Check the next stone. It should be Wilton."

She moved to the next grave, bent over, read the engraving, and said, "You're correct. And I see why you knew. They died three weeks apart. 'Wilton William Sumner, Born August 8, 1854, Died June 24, 1885.'"

Trotter had finished his row and began working toward Dennia from the opposite end of her row. He stopped at a grave two plots from where Dennia stood. "Try this one. 'Markum Fredrick Sumner, Born March 18, 1849, Died March 20, 1897.'"

"That's number eight." I checked off the name on the list of Sam's children. "That means eight of the eleven are buried here. Old Sally said 'go to the place where we lie, but not I.' With that many children buried here, this should be the spot. She died in 1907. Seven were already here. Now, all I need are some huge water containers or a big rain. I'm that close."

Trotter looked at me like I'd lost my mind.

"Oh, ye of little faith," I laughed. "I've picked out three candidates and have eliminated some others already."

He shrugged his shoulders and said, "So now what?"

"Pray for rain."

"What if it doesn't rain?" He looked like he thought I was playing a joke on him.

"You and I will have to work a lot harder. We'll have to water this whole graveyard."

Trotter shook his head, "How we going to do that?"

"Form an old-fashioned bucket brigade," I said.

Dennia suggested, "How about a thousand-gallon tank and a pump. I have a rig I use to fertilize. You can borrow it."

"Thanks, Dennia, that will be great," I said.

"Good, that gives me the opportunity to be nosey." Dennia's smile created small lines in her face where the dust adhering to her features separated. I sincerely hoped she stayed nosey.

CHAPTER 54

Trotter held his truck on the road as we traveled the 112 miles from LaBelle to Kenansville. I dozed intermittently. My cell phone vibrating in my shirt pocket woke me.

"Hello," I managed a sleep-addled word.

"Sly, where are you?" Clareen's voice was excited, almost frantic.

"We're just driving out of Okeechobee City."

"You need to get back to the Ranch fast!"

"What's going on?" I was fully awake.

"Someone was sneaking up on the ranch house. One of your hands saw a man and went after him. Another man he didn't see shot him! Herman Wilson and one of his boys were at the house. You know Herman. He always carries an arsenal. Skip and two of the boys checked Cindy; she's fine. However, the bastards cut the power lines to the house."

"Clareen, did anyone call the sheriff?" I put our conversation on the speaker so Trotter could hear.

"About half the county. I did. Herman did. Cindy did. Skip did. I'm sure there's a dozen cars there by now."

"Who got shot, and are they okay?" I crossed my fingers and prayed.

"Curly Mathews. The bullet just grazed his thigh. Herman said Curly was more mad than hurt." Clareen anticipated my next question. "No one got a good look at them. Curly said the one he saw was a silhouette and was crouched way over. He never saw the one that shot him."

"Do they know how many there were?" I asked.

"No. I asked if they saw a vehicle. Nobody did."

"Did anybody check the gate?"

"Skip and Herman were going to, but the sheriff's office said to stay at the house. Hold on; my other phone is ringing." I heard Clareen speaking to someone. In a minute, she returned, "Sly, you still there?"

"Yes."

"That was Cindy. Everything is okay there. They had to wrestle Curly into the ambulance. He didn't want to go to the hospital. Herman said the worst thing that happened was they cut the power lines and used bolt-cutters on the gate padlock. Skip said the gate was open, but he didn't think we lost any cows. One other thing. They only cut the electric line to the house. They climbed the pole where it branches off to the outbuildings and the Foxxes' place. The only line cut was the 110-volt service. Two-twenty still is alive in the house."

"They just wanted the lighting out." I thought for a second and asked, "If Herman's still there, ask him about making a call to the power company and ask one of his friends to fix us up."

Clareen acknowledged, "He is there, and I'll ask him. Skip was asking what to do."

"Nothing! The people who are doing this are dangerous! I don't want any more of our people hurt."

"I'll tell him. He won't like that, but. . . . When will you be at the ranch?"

I looked at Trotter and asked, "How long?"

"Forty-five minutes, an hour at worst."

I asked Clareen, "You hear that?"

"Yes. I'll call Cindy, so you don't have to. Call me when you arrive, okay?"

I said, "Will do."

Clareen finished the conversation. "I hope that the boxes of gold you're hunting end up being the size of dump trucks. Won't be worth it if they aren't."

CHAPTER 55

"Wow, there was a lot of excitement here last night!" Russ is a positive guy who tries to see everything in the best possible light.

"You're right about the excitement. I wouldn't use the '*wow*.' I hope you weren't bothered too much," I said.

Russ shrugged his shoulders. "We slept through the shooting part of it. Skip woke us up to be sure we were okay."

Val asked, "Why would they want to break into your house? Surely not to loot it. They were on foot, so they had to be looking for something small and something specific."

"I'm sure they were. They were looking for Sally Sumner's letter with clues to finding the treasure. The one you have a copy of. By now, they have figured out I have it." Pausing, I spoke of something that bothered me, "We've got two groups searching for the same thing, but they feel like one. There are connecting wires between all that's happening. I'm sure, but how? That's the question." I took a deep breath. "I'm having trouble matching the ends."

"I think we have some solder to connect the wires," Russ said as Val started looking up information on her laptop.

"There's a flash drive where all the info is stored. But you might want to get something to take notes on. . . . I know that's the way you prefer to work," Russ said.

I pulled a legal pad from my desk drawer, picked up a pen, and nodded to Val and Russ.

"The best way to explain this in the least amount of time is to answer some of your last questions first." Val looked at Russ and nodded.

Russ scanned his computer's screen, then smiled at me. "The lady from the little theater in Beaufort made our tasks possible . . . even easy. That little theater was a catalyst for the whole thing." He punched a few keys, smiled, and said, "Ready?"

I nodded.

"Once I oiled up Margie's memory—what's her last name, Val?' he asked.

"Spelling," Val and I answered in unison.

"Yeh, anyway, she put the whole thing together like she was laying bricks for a wall. She really knows about putting together a play and all that goes on behind the scenes. Old Margie—" Val's withering stare told him to move along. "And now, getting back to our interest. When I mentioned Edward Kraggen, I punched a hole in the information damn." Russ scrolled through his notes. "Okay. Edward Kraggen and his wife, Venus, joined the little theater slightly before the Sumners. Margie said that Venus was the one who was interested in acting. . . .Edward had the talent to do it. They were originally from Green Mountain, North Carolina. Venus had worked for the University of Tennessee as some type of assistant to professors in their criminology department. She described corpses and made the whole company nauseous. Most everybody liked Edward; Margie's description was he was a great big old St. Bernard. The Kraggens were older than the Sumners by several years. They were friends for a while, but Margie thinks that tales Venus told about corpses made Helen shy away. She believes that Venus recruited the Crisps and the Tedders to join the little theater."

I asked, "How did that come about? That would make for an interesting connection."

"Let's see," Russ scrolled some more. "Margie said Mark Sumner was asked about his family tree. He told a story about a treasure buried with a relative that no one could find, the names of some of the families involved, and the thing that interested Venus, Helen had a claim on the money if it ever was found. Within two months, the Crisps and the Tedders joined."

Russ adjusted the text on his screen. "It was sort of strange. The Sumners, Tedders, and Crisps all became friends. They had a falling out for a while when Harn made a pass at Helen, but it got smoothed over. Least, that's what Margie thought. The Kraggens seemed to be the odd couple out. The Kraggens moved back to North Carolina a couple months before Helen and Mark left. But Margie said they stayed in touch with her and the Tedders and Crisps. Venus told Margie they would be back in Beaufort very soon, but they never came back. As far as the other three couples, things stayed the way it had been. Margie believed they remained good friends. With the exception of the day before the Sumners disappeared, the rest of them were close until the Sumners vanished."

"Did Margie tell you about that last day?" I asked.

"Not much. Everybody was mystified. The Sumners were normal and happy the day before. Next day they came in, hardly talked to anybody, except to tell them they were going to leave town. . . . They gathered up their things to take with them. Margie noticed they made a point to avoid the Crisps and Tedders. That's all." Russ nodded to his wife. "Val has the next part."

"Val, what do you have?" I asked.

"I have some things that make great sense and others that seem crazy." She glanced up from her laptop, "You ready?"

I nodded.

She said, "If you get behind taking notes, don't sweat it. You'll get a flash drive from me too."

I held up my pen, grinned, and she shook her head.

Val concentrated on the laptop's screen. "You wanted background on all four. I did the Sumners because I knew you'd want that next." She peeked at me over the top of the screen. "I'm going to skip the details I don't think have a bearing on your treasure hunt." Val's eyes returned to the screen. "Mark Sumner. You know he's a direct descendent of Sam Sr.'s. Born and raised in Okeechobee County. Football star but didn't have the grades for a scholarship. Known as a hard worker. Graduated high school and went straight into the Marines. Trained at Pendleton. Was transferred to Paris Island. As soon as he got here, Helen started visiting him. She was his high school sweetheart. You've heard the rest.

We know that he died at the Sandfly Road home. Anything after that is fake. Questions?"

"None."

"Helen Quarreles Sumner. She was born and raised in Okeechobee County. Was class valedictorian, queen of everything, voted by her class as 'most likely to succeed,' and voted by the boys of the class as the girl they'd most like to be stranded on a deserted island with. Helen was president of the Thespians Club. Great singing voice. Graduated high school and went to the University of Florida. Did great. Outstanding GPA. Something happened halfway through her junior year that made her decide to quit. She almost immediately rekindled her relationship with Mark. She moved to Beaufort. Very stable life. Seems as if she and Mark lived for each other. They were like any young couple. She did very well on her jobs. You know about the theater thing. Then the disappearance. After that . . . you have a complete 180° turn in her behavior. Up until she showed up in Bartow, she never stayed anywhere longer than two years, never kept a job for half that time. I called a couple of employers. . . . Their comments about her weren't stellar."

"What do you have on her when she moved to Bartow?" I asked.

"She just showed up one day. Within a month, she started to visit Ellen O'Neal. Took a clerk's job with the courthouse. Eight months after she came, the state people decided they needed to Baker Act the O'Neal woman. Ellen fought it. Helen became her champion. End of the story is Helen Sumner got custody of O'Neal. Helen quit her job with the county to take care of her great aunt. As far as the records go, they are living at the farm. A Mark Sumner is living with them. He has a job as an accountant with a local property management firm."

I said, "Where he has access to land records state-wide. The pieces are fitting."

Val started to talk about the Tedders. "Harvey Tedder. He was born and grew up in Florida. He graduated from Plant City High School. Went to Polk Junior College and got a degree in accounting. He met his wife there. He worked for a big company in Orlando. Some of his work buddies concocted a scheme to use company facilities to make after-market seats for boats. Harvey made the records of the stolen materials and labor go away. They got caught, and he did almost two years. He joined his wife, who had moved to Monroe, North Carolina. They met the Crisps there.

Anyway, he did delivery work, was a salesman at a Home Depot, and eventually worked in a tax office as a clerk. When the Crisps moved to Beaufort, he and Gretchen went with them."

I said, "Skip everything up until the Sumners disappeared."

"Well, they were gone in a month. Both couples moved back to Monroe. Russ told me, Margie said she thought Harvey wasn't a bad guy when you separated him from Harn Crisp." Val scrolled through some information. "There's a lot of interesting shit here that I'm going to cover with the Crisps. Harvey Tedder has kind of disappeared. Once in a while, a credit card in his name pops up. Application for a gun permit—I guess he forgot felons can't own a gun. Every time he surfaces, it's in the same general location that Mark Sumner is supposed to be in."

I raised my hand and said, "Move on."

A slight smile formed on Val's face. "Gretchen Cobb Tedder. She was born in Harrisburg, Pennsylvania. Her family moved to Lakeland, Florida when she was a sophomore. Decent grades, very attractive. She got a GED instead of a degree from the local high school. When I checked around, I found she dropped out of school because she was pregnant. Evidently, she had a recurrent problem with that. Anyway, she went to Polk Community College, met and married Harvey. When Harvey had his problems with the law, she moved to Monroe and stayed with some family friends. A few months after she got there, she met the Crisps. A little while later, she ended up with her third abortion. I guess the third time was a charm. She's had zero problems in that area since."

Russ cleared his throat, "Margie told me that Gretchen was a real flirt. It caused some problems with Harvey."

"I don't care about her sex life," I said.

"You might. Wait until I cover the Crisps."

I nodded for her to continue.

"After the Tedders moved to Monroe, she got a job as a hostess in a restaurant. Then she worked for a shirt factory. About six months in, she quit her job, and she and her husband left Monroe. If you don't mind, I'll cover the rest of it when I cover the Crisps. And, this is important, I'll cover the Kraggens at the same time."

"I don't need to know about their jobs and lives. Val, boil it down to the parts that affect the relationships and any impact on my project, if you can do it."

"The Crisps. Thelma is ten years older than Harn. Thelma worked for Harn's father as a makeup specialist in his funeral house. That's how they met. I think Thelma thought Harn would inherit the business. Buzzzzzzzz. That wasn't going to happen. His dad kicked him out. Harn is a maggot-infested pile of manure. A good-looking one, but a pile just the same. He had trouble dating for that reason. Folks knew him. Thelma had moved to Monroe from Green Mountain. Guess what? Thelma is Edward Kraggen's older sister. I tried talking to the Kraggens' parents. They wouldn't. So . . . I found their next-door neighbor. Her words were brief but descriptive. She said Edward was a good guy but easily led. He never got into serious trouble. Not so, for his two-year-older sister. Brenda, the neighbor lady, gave one example. When Thelma was in high school, she tied up one of her classmates, stripped her naked, and made her sit on the opening to a beehive. The girl spent three days in the hospital. Brenda told me she'd sooner spend a night locked in a room with a dozen copperheads than with Thelma. Thelma was forty-eight when she moved to Beaufort. Harn is ten years younger.

"Edward Kraggen and his wife, Venus, are an interesting pair. Edward and Thelma are from Yancy County, North Carolina . . . that's Green Mountain. Being so large made him a freak. He wasn't enough of an athlete to play basketball past high school. A promoter tried making him a pro wrestler. That didn't work. He was too good-natured. He worked on the family farm until he met Venus. She met him when he made a trip to an agricultural seminar in Knoxville. They got married and moved to Monroe. You know about her background in the criminology department at UT. She took a job working for . . . ding-dong, the Crisp Funeral home. Edward was a dispatcher for a trucking company. He got promoted, and they moved to Beaufort. Does that connect the lines for you?"

I grinned, "It sure does. Val, you and Russ are fantastic! You'd be great private investigators."

"No way! We don't want to have to deal with these types of people. We're happy doing what we're doing." Val pushed away from her computer.

Russ smiled smugly and said, "You haven't heard the best part. Some things really tie up the package."

He looked at his notes. "Evidently, Gretchen and her sex life created an explosion. According to some police records, she swore out a sexual assault charge against Harn. She was bruised and battered. Harn said it was consensual. In the investigation that followed, Harn produced multiple tapes of the two of them in the act . . . and she was a very willing partner. Within days, Harvey and Gretchen left Monroe. You know what has happened since."

"One becomes two," I said and whistled.

Russ held up his index finger, "And, three days after the Tedders left, Thelma Crisp vanished. She raided her's and Harn's bank accounts, took everything of value, and supposedly left town. The problem is, there is less evidence of her existence being alive than there is of Helen and Mark's. It boils down to two possibilities. She went deep underground to keep from being found, or she is *really* underground."

"There is a pattern you'd be blind not to see." I shook my head. "Harn is one violent character."

"Last, but damned important." Russ looked up from his laptop. "I called the company Kraggen worked for in Beaufort. When Edward Kraggen quit his dispatcher job, he said in six months he'd never have to work again. He said, 'There's a songbird that will sing me a fortune.' He claimed he'd be back to buy a couple rounds of drinks for his friends. That never happened."

I smiled and nodded.

Val asked, "Do you need me to go over more information on the Crisps or the Kraggens? The details of what I found are on the flash drive."

"I don't need you to go over any more. The wires look like they're connected. Like you say, I can always use the flash drive."

Confidence is knowing what obstacles you'll face and who the obstacles are. Over-confidence is not being aware that other possibilities could exist. I try to keep that in mind.

CHAPTER 56

The stack of correspondence on my desk was impressive. And depressing. And time-wasting.

I heard Clareen answer the phone, and I hoped it was for me. Clareen yelled, "Pick up, it's Nina Dupree from the Beaufort PD."

Nina's dulcet tones asked me how I was before getting to business. "We received the DNA results from our state crime lab. No surprise. Our skeleton is Helen Sumner. We got our matching samples from her sister and brother. Her parents are dead."

"Well, that proves what I already knew. My Helen Sumner is an imposter."

Nina said, "Yes, and you are probably dealing with one of the individuals that had some part in the murder."

"One that, based on what you have for evidence, you can't get extradited from Florida."

"That's it. I could get my claws on her with papers issued based on suspicion or as her being a material witness. Any ideas on how to get her here?"

I thought for several seconds before saying, "I might. You'll have to have two sets of papers. One for Helen Sumner, even if she isn't, and a set for Gretchen Tedder. I'd have the same set up for Mark Sumner and Harvey Tedder. I'm ninety-nine percent sure they are living with the primary client I'm working for. There may be a way to get them out of my hair and put them in one of your cells."

"I'm all ears," Nina said.

"Do you have the ability to set up something with a bank near the Georgia – South Carolina border? Just inside your state line?"

"I'm sure something can be arranged. What do I need to do?"

While she answered, I scribbled a few notes. "Okay, here goes. One, you rent a safety-deposit box in Helen Sumner's name. Two, go to the key store, make a copy of any safety-deposit key, put it in an envelope, and put it in the deposit box. Also, put a note in it that says, "Big O, State Bank." That's a real bank in Okeechobee. Three, arrange to have a person on site after I tell you I've baited the trap. Four, I'll disclose I've discovered that Helen must retrieve that key to give me access to the last thing I need to solve the clues needed to recover a treasure. You wait for her to show up. You have her on a fraud charge because you can prove the real Helen is dead."

"I don't know if I can plant that and get away with it," she said.

"Have a friend outside the department?" I asked.

If it's possible to hear a smile, I heard one. "Matter of fact, I have a good friend who is a loan officer in Anderson. With the proper explanation, it will get done."

I returned the smile, "When you're set, let me know. It may take me some time, but I believe this will work."

Chapter 57

"No black HUMV," Trotter told me as he sat in the side chair next to my desk. "Not at Friedman's Lane. Not at any places I checked."

"Did you see any other vehicles that looked suspicious?" I asked.

Trotter shook his head. "Nope."

I couldn't believe they had simply given up. "What about deer stands or some kind of a blind?"

"Boss, I'm not Davey Crockett."

I grinned. "That is a bit much. You have any idea how they might be keeping tabs on us?"

Trotter pinched his eyes shut, put his elbow on the desk, placed his head on his hand, and mumbled, "How would I do it?" His face shifted to a faint smile, and he pretended to be snoring.

"Smartass," I said as I knocked his arm out from under his head. I tried again, "Well?"

"Honestly, I can think of many ways to do it." He counted methods on his fingers. "A remote camera hidden on a fence post, a drone, someone posted in the fields wearing camo and hiding in the weeds, a car on Canoe Creek Road that's close enough to watch the intersection of Lake Marion Road. Want more?"

"You made your point. I'm planning for our trip to LaBelle, and I don't want our violent friends following us." I doodled on the legal pad in front of me, passing time as I tried to figure a way to keep from being followed.

"How about driving a vehicle to Herman's garage sometime before we make the trip and leave it. The day we go, we drive in the Jeep; they know that best. We leave the Jeep and take off in one of our trucks. If they are watching, they see us go in the garage but not come out." Trotter looked like he'd solved the problem.

"Pretty good, Trotter. That works if they don't know the rest of our vehicles. Plus, we have to drive one way or the other on Canoe Creek Road. They can post someone on either side and spot us before we can make another turn. Let's add a couple things to your idea. I'll rent a car in Okeechobee city. We'll park one of our trucks there. We drive back the rental car and leave it at Herman's. When we leave, we drive the rental car back to Okeechobee and pick up the truck. In case they spot us or figure out what we've done, I'll turn like I'm going to the office. We'll pull off and check to see if anyone is following us."

"Sounds like a plan," Trotter nodded and agreed. "Aaaaa, what if they are?" he asked.

"We make a plan 'C' up on the spot."

There were two and a half weeks left before June 1. I picked up the phone on my office desk and called Dennia's home number. It rang a few times before her smooth voice answered, "Hello, Sly, I hoped you'd call."

"Good to hear your voice." I was tongue-tied.

"Are you coming down soon?" she asked.

"Yes. In fact, that's what I'm calling about. If your offer is still open on borrowing your tank and pump rig, I'd like to take you up on it." I thought, *Please say yes.*

"Certainly, I'm looking forward to it." She hesitated for a couple of seconds, then asked, "Is Ken coming with you? I know that's the first thing Lily will ask. She's pestered me to find out when you were coming back."

"Trotter will be with me. We plan to come on Sunday afternoon. That will give us two days to do the preparation work. If everything works the way I expect, I'll be ready for my June 1 deadline." I asked, "Can you recommend a place to stay for a couple nights?"

"My ranch. I have several spare bedrooms, the fertilizer rig won't be the problem it might be at a motel, it will save time because I'll cook, and Lily will be forever grateful to me—well, for a month or so. Besides, my house is closer to the graveyard than the closest motel."

I had to get a grip. Sounding like a sixteen-year-old wasn't something I wished to do. "That's most kind of you. It would certainly expedite what we intend to do."

"I'm looking forward to having you gentlemen as guests." She added, "Besides having the tank filled with water and ready to go, is there anything else that you need?" Dennia sounded enthused by our visit. My spirits lifted an octave.

"One thing that would help is a couple of phone numbers." I checked two items on my to-do list. "I need a number for Oscar, the graveyard guy I met last time, and I need a number for Hendry County Permitting. We are probably going to have to dig at some point."

"I'll send the numbers to you in an email. You'll need directions to my ranch and the code for the gate keypad. They'll be in the email also." She took an audible breath and added, "Don't worry about the permit. I have an excellent *business* relationship with three of our five commissioners."

I noted the heavy emphasis she put on the word business in her last comment.

"Is there anything we can bring with us you'd like?"

She laughed, "Your patience. Ever since your man Trotter has been here, Lily is obsessed. You better warn him. My heifer is looking for her bull. I go through this about every six months. Don't worry; she's smart enough to keep the fence between them."

"Aaaaaa. Trotter isn't—"

Dennia laughed and said, "Remember, I've seen Trotter. I know what kind of bull *he* is. She's been warned."

CHAPTER 58

"Sorry, Sly. Your rental car is parked out back. I had so much business, I filled the garage with cars. It was inside for two days, and I put it where no one could scratch it up." Herman stood next to me as I sat in the driver's seat of my Jeep, and it idled at the garage's front doors.

"Thanks, Herman. I'm sure there was no harm done." I patted the steering wheel of my Jeep. "Think I can hide this old girl inside the garage for forty-eight hours? You can move it outside after that."

"Not a problem," Herman pointed to the last of four bays. "Pull 'er in there and go all the way to the rear."

It took a half-hour to transfer our clothes, tools, cameras, and electronics to the Ford Focus I'd rented. It was white, small, and in every way the antithesis of the vehicles we usually drove. Trotter walked to the road and carefully looked for the black HUMV, the silver Toyota, or any other suspicious vehicle loitering along Canoe Creek Road. He saw nothing.

People are often surprised to learn that Florida is ranked as one of the three top cattle-producing states in the union. If they need convincing, send them down US 441 or Florida 60. Pastures line those roads for miles and miles. Herefords, Angus, Brahman, Charolais, Simmental, Ona Whites, and many other mixed breeds graze peacefully by the hundreds. Clustered in other areas of the state dairies featuring large herds of Holsteins flourish.

Today's Florida is a heavily populated state whose livelihood relies on various economic engines. Tourism pops to most peoples' minds first and rightly so. Agriculture is up there; Florida fields provide produce and fruit on our tables, particularly in winter. Cattle quietly continue as a top contributor. Space provides jobs and prestige. It sports a multitude of satellite and light manufacturing facilities.

Just one hundred years ago, Florida remained an "eastern frontier" by the rest of the United States standards. Backward, poor, sparsely populated, and occasionally violent, cattle remained king, and the ranchers who owned them were one of the two dominant factors in shaping Florida and its politics.

Trotter and I drove roads lined with land that was very little different from 150 years ago or even much earlier than that. When we arrived at Yeehaw Junction, I made the turn on to Florida 60, drove for a couple of miles, and pulled into a farm lane that was lined with cabbage palms and palmettoes.

This would be the test: if we waited ten minutes and there was no sign of our being followed, it would be safe to proceed. Ten minutes elapsed. No black HUMV, no silver Toyota. No other suspicious event occurred. We resumed our trip, convinced we had avoided being tracked. A major problem had been avoided, we thought.

"Where are we going to eat?" Trotter never forgot his stomach. We were a few miles from downtown Okeechobee. I looked at the time display on the rented vehicle's dash. Eleven-fifteen. I knew the time it took to get from Okeechobee to LaBelle: an hour, maybe a few minutes more. It wouldn't take long to turn in our rental, maybe fifteen minutes.

I offered what I thought would be a pleasant alternative to Trotter. "Think you can keep that gut of yours in check for an hour-and-a-half? We have time to drive to LaBelle, eat at Betty and Billie's, and still be at the ranch before two."

Trotter looked at his belt line. He asked it, "What say, el Gutto?" He made a face, shook his head, and said, "El Gutto says, no way!"

"I don't believe it! Your stomach is more important than seeing the girl you told me you're going to marry?"

"She doesn't work today. Graham Bell invented telephones." Trotter's smile was as good as saying, "Gotcha!"

"What does that cavern inside your body want? We eat here unless you want very little choice. After we leave 'Chobee, there isn't much until LaBelle."

Trotter shrugged his shoulders. "Turn the car in. We might see something." He turned toward me and added, "We should get gas. Rental companies hold you up."

We had reached the town and were driving by the older business section. The highway passed the large and elongated town square that stretched for several blocks. At one end of the park were obligatory military tributes that are the fabric from which small towns are made.

Eventually, we turned right. We entered the new center of business, and within a few blocks, Trotter turned into a gas station to fill the tank. I slid out of the passenger's seat, credit card in hand, to pump gas.

When I opened the cover to the fill tube, I dropped the credit card. After picking it up, I glanced inside the alcove, where I would place the pump nozzle. A strange-looking device was attached to the metal on top. I read, '*Optimus 2.0.*' The name was familiar. Suddenly, I stiffened. It was a tracking device. If it wasn't part of the rental agency's security system, our enemies knew right where we were!

Florida Economy Rentals didn't use any tracking devices in their vehicles. We were compromised. After we returned the car, I spotted a highway patrol cruiser parked in the lot. I eased up to it and placed the "bug" in one of its wheel wells. I hoped it would drag those following us off on a futile chase. We left Okeechobee in Trotter's truck with full stomachs and depleted confidences.

CHAPTER 59

"We make the next turn." Trotter nodded and moved his truck into the left lane. Florida 78 separated from super-highway US 27 for the last twenty-five miles to LaBelle. I knew the intersection because it was one of the places I had discovered from my pursuit of history around the state. It lay in the heart of sugarcane country, a land so flat that a carpenter's level seemed unneeded. The fields were in the early stages of growth, only a foot or two high. You could see great distances in any direction.

My familiarity with the corner was the historical marker that stood high and stark on the road's shoulder. It commemorated the life and burial place of Billy Bowlegs, a Seminole Chief that returned from Oklahoma to his native soil for his final rest. He was buried in the Ortona Cemetery, one of the places I initially suspected the Sumners might be interred.

I scanned the road behind us carefully, looking for one of the suspect vehicles. There wasn't a black HUMV or silver Toyota that I could see, though the traffic was heavy enough they could have been hidden in it. I said, "Keep your speed at forty-five. I want to see if anything shows."

Trotter grunted his agreement and stayed far below his usual seventy. I kept my eyes fixed on the intersection. We'd traveled three-quarters-of-a-mile when I was satisfied no one was behind us. I said, "Let her rip." Trotter accelerated sharply.

We were about to round a curve that would end our ability to see far behind us. I took one last look. A black HUMV was just completing the turn on to the road we were on.

"Time for plan 'C.' I can't believe the bastards found a way to follow us. They are good, I'll give them that," I said.

Trotter glanced at me, lifting his eyebrows and shoulders at the same time.

"I think there may be something that will work. Keep running at sixty, so they can't miss us. Up ahead, you'll come to some curves, first right, you go a mile, then left. The Ortona Cemetery is ahead on your right. There's a sand road that parallels the highway. We want them to see us go in. Some oaks will screen us from their view. We must be in a position to speed out of the other end when we see them turn in. Then. . . . then we see how fast this truck will go."

"If you're talking racing them, I'll whip their asses." Trotter always said he was born to be a NASCAR driver. We'd soon find out.

As we negotiated the second curve, the HUMV moved closer so they wouldn't lose vision. Our tires thumped as they left the highway and traveled the sand road. I told Trotter, "Get this thing to the other end of this road as fast you can without wrecking us. I want us to tear out of here just as they pull in."

We passed the Billy Bowlegs Monument and sped to the exit. I told Trotter to stop where I could see the HUMV leave the road to follow us. The tension in the truck's cab was palpable. "Ready!" The HUMV slowed, but would it turn? It did! As the first half of the vehicle disappeared behind the oaks, I screamed, "Go! Floor it!" The truck's tires spun and peeled rubber as Trotter turned the F-150 into a T-bird. I looked at the speedometer. One-hundred-fifteen. I kept watching out the rear window. The road behind us was empty. Raw speed worked when stealth failed.

I continued to watch as Trotter raced away from our tail. When we reached the point where the road ended on another highway, we cut our speed back to normal. We watched. No HUMV appeared. We were free to go to Dennia Hays' ranch. I sincerely hoped we'd seen the last of our shadows for the next few days. I hoped, but I didn't believe.

CHAPTER 60

We were definitely at the right place. An elaborate wrought-iron arch spanned the paved drive lined by white wooden fences. The name 'Hays' in wrought iron letters in the arch at its apex eliminated all doubt. Two horses reared on their hind legs to support the name. Iron lacework comprising the rest of the arch suspended them between two ten-inch diameter poles fifteen feet high. The drive curved into a mini forest of thick, old, Spanish moss-encrusted oaks. It confirmed that Gardenia Hays wasn't on any poverty lists.

We stopped at the ornate gate made of steel bars with a mural of a farmhouse surrounded by horses, cows, and other farm animals mounted in its center. Located on an 'island' in the center of the exterior entrance was a mailbox nestled in a concrete stallion's outstretched legs. Next to it, and situated for the convenience of a driver in a vehicle, was the keypad . . . complete with a video camera and a screen.

Trotter powered down his window, pushed the numbered buttons on the gate monitor, and waited for a response. It was instantaneous. The gate began swinging inward before Lily's familiar face and voice welcomed us with, "Hi guys, come on in."

As he drove his truck through the gate and onto the Hays' farm drive, Trotter blinked his eyes and said, "I don't think we're entering a ghetto."

"Damn! I ain't believing this!" Trotter's mouth remained ajar. I understood why and made a quick check to be sure I kept my trap shut. The house in front of us was huge, built in the style of the early 1900s ranch homes, but in a grand fashion. Multiple cupolas suggested that the house was engineered like one as well. Before AC, Floridians of means used verandas, high sloped ceilings, and central vertical shafts/ducts to connect to cupolas to create convection cooling.

The horse barn looked as though it had been transported from the blue-grass earth around Lexington. Several bungalows and outbuildings surrounded the mansion. White purity covered everything, and forest green trim accented it all. My first look left an indelible impression. If I didn't know I was in rural Hendry County, I would have thought I was sitting in front of an estate in Naples or West Palm Beach.

Trotter drove on to the circular drive fronting Dennia's home. Everything inside the island created by the driveway was meticulously landscaped, as were the grounds around the house. A man in a western-style blue shirt and jeans emerged from the front door. He greeted us at the edge of the drive where Trotter parked. He said, "Hi. I'm Art. Welcome to the Hays Ranch. Let me take your luggage to your rooms."

We followed him up the stairs to the veranda, through double doors with Tiffany glass windows, into a world of what can only be described as wealth. Art stopped and pointed to a series of sliding glass doors. A large swimming pool was outside, surrounded by gardens, a cabana, and a bar area with several lounge chairs. Lily and Dennia were dressed in sundresses and were seated at the bar. A TV monitor mounted on a wall was showing the front gate. "Ms. Lily asked me to have you join them by the pool." Art smiled and pointed to the glass doors.

Trotter looked as uneasy as I felt. We were entering uncharted territory.

The four of us sat at the bar sipping mixed drinks. An air of social distance settled over Trotter . . . and me. I considered myself affluent . . . until Trotter parked his pickup in front of the mansion. Dennia and Lily immediately detected strain. I wasn't sure they knew what was causing it.

Dennia said, "I'm not sure what you wanted to do today. Oscar called to tell me he moved up cleaning the right-of-way next to the graves you're interested in. He said he hopes it saves you some time. We can ride over there if you wish. He did say he didn't want us doing any work in the graveyard on Sunday."

"The last thing I want to do is get the caretaker upset with us before we start. We'll stay away," I said.

"I know what I want to do," Lily said. She looked at Trotter and asked, "Do you ride? You don't have to be a jockey. We have horses that are so eas—"

"I ride a few days a week under normal circumstances," Trotter interrupted. "Remember, we live on a cattle ranch."

"Good! I want to show you our ranch. I'll get jeans and a shirt on, and we'll go riding." She looked at Trotter critically, "Those are nice boots. If you have old ones, you might want to change them. Some places I'll show you will be on foot and will be wet."

"I've got waterproof work boots. Your man Art took my suitcases in that wing." Trotter pointed in the direction we saw the man disappear. "I'll go that way. Where should I meet you?"

"Your room is the third door on the left, going down the hall. I'll meet you at the front door. That's the closest way to the stables," Lily said. She looked at me and added, "Mr. Harrell, your room is right across the hall." She pointed to a sliding glass door to the left of the pool. "You can get in from there."

"Thanks," I mumbled.

Dennia warned them, "Chiara will serve our supper at six. Don't be late." She looked at me, "I hope you like home-cooked Italian. Chiara is from Modena."

Trotter and Lily were disappearing as we spoke. I yelled at Trotter as he passed through the doors into the vestibule we'd first walked through, "You take good care of the lady."

He glared at me over his shoulder.

After they both disappeared, Dennia smiled and said, "Don't worry about Lily. She is definitely not a delicate flower. Cactus Rose or Skunk Cabbage Blossom are more appropriate names for her."

My face betrayed my doubts.

"Sly, I can assure you I have no worries. I won't for sixty days or so. Then. . . ." Dennia changed the subject. "Would you like to take a look at the tank and pump rig? It's in one of the outbuildings."

"I sure would."

"Well, let's go do it."

CHAPTER 61

The tank and pump were shiny stainless steel, mounted on a tandem axle trailer. It might have been the first farm trailer I'd ever seen without a spec of rust, no dirt from its last use clinging to its surfaces, and with tires that weren't old, worn, and fissured.

Dennia walked around to a Briggs and Stratton ten-horse motor. She said, "The gas tank is a little small; we should carry an extra six gallons." Dennia rubbed her hand on the stainless tank. "I have a bad news, good news type of thing. Roger, that's my ranch manager, told me I gave you the wrong information. The tank is not 1000 gallons. Bad news. The good news: it is actually 1200 gallons. No harm done."

"The rig is perfect!" I looked at the pump and tank with admiration in my eyes. "I believe I'll be able to do what has to be done in one fill-up."

"Don't worry about refilling if we need to. I have a permit to pump out of the river, and there is a spot I can get to it a little over a mile away." Dennia paused and looked at me for several seconds. "Do you mind telling me what flooding those graves with water is going to do for you?"

"Not at all. I don't want to bore you, so I'll give you the short story. I have a copy of an old, old letter providing clues to finding an inheritance for my client. The most important clue is finding a grave with greener grass growing over it. The woman who wrote the letter lived in the Northwest part of the Florida peninsula. In that area, a lot of the soil wasn't very productive, mostly ball-bearing sand. Water and fertilizer leeched right through it. So ranchers found a way to improve the yields of their dooryard gardens. They dug up the area under where they were going to put the garden. When they had two feet or so dug out, they placed large flat rocks in the bottom. They made the rocks act like a cup by being sure the middle was lower than the edges. Then they mixed the sand with good soil and filled it in back over the rocks. In effect, they made their gardens in an outsized flowerpot. It held fertilizer and water in place in the cup. The lady who wrote the note knew this and had the ability to build such a thing over the grave. That's what I'm looking for."

"That is ingenious." Dennia's eyes were bright. "It's like people who make their gardens in sunken wooden boxes. So you make the grass greener . . . you find the inheritance. Would adding a little liquid fertilizer help the process? I have plenty here to spare."

"Yes, it probably would. Under any circumstance, it will be a two-step process. If I'm correct, old Sally had that done to one of the graves. I'll have to wait a week. It will take that long for the water and fertilizer to penetrate deeper, leaving the grave with the rocks under it to remain greener."

"May I watch? Your whole project fascinates me."

"Oh, yes, I'd love to have you . . . there." I added the last word quickly to protect my thought. Her knowing smile told me I didn't do very well.

Wine and bourbon flowed after Dennia and I returned from viewing the tank and pump rig. Our eyes locked. I remained silent, for I knew what I chose to say next would probably chart where our relationship would head. I decided to be honest, completely honest. I leaned forward, maintaining the hard eye contact we shared. "Dennia, I'm not going to try to guess what you might want to hear. Instead, I'll tell you what I'm thinking and feeling. You are a beautiful, sensuous woman. If I told you I never thought about. . . . I won't spell it out, I'd be lying, and you would know I was. Am I curious about your business? I now see one of many? Yes. Does it consume me? No. In fact, I've seriously thought about asking you if you'd franchise . . . after seeing your digs today."

Silence, complete silence. Absolutely no change in her expression. After a long thirty seconds, she said, "If you're asking, yes, I'm attracted to you. Let's just let things happen. There is time for history later. Honestly, I'm fascinated by your past. There's time for that too."

CHAPTER 62

"Let's move it to the next row." The two-inch hose was perfect for the purpose for which we used it. Its end was a twelve-foot-long section with holes punched in it every few inches. Water flowed through these and drenched the soil beneath. We had arrived two hours before and already had soaked half of the parched earth in the section of the graveyard in which we were interested. Trotter and I pulled the hose to the beginning of the next row of graves. Our most significant concern: to do absolutely no damage to stones or memorial items.

"How's that?" Trotter sighted down the row, trying to keep the hose in a straight line and distribute the water as evenly as possible.

"Good," I answered. The ground we had already irrigated hungrily consumed the water. Puddles had nearly disappeared. Drought conditions existed, and I wondered if we should flood the earth twice. Dennia leaned against Trotter's F-150. I shouted, "Dennia, would you check the gage? Tell me how much water's left?"

She disappeared behind the tank and reappeared in a few seconds. "You have 830 gallons left."

"Thanks, I think we'll do as much as we can twice. Maybe go a little lighter the second time." Things were going so smoothly; it caused me concern.

I glanced at Dennia. She served as our lookout, with instructions to let me know if we appeared to be under observation. I expected that we'd attract local gawkers. She said she would know most of them and explain them away. So far, she'd had no reason to raise the alarm. In fact, she said there was a surprising lack of interest in our activities by the cemetery's neighbors. That was fine with me!

Usually, when I'm with Trotter, I don't need to check the pocket watch I carry. Yes, I have a fondness for antiques. He's a better custodian of time than Big Ben, the iconic London landmark. His stomach is more accurate. I thought we'd finish around two, but we were doing far better than that. Nine-thirty-seven. I pulled the Walmart special from my jeans pocket. We could afford the time. "Let's take a break," I announced. The pump went to idle, and Trotter was on the way to the truck and his cooler. Trotter is a Coor's man.

"Come join me," Dennia waved an invitation. She was seated on the trailer tongue. The woman wore a faded pair of baggy jeans and a tee proclaiming, "What's for Supper? – Florida Beef!" I couldn't help thinking the woman would look good dressed in a cardboard box.

I eased my butt on to the bar and smiled. Trotter grinned and walked around the front of his truck. I said, "I like your tee shirt. Lots of people need to take your advice."

"I know you have a place at Kenansville. How many cows do run there?"

"Right now, I'm down to around 950. I usually have from 1000 to 1200. A third of my herd is White Ona Angus. Herford's, Charolais, and I keep a small herd of Andalusians . . . the descendants of the cows the 1500s Spanish brought with them. They were the parent stock of the Florida scrub cows that founded the cattle business in the state. But you know that."

"My husband used to talk about Florida's cowboy tradition and all that went with it. Cattle, people, wildlife, and the style of life that went with them. I miss it. He died seven years ago. A lot of the little everyday things a friend or partner does don't get noticed until they disappear." Dennia smiled. "He was a good man. I was lucky. But life has to go on." She tilted her head to the side. "I don't know if I can ask, but have you ever been married? I know you're not now. You don't seem the single type."

Shaking my head, I said, "I've never found a lady who was willing to put up with me."

She smirked instead of answering.

"When I first got out of college, I got into a job that wasn't conducive to having a wife. I seldom was home. It was a little dangerous, maybe a lot dangerous, and I moved around so much I never had time to establish relationships of any type. I went from that job to one where I didn't have a home, and that job was a lot dangerous. One day I woke up, more than twenty years older, and most of the women that attracted me, and them to me, were either married or not interested in marriage . . . at least to me."

"What did you do? I mean, what kind of work?" she asked.

"I can tell you I worked for a national defense contractor and the US Department of Justice. I cannot tell you what I did for them." I smiled, "Quid pro quo, Dennia. How did you end up running a major ranch and an erotic dance establishment?"

"Aaaaa, Sly, we have a visitor," Trotter said as he walked up to us.

Dennia looked past Trotter. "It's only Oscar. . . ." she hesitated, "but he has a visitor I don't know."

I stood and said, "Hi, Oscar."

He smiled and waved. Oscar didn't have to tell me who was with him. I can smell reporters.

"Hi there, folks. I have someone to introduce you to. This here is Norma Reeves. She's a reporter from the Ft. Myers Newspress. I told her you were doing a historical project on old graves, and she wanted to meet you."

She extended a hand, and I shook it. She asked questions, and I lied liberally, hoping my explanation that my primary interest was researching old Florida families was good enough camouflage. When she asked if my "other business" was involved, I laughed and lied again with a hearty, *No!* When the lady made several attempts to push me into compromising statements and failed, she left. My golden retriever, Mandy, is a great judge of character. I'm sure, at the sight of Norma Reeves, she would have raced away, her tail tucked tight between her legs, whimpering as she sought a hiding place. We watched the reporter and Oscar return to his truck.

Trotter said, "Let's get this done."

CHAPTER 63

We sat around Dennia's pool, relaxing. By 2:30 in the afternoon, we had thoroughly doused and re-doused the graves. It was now 3:30, and the tank and pump rig were cleaned and back in its accustomed place in one of Dennia's outbuildings. Our first rounds of bourbon and wine became half-empty glasses, and we basked in the satisfaction of completing a job without complication.

Dennia and I were satisfied with small talk. Trotter picked a chair and positioned it on the edge of the pool. He kept one eye on the big screen TV and the other on the sliding doors. . . . Lily's shift was over at four, and Trotter was impatient.

Dennia asked, "So what do we do tomorrow? Do we water the graves again?"

"No, we did exactly what needed doing today. If what we're looking for is there, it will be best if the ground dries out this next week. It will make the grave with the rocks under it stand out more. The grass will be greener and thicker over it." I shook my head. "There isn't much I can do tomorrow. I want to be sure that my drawing of *all* the gravesites is correct. Adding the GPS location and bearings on the layout and orientation of the graves could be needed. Make some observations regarding some of the sites I think are the most likely hiding place. Sometime, I'll have to visit the county courthouse to see about permits."

"Don't worry about the permits. I had a friend in the codes enforcement department produce four of them, leaving the exact sites vacant. You'll have to fill in that information. They're all signed by a commissioner, so we're nice and legal. If you need to dig more than four holes. . . . Then, Houston, we have a problem."

"Then we don't have a problem. I'm bringing our GPR unit down with us next week. We'll know right where to dig."

Dennia was puzzled. "GPR unit, what's that?"

"Ground Penetrating Radar. Instead of sending radio waves into the air, it directs them into the ground. We can see what's underground deep enough to avoid digging up a grave that doesn't have what we want."

"How deep can it produce images that you can use?" she asked.

"It depends on the type of earth. The sand we'll be using it over . . . five to ten meters. That's a hell of a lot deeper than we need." I stared at her for a few seconds. "I don't know how to thank you enough. Getting the permits cleared with your county people, that's a fantastic help."

"It wasn't a problem for me; it might have been for you." She waved her hand. "It was no big deal."

I weighed whether to make the next remark or not. I decided, what the hell, and said, "The only bad part of that is it gave an excuse to prolong my stay a few more hours."

"You don't need an excuse." Dennia didn't smile.

Before I could say anything, there was a huge splash. Trotter had been pulled into the pool by a mischievous Lily, who swam up silently behind him.

CHAPTER 64

We paralleled the Hoover Dike that circled Lake Okeechobee. Trotter sat behind the wheel of his F-150, humming along with the country songs he played on his music system. He listened to Brad Paisley through 'muffs' that covered his ears.

Sugarcane filled the fields on the west side of the road, the dike the east. Hoover built the dike to prevent a repeat of one of the worst natural disasters in US history. In 1928, a colossal hurricane swept over the lake, traveling from north to south. Water piled up in front of the storm and destroyed South Bay, Belle Glade, and Pahokee. The result . . . 2,500 killed, the towns obliterated, and the agriculture economy in the area set back years.

Trotter's focus on his music, the monotony of the cane fields, and the forty-five-foot wall of sand that is the Hoover Dike made me look for a way to constructively spend the time in the truck. We passed the Glades Correctional Institute. The prison reminded me that those who had been involved in the murders of the Sumner couple should reside in one. It was my time to contribute to putting them there.

I looked for the phone numbers of the Beaufort Police Department and Detective Nina Dupree. Hoping the detective would be in the office, I tried her number first. In her mellow coastal Carolina drawl, she answered, "Detective Nina Dupree, Homicide Division. Can I help you?"

"Hey, Nina. It's SJ Harrell. If you have everything set up to throw a net over a couple of the folks in the Sumner murder case or whatever you're calling it, I'm ready to send them your way."

"Hey, SJ. Yes, we have everything ready to go. Just so you know, I contacted your office and had the lady that runs it send me one of your letterhead sheets and envelopes. Clareen addressed the envelope to the bank, typed the message on the letterhead, and even volunteered to forge your name on it so I could claim as little part in it as possible. She's great!"

"She is. She knows it. And I take good care of her." I asked, "Is the safety deposit box set up?"

"Yes. A friend at the Anderson Bank & Trust has the whole thing done. My team is ready to leave, and I'm going to be there to supervise. The envelope is already in the deposit box, and if Clareen doesn't have the key for the fake Helen already, she'll have it today."

"Good, I'll set everything in motion. You need to have somebody there right away. I'll get the key to her as soon as possible, and the way I'm framing the story to get her to Carolina, she'll have to get there practically overnight. She'll think I can't go forward on finding the treasure without it."

"Thank you!" Nina hesitated a second and added, "Be damned careful. I'm betting Harn Crisp is one of the dudes behind that second group. He's ruthless. I believe he's a killer. The one that killed the Sumners, and I think he might have killed his wife too."

CHAPTER 65

I had Helen Sumner, the person who was posing as her, thoroughly confused. That was precisely what I wanted. I purposely sounded as accusatory as I could, "Why are you holding out on me when you want me to find the inheritance? I'm having trouble with that."

"I don't remember. I really don't!" The woman was frantic. I could imagine what her face looked like.

"Do you know how shocking it was when we finally deciphered the note only to find there was another? And that you had retained possession without letting us know it existed? Your husband's note is a showstopper if I don't get it. I tried on my own. I had the key stolen from the police evidence locker, but I can't use it! You're the only person that can."

"Just a second," she said. I heard snatches of conversation in the background, including a voice I didn't recognize saying, "It could be. . . . I'm so confused. . . . Yes, she might have. . . . I don't know." When the woman masquerading as Helen Sumner returned to the phone, she said, "Mark said he put it there in my name. I'd forgotten. We didn't think you'd need that at all."

"I do. June 1 is practically here. I need you to drive up, get it out of the deposit box, and get it back to me. Where can I meet you on your way up to give you the key?"

"Just a second." There was discussion in the background. Then she said, "How about in the parking lot of The Catfish Place? The restaurant where we met?"

"Fine, let me speak to Ellen," I said.

"Why do you need to?" she asked.

I tried to sound as angry as I could, "Because I fucking want to! I'm about to deep-six this whole damned exercise."

"Okay, okay, okay." My scared imposter muffled the phone for several seconds before Ellen's voice said, "Mr. Harrell, I don't understand. What is happening?"

"The people with you evidently haven't been completely honest. When they leave, do you have someone who can stay there with you?" I asked.

"Yes, my nurse."

I lowered my voice a little to make it hard for anyone to overhear. "Ellen, I want you to stay where you are . . . don't go with your niece, understand? There is a chance you can't trust them. I know it is hard."

"I understand, Mr. Harrell. Recently . . . well, I do understand."

"Good, can you give me a phone number to reach you at?"

"You can call me on this one. It is my phone. They have two that belong to them. I'll call you if anything isn't right here." There was a pause; then she asked, "Do you think we will really find the gold?"

"Absolutely."

After I ended the call, I found an eavesdropper. Cindy asked, "How could those people believe the crap you fed them?"

"Easy. Greed and panic eliminate the thinking process."

CHAPTER 66

I watched the gray BMW with Gretchen and Harvey Tedder drive west toward the Sunshine Parkway. I recognized Harvey from his photo. Purposely, I presented an image of a mad, distrustful partner. It did what I hoped; they were anxious to get away from my presence as quickly as they could.

Their response when I asked them how soon they could return: three days. I growled my approval. They would quickly find out they weren't likely to be out of a jail cell for a long, long time.

I expected the negative and curt response to my question regarding where Ellen lived. Those words thoroughly disturbed them. My take was they were fearful of being 'cut out' of the money that they'd struggled for so long to obtain.

It was midday, Wednesday. I did my own calculation. They couldn't get to Anderson until long after the bank closed today. That meant the earliest they could show to get the 'red-herring' Nina had placed in the safety deposit box was Thursday at ten. I anticipated their eager arrival at the bank's doors as they opened. Nina was going to keep them from making a call back to Ellen for hopefully the rest of the day. She said she would plant the idea in their mind that they were in real jeopardy, particularly if additional witnesses came forward. If they elected to stay isolated from their old friends for a week, I'd be finished, *or they thought I would.* It gave me a sure eight hours to convince Ellen she was better off taking my counsel. The time clock to the end of the adventure was ticking.

The number I called on my cell answered. I said, "Nina, they are on the way."

CHAPTER 67

Trotter and I sat in my boat as a gentle wind shoved us along Lake Marian's shore. This shoreline was one of our favorite spots on the lake for bass. The lake formed a large cove of uniform depth that was seventy percent covered with lily pads, hogwort, and water hyacinths. Patches of flags, bullrushes, and cattails grew through the heavy cover. On a good day, you could expect a largemouth to crash up through the vegetation to inhale the weedless baits we used.

Our trip was a combination planning trip/fishing excursion. We'd both just caught and released nice fish when I suggested, "Let's take ten?" Trotter nodded and set down his pole. I prepared to followed suit. "Where did we leave off?" I asked.

"You were telling me about your call with Ellen O'Neal." Trotter reached for a Coors. He always asks, "Want one?"

"No, thanks." I'm strictly a bourbon man. I finished winding in my lure and laid my rod down without much thought; the spoon dangled in the water an inch under the surface. "Ellen O'Neal. It went much better than I could possibly have hoped for. I started the conversation very gingerly. The woman brought up concerns she had about her housemates. She told me some of the things that she believed both should know. They didn't have the foggiest notion about them. Ellen tested them by telling a story about a trip they supposedly went on to New Orleans. Only they didn't. Both imposters provided a wealth of details about a trip that never happened. She was perfectly willing to disassociate from them." I paused. "You know, that bothered me. All she was interested in was discussing the treasure. I planned to tell her that Helen and Mark Sumner were dead, and she'd been living with imposters. I didn't. My gut said no. I can't tell you why. Maybe I thought she'd freak out. Telling her later won't hurt. Nina Dupree said she'd make it as difficult as possible for the Tedders to call Ellen. She's going to tell them she was looking for someone to furnish her the motive. That should keep them from exposing their connection with anyone who knows about the treasure. It lifts the charge to Murder one. Nina said she'll notify me before the Tedders call Ellen . . . *if they do!* The only thing I couldn't get out of Ellen was where she was living. She is scared shitless of the people after her and the gold."

Trotter said, "Her fears are certainly warranted. I hope she never finds how real they are."

"I do too." I leaned back in my seat. "We need to take an arsenal with us next time we go to LaBelle. I want to be sure we have two MAC 10s, shotguns, AR-15s, and handguns. We don't need to be outgunned. Wilson said he saw an AK-47 in the HUMV. So. . . ."

"I'll have them ready to go with plenty of ammo. What other equipment you want to take?" Trotter asked.

"The GPR unit. I want a computer with CAD software loaded on it and a printer. Same hand tools as last time." I grinned. "I'm taking a bathing suit, so if I get dunked, half the stuff in my billfold isn't ruined."

Trotter had a wry grin, "Wise precaution."

"Speaking of precautions, Trotter, we need to be very careful. I want to be sure we distance both Hays ladies from what we're doing down there. Dragging them into the middle of what could end up as a banana republic war. . . . I want to be sure they stay out of danger."

Trotter put his elbows on his knees and stared at me. "It's a little late for that. Don't you think the bastards behind what happened to the Sumners and Burrows will try to extract information from anyone they think they can?"

"Yes. We hadn't got home when I realized that. One of us should have found a reason to stay down there. That's a mistake we'll rectify today. You're going back this afternoon. I'll call Dennia and make up a story on why you need to be there to safeguard what's in the graveyard. You can take what we'll need next weekend. We'll both leave the ranch at the same time this afternoon. You drive one of the company pickups . . . be sure it's white. I'll drive my Jeep. I'm sure they'll follow me, but if they don't, it is on you to lose them. Under no circumstance lead them to the Hays' ranch."

Trotter nodded solemnly.

"One last thing. Trotter, be damned sure you keep it in your pants! This affects me. I don't want you screwing up things for me with—"

My fishing rod rubbed against my leg. A bass had struck the lure as it wobbled along the surface. Pure luck allowed me to grab my pole before the bass pulled it into the water, weeds, and never, neverland. Trotter mumbled, "You have to be the luckiest man alive."

CHAPTER 68

"I'll be gone at least a week, Clareen. When I leave here, I'm going to the ranch, then to LaBelle. When I return, I hope we all will be a hell of a lot richer."

Clareen gave me an '*I know what you're really doing*' look.

I said, "I do like the woman. That isn't it. I pulled some innocent people into this Sumner affair. If something happened to any of them, my conscience would never let me forget."

"You have Trotter there already. He's good at what he does. You need to be there? Tell me that Dennia woman doesn't figure into it in some way."

Clareen is a truth serum. I couldn't avoid being honest with myself. "Yes, I guess she does."

"You like this one. It's been a while since I've seen interest, much less like. When this business is over, you need to bring her around," Clareen said.

I nodded and tried to look grim. "You feel the need to approve my dates?"

"With your track record, yes. Sly, if there's a tree loaded with sweet tangerines, you'll pick the one lemon mixed in. Anything you get serious about, run her by Cindy and me." She shook her head sadly. "For a man that's so smart on everything else, you were last in line when the good Lord was handing out woman-picking sense."

When I didn't reply, she asked, "Is there anything special I can do to help?"

I thought for a few seconds before answering, "Yes, a few things come to mind. I want you to check with Nina Dupree, she's—"

Clareen interrupted, "I know who she is."

"Okay, I need to know the instant something happens with the Tedders, the couple—" Clareen nodded, indicating she knew who the Tedders were, so I continued, "I need to know the second they are in a situation where they can contact Ellen O'Neal. Get in contact with me right away if that happens. Report any weird phone calls, the HUMV, or other mysterious vehicles hanging around; make sure you carry your gun with you; and expect there might be an attempt to break in here. Get me if Ellen calls. Tell anyone who calls I'm on a historical fact-finding trip. You don't know when I'll return. Check in with Cindy at least twice a day. I want to be sure everyone's safe. I'll call you once a day." My mind turned over what else she could do and concluded, "That should do it. I'm a cell phone call away if it doesn't."

Clareen nodded. "Trotter sent me a picture of Lily. After seeing her and hearing him talk, do you think this is the one that will make the dog give up hunting quail?"

I shrugged my shoulders and said, "I really don't know." She could have asked the same question about me.

CHAPTER 69

"Tell the Foxxes where I'll be. Tell them not to tell anyone where that is."

Cindy nodded, writing notes as I spoke.

"Make sure you have Sheriff Clark's number on your speed dial list. Any type of trespassing by anyone we don't know . . . you call him."

Cindy checked her notepad and said, "Herman Wilson called and wanted you to contact him. Something about a fox in the henhouse."

"I'll call right now."

"Are you leaving soon?" she asked. She motioned to a window, "It will be dark soon."

"No. I'm taking one of the pickups I usually don't drive, and I'm leaving after dark. To be sure I'm not followed, I'm going to take Lake Marian Road, and I'll drive the back way all the way to Highway 60."

"Goodness, that's all washboard roads and sand ruts. It will take you an hour just to drive that." Cindy frowned. "You'll need a couple extra soft drinks and a sandwich." She vanished into the kitchen.

Herman answered his cell phone, "Me and the boy caught forty of the biggest old shellcrackers you ever saw the other night. But Sly, that ain't what I called about. I feel bad, but we figured out how that bug got planted in that car you rented. Irene's been complaining about this woman that comes in twice a day and sits at the counter drinking coffee and talking to folks. She was running customers off talking about decaying bodies and such. I wouldn't run her off because she spent money every time she come in. Well, I was a watchin' her today, and guess what, that black HUMV picked her up, and they screeched out of here like their tails were on fire. I mentioned it around, and Henrietta said that woman asked if the Focus you rented was yours. I imagine we both can figure the rest. I'm plum sorry."

I had stored the last of my papers in my desk when I decided it would be a good idea to call Trotter. I'd see if I could bring anything he'd left behind. Before I could lean back in my chair, Trotter answered. His hello was grouchy.

"Hey Trotter, you need anything from here? I'm leaving in an hour."

"You have a bullshit deflector? Bring it if you have one," he growled more than spoke.

"What's wrong? Are Dennia and Lily okay?" I stood up without realizing I did.

"No, no, no. The girls are fine. They couldn't be better."

"What's wrong?" I repeated.

"Just wait until you get here. There's not a damned thing you can do, and you'll stew about it all the way down." Trotter typically isn't evasive. That bothered me. "Believe me, there's nothing you can do. It isn't going to keep us from going after the gold. When do you think you'll get here? Ten-thirty?"

"It probably will take me an hour extra. I'm going to drive the farm roads to Highway 60. That will be slow going, but I won't be followed that way. I know it will be late . . . eleven-thirty."

Trotter remained silent.

I asked impatiently, "What in hell is going on?"

"You don't have to worry about being followed. I spotted the HUMV at the ranch gate a couple hours ago. Before you ask why, I'll tell you. That damned reporter put a big article in the newspaper yesterday. This place and the cemetery are a zoo. Dennia used her influence to get local security posted at the graveyard. There's a deputy there around the clock. Oscar isn't making it easy. He's getting his fifteen minutes of fame and enjoying every second." Trotter sighed into the mic. "There's nothing you or any of us can do."

"Shit. Was there any mention of treasure, gold coins, anything?" I asked.

"No. Thank God for that. The Reeves woman added her imagination to the story. She said your interest in historical and archaeological artifacts are well known. She said, I quote, 'It's exciting to speculate if Mr. Harrell will discover an important historical item during his quest.' It was a featured article. Must have been a slow news day. We've had two TV stations call for information. We told them that we couldn't comment. They have to speak to you. Be ready."

"Change of plans. I'll leave as soon as I can. Do you need anything?" I asked.

"Nothing." Trotter answered and added, "I want to warn you. A few news people are hanging around the gate. Also, your lady has five of the nastiest looking Dobermans I've seen since I was in service. Keep a lookout for them."

"See you in a bit." I hung up and spent the next five minutes cursing under my breath.

CHAPTER 70

As I pulled through the Hays' ranch gate, I ignored the rabble of reporters and cameras gathered around the outside of the fencing. They screamed questions, most of which made no sense. I was glad to be past them but unsure about what might be waiting for me at the house. By the time I reached the circle in which the driveway terminated, I was apprehensive and agitated. The last thing I wanted had occurred: something that could destroy my new relationship.

The lights switched on and illuminated the veranda. Art was already outside and walking to my pickup. Shadows shielded his face, so I couldn't see his emotions. When I opened the pickup door, he said, "Where's your suitcase and anything else you want inside?" I pulled my two bags from the truck bed and handed them to him, saying, "Thanks, Art."

He looked relaxed and said, "That is a circus out there, isn't it?"

"Yes, I'm sorry about that. Is Dennia upset?"

"Not at all. You don't know Missy Dennia yet. Nothing like that bothers her. Only three things I know get to her." Art moved his hand over his mouth as if he'd said too much. "Sometimes, I talk when I shouldn't." He led me to the Tiffany stained glass doors, where a blurred figure was visible standing inside . . . waiting.

I was astonished. Trotter was right: neither Dennia, nor Lily, were perturbed by the unwanted beard on the face of the entrance to their home. Dennia's first words were, "I'm glad you're here." She took my elbow and guided me to the bar. It was a more decisive vote of confidence than a flurry of words. Trotter winked at me. I nodded just enough to acknowledge he was right.

When I offered my apologies about the upset I'd created, they dismissed them as unnecessary and acted as though nothing had occurred. They were more interested in my story about the tracking device and how it ended in the rental car's gas cap compartment.

"Trotter, have you been to the graveyard?" I asked.

"Yes, all four days I've been here. Thursday, Friday were calm. The newspaper article was printed Saturday. People started to show up late in the afternoon. Most just drove by. A few wanted to get out and snoop, but I kept them out. It was difficult. Oscar claimed he'd get someone to stay overnight to keep people from stomping all over the place. I doubted that. Dennia and I went over to be sure. There were a dozen-and-a-half people in the graveyard, and Oscar was conducting a tour. Dennia called in a favor from the sheriff. There's been at least one deputy there since. Today, the place was a zoo! Cars lined the road for a couple blocks. Oscar was giving impromptu history lessons. It was crazy. A couple of people complained there wasn't much to see. Hopefully, that will get around. Maybe things won't be bad during the week."

"Is there any good news?" I asked.

"Yes and no. Two of the graves have thick green grass on them. The one that is the best candidate isn't a grave one of the Sumners are buried in. The second-best candidate is. The rest all look the same."

"On the phone, you said you saw the black HUMV. Tell me about it."

"Not much to tell." He pointed to the screen that showed the area around the gate. "Around four this afternoon, it drove past. I went down there. Watched to see if it came back. It drove by twice. That was in twenty minutes. It never stopped. I stayed down there for an hour. It didn't return. There were three in the car. Two men, one woman. The men were Kraggen and Crisp. From the photos I saw, I'd guess the woman was Kraggen's wife."

Dennia turned to me. "They're after the same thing you are, aren't they?"

"Yes. They are violent individuals. We've tried to keep them from finding us here. We were fine until the reporter wrote her story. I'm sure they heard the TV coverage with my name singled out. Dennia, I didn't want to expose you and Lily to this."

"How could anyone guess that Oscar would call a newspaper reporter? The old fart wanted some excitement. Managing a cemetery doesn't offer much of that." Dennia looked at Lily. "We're big girls, and we can take care of ourselves. Right, Lily?"

Lily agreed, "Right, Mom."

I nodded and thought for a few seconds, then said, "I don't want to put you in more danger. Trotter and I will get out of here tomorrow morning."

"No, you won't!" Dennia's expression was deadly serious. "Through no fault of yours, the publicity has involved us. Those people you worry about don't know how deeply we're involved. They may believe we know everything. Moving out won't change that. I'll feel a hell of a lot safer with you two here. I have eight tough ranch hands and five of the meanest dogs in the county around us, but Sly, please stay. Besides, if you think you'd feel bad if something happened to us, think how badly you'd feel if you weren't here to protect us."

"She's right, Sly," Trotter agreed. He's slid his arm around Lily.

Dennia took a sip of her drink. "What can we do to get this finished?"

"The only thing we need that we don't have right now is a backhoe. We won't need that until we locate the treasure. If we get lucky, that might be tomorrow. If not, we'll have to wait another week until after June 1. Either way, we need that piece of equipment. That is, unless we dig it up by hand. . . . I don't think so. There shouldn't be a problem renting one. What *is* a problem is the minute we rent it, and pull it in here, we announce we're going to be digging. The rumor mill will crank up; there'll be nosey reporters wall to wall . . . it will be a mess."

Dennia finished her drink. "You won't have to rent the equipment, and you won't have to pull it back here. I have a friend who has a farm less than a mile from the Denaud Cemetery. He has a new backhoe. We can borrow it for as long as we want, when we want. Can either of you operate it?"

Trotter raised his hand, "I've operated about every kind of construction equipment."

Dennia said, "I'll make the call."

CHAPTER 71

"It isn't as bad as yesterday," Trotter said.

We approached the graves on the road lined with local curiosity seekers. Lily counted eleven cars. The deputy, who looked harried, was in the process of shooing a group of five people away from the barbed wire fence. Yellow tape strung around the circumference of the cemetery did little to deter gawkers. People from the cars packed the right-of-way adjacent to the graves. I hadn't expected to perform in front of an audience. There wasn't any way around it; we'd do the preliminary search with a crowd looking on.

Dennia commented, "I know about half of these people. Looking at license plates, most of the rest are from Lee County; that's Ft. Myers. That article did cause a commotion." She pointed to the deputy. "I know him." The crew cab door opened, and she climbed down. "I'll go get Rufus to clear a place for us to park."

The Ground Penetrating Radar functioned correctly. We could examine various levels beneath the surface. Coffins and their contents appeared on the screen as we

DL HAVLIN — 236

rolled over each of the Sumner graves. The caskets were there. The grizzly skeletons were there. And . . . nothing else. I re-examined the Sumner grave that Trotter had found with greener grass. I rolled over it again . . . and again . . . and again . . . with the same result. Einstein's quote that repeating the same thing over and over and expecting a different result is . . . well . . . stupid. There was no treasure there.

I fully expected to find the Sumner grave with green grass to have the rocks buried a couple feet beneath the surface. There was no trace of the cup that retains water and nutrients. When I learned that Sally Sumner grew up in a place where that practice was common, I was sure I'd discovered the key to finding the inheritance.

Trotter looked at me for some ray of optimism. I couldn't muster even one. I stood with my hands resting on my hips. What was I doing wrong? I decided to take a look at Sally Sumner's clue letter.

"Where are you headed? Dennia asked. She walked beside me.

"To the truck. I want to read the instructions old Sally left for her female descendants."

I opened the pickup door, opened my briefcase, and removed the file folder containing the letter. The words written on the paper appeared in my mind before I opened the folder. I thought I'd memorized the entire document. What hadn't I interpreted correctly? What had I failed to do? To understand?

The first paragraph had no bearing on finding the treasure. The second did. "Find the one I bore that lies still who earned nothing yet received all." That had to be Sam Sumner Jr. But how? Every bit of research told me his body was never found. I passed over that as being impossible to interpret.

The third paragraph wasn't any help either. "Daughters, read this!" Those words told me what followed were the critical instructions in paragraph four. We were at the place where the Sumners were buried, not where Sally was interred, and close to the old cattle trails . . . within two hundred yards. The next sentence said, "Stand three paces from the stone of one of the unworthy ones, the grave with the greener grass." I'd stood three paces from the Sumner stones . . . but they were not the grave with greener grass. It struck me. I had not followed the exact instructions! I slapped my forehead with my palm.

"What's wrong?" Dennia asked.

"I did what most people do when they open a box of a new piece of equipment and try to operate it. I didn't read the instructions carefully enough." I started back to the graveyard. "Let's go do what she said."

The next minute would dash our hopes or exhilarate us. I lined up the radar unit at the foot of the grave that had the greenest grass in the cemetery section that was critical to us. "Ready?" I asked.

Trotter said, "You're running the show."

I turned on the unit and began adjusting the depth of penetration. The screen remained blank until we reached twenty inches. Rocks appeared at the outer edge of the grave. The next few inches disclosed the stone forming the pocket I had expected.

Trotter watched the screen and said, "Holy shit, we got it!"

"Things are looking good, but let's not get too excited. And for sure, we don't want those around us to see we found something," I cautioned.

"Can I see?" Dennia asked.

I stood away from the screen, "Sure."

"I can see it is different here than the other graves, but I don't see what you're excited about."

"Let me adjust this a bit." I turned the dial regulating wave penetration, which would send the signal deeper. They disclosed something that made me stiffen. A skeleton lies beneath the rocks, not in an orderly fashion within a coffin. It sprawled haphazardly, as if simply dumped into the open pit. I looked at it in disbelief. Trotter and Dennia gasped.

Trotter turned around and read the information on the gravestone. "Alice Smith, there's no birth date, died June 2, 1899." He looked up. "That's a few days after Sam Sumner Sr. died."

While he was speaking, I bent over and adjusted the radar to penetrate deeper. At the standard burial depth, a coffin containing a smaller adult skeleton showed on the screen. That skeleton had not been placed in the coffin with any reverence. It was in an unusual position on one side.

"What in the world?" Dennia said.

I straighten up. "Well, I think we just discovered the bodies from a murder that took place 125 years ago. Meet Samuel Sumner Jr. and his mistress."

CHAPTER 72

The gravestone in front of me was notable for what it didn't commemorate. It was large, which made its lack of inscription more conspicuous. I guessed its height as three-and-a-half feet and its width as two feet. In fact, it was one of the larger markers in the section of the cemetery where it stood. The stone's rounded top had a distinctive three-inch hole centered six inches down.

The stone looked unfinished. Its rounded top, the hole, and the positioning of the meager inscription gave the appearance of providing space for significant flourishes and messages. The impression? That stone probably looked the way it did due to the haste and stealth required to erect it.

"Alice Smith, I wonder if that was your name," I spoke to the marker, not my companions.

Dennia asked, "Do you think it was?"

I hadn't realized she was only a few feet from me. "I don't know, but I doubt it. It would be the height of arrogance to murder someone and hide their body under a gravestone with their name engraved on it."

Trotter walked up and said, "That's the third time I've run the GPR over all the Sumner graves and the ones on either side. I haven't found anything worth looking at. Except for what looks like some small items, a piece of metal, something like that, there is nothing. I even tried to penetrate under the coffins. I think we have been performing a goose chase, or we need to wait until June 1."

I was sure the treasure was either in the graveyard or had been. Sally Sumner's explicit instructions were to do the recovery on June 1. I decided we should wait to do anything further. "We're doing the Einstein thing. We'll wait until June 1. There is one last thing I want to do. I'm going to run the radar unit over the grave with greener grass. Trotter, record the images of each block. There may be some sort of clue in the skeletons or the grave we haven't figured out."

"Are you going to quit soon?" Lily asked.

"Yes, it won't take fifteen minutes to finish," I said.

She nodded in the direction of the road fronting the cemetery. "Isn't that the black HUMV you've been watching for?"

"Yes, that looks like it." I asked Dennia, "How long is the sheriff going to keep a deputy posted here?"

"A couple more days. Do you think we need the deputy longer?"

"Not until after June 1. Then we'll need one badly or not at all."

CHAPTER 73

Driving the roads from Kenansville to LaBelle was so routine that my truck tugged at the steering wheel at each required turn, or so it felt. This trip should resolve the issue. Or would it? As I drove the last portion of the cow pasture-lined roads, I remembered my conversation with Russ Foxx regarding Sally Sumner's letter's cryptic clues. Three items that were parts of the instruction were still a mystery, with only guesses about their true meaning.

The first nebulous clue was, "*the son above will point the way to the son below.*" We believed that the clue referred to what I'd thought was the random position of Sam Sumner's arms, both pointed to one of his brothers at a lower level beside him.

We had no clear answer for the clue that stated, "*Goins lies there, beneath a cloud that covers many points.*" We believed Goins was the word coins disguised. The cloud and many points were a mystery in substance, if not meaning. Russ and I agreed the clue warned of a booby trap.

The last clue was a complete mystery. *One of a dozen eggs may be bad, check for it to the last.* It made no sense to either of us. We set it aside, hoping something would become evident as the search progressed.

I passed the Ortona Graveyard and remembered our experience with whom I believed to be Harn Crisp and the Kraggens. I was confident they would attempt to seize the treasure. The question was, when?

If I were them and was comfortable performing violent acts, I saw them waiting until we'd found the cache, and they'd try to take it from us. I decided I should plan for that eventuality. Trotter stayed in LaBelle for the last week to protect the treasure and to protect the Hays. There had been no attempt on either. I wondered if our competitors had given up. Naw, not likely! In twenty-four hours, we'd all know. *I thought.*

"We don't want to show up early. I need to be there to have everything ready to go at three. It should take less than an hour." Trotter looked at me like I'd lost my mind. I was notorious for arriving extra early to any event with which I was connected. "Trotter, if we get there early, we'll draw flies. The type that drive HUMVs."

"What if the scum bags in the HUMV are already waiting?" Trotter asked.

I looked at him for several seconds before asking, "You know we can't do a damned thing but let them watch. What's bugging you?"

"I don't do waiting well."

He needed some 'busy' work. "Let's put your combat training to work. Find a place with some defilade we can get too fast if those turkeys decide to start shooting. You pick the weapons. I'm adding to your job. Each time we go there, you put a locked case of guns at the place you pick. We each need a key to it. When we're done, you retrieve the case. Let's call it insurance."

Trotter and I lifted the Ground Penetrating Radar unit out of the pickup truck's bed. I asked Dennia, "Are they still parked in the same spot?"

"Yes. One man is leaning against the HUMV, watching us with binoculars."

"Dennia, would you keep watching them?" I asked.

"Sure."

"If they move from that spot, tell me right away, and you and Lily leave. If you can call your friend at the sheriff's department and get a squad car here . . . that would be great," I said.

"That won't be a problem," she removed a small set of field glasses from her purse. As Trotter and I set the GPR unit inside the barbed wire fence surrounding the cemetery, she said, "There is a man and a woman inside the HUMV."

"That accounts for them all," I said.

Trotter put his hands on his hips and prodded me. "We going to do this?"

I took a last glance at the HUMV, and Trotter saw me do it.

"There's no way they're going to stage some wild ass commando-style raid during daylight with a dozen cars and three dozen witnesses standing around. If they make a move, they'll let us get the treasure out of the ground or just about so. They have to move fast to be able to get it away from us. They aren't stupid." I knew that was true.

Trotter turned on the GPR unit. "You have the O'Neal woman's note?" he asked.

I said, "Yes," as I followed the first instruction and went to stand at the foot of the grave with greener grass, three paces from the stone. Trotter and I agreed we would make our assumptions about the instructions we couldn't decipher. I began reading the portion of the note with clues and acting on what we thought they meant.

I read the second paragraph.

Unworthy man gains for he is man. Find the one I bore that lies still who earned nothing yet received all. All that was given was removed. That which was removed will be given.

"We agreed the 'unworthy man' and 'find the one I bore that lies still,' refers to her son Samuel, Jr., and that we assume he is the skeleton buried under the rocks." I looked up at Trotter.

He said, "Yes."

I read the last paragraph.

Daughters, read this! The first day of June go to the place where we lie, but not I. The one where the cattle pass. Do as these words here say. Keep the sun in your front. Stand three paces from the stone of one of the unworthy ones, the grave with the greener

grass. As a clock's arms reach three o'clock, the son above will
point the way to the son below. Beneath the pointed place is the
plate with many strikes. Start as it says and count the strikes. Goins
lies there, beneath a cloud that covers many points. Beware the
cloud but find all that is yours. Remember as I taught you, one of
a dozen eggs may be bad, check for it to the last.

I began reciting to Trotter my interpretations of the remaining clues. "First clue is 'The place where we lie, but not I,' refers to this graveyard. 'The first day of June go the place,' that's in there to be sure rainy season has started, and the grave will have the greener grass. I would have thought it had something to do with the sun's position, but that doesn't work with the later clues. We're close to the old cattle trail. I'm standing with the sun in front of me. The son above is Sam Jr., pointing to the son below, which is the skeleton of Markum Sumner. The arms are in the three o'clock position from where I'm standing. Beneath the pointed place means where Sam Jr.'s arms point to where the final clue is buried. It's a plate of some kind with directions to the gold."

"What about the twelve-egg thing?" Trotter asked.

"I have no idea, do you?" I asked.

Trotter shrugged his shoulders. He turned on the GPR unit and quickly moved the unit to show the skeleton beneath the rocks. The image on the screen showed both arms pointing to my right at a ninety-degree angle as I stood in the spot dictated by the clues.

I helped Trotter line up the unit in the exact direction the boney fingers pointed. He inched the unit forward until it had passed entirely across the adjoining grave. Nothing appeared on the screen! Our disappointment was crushing. We had assumed the plate would be buried at least two feet deep. I told Trotter, "Let's start over. This time we'll start a few inches from the surface and work down six inches at a time."

He'd made the first pass without success. Trotter had only covered a quarter of the next pass when he stopped and yelled, "I got something!"

We stared at the screen. The object was flat and appeared to be stuck into the earth vertically. It looked to be a four-inch by six-inch object a quarter-inch thick. The gray blur on the screen held real promise. "I see how we missed it the other day. We were looking too deep, and it has a very small profile."

Lily appeared next to us with a shovel in hand. Trotter carefully marked the spot; I dug around the object to be sure I didn't damage it. I spent as much time to unearth it as I would have taken to excavate an important fossil. Finally, I removed the dirt from a flattened beer can!

"We're missing something," I said. The four of us sat on the ground around the Ground Penetrating Radar unit. We had spent the previous two hours painstakingly moving the GPR back and forth over the next grave, then the one next to that. We adjusted the penetration depth to add a few inches at a time. When we reached a depth of a foot below the coffins, I realized we were wasting our time. I asked myself, *Have we exhausted every possible solution?* The bitter thought that I bought a fairy tale and tried to make it reality, laughed at me. I'd involved innocent people . . . for this? Then I remembered one of my discussions with Russ Foxx. He was right. We wouldn't know we interpreted the clues correctly, or even had them all, until we had the original letter Sally Sumner had written. It was a long shot, but it was the only shot we had.

"We are missing something," I said. "We're suspending the search until we have the proper document to search with." Trotter, Dennia, and Lily all looked at me like I was crazy. I explained, "We have a copy of Sally Sumner's letter, not the original."

"Didn't Helen Sumner or whoever say you got an exact copy?" Trotter asked.

"The whoever is the problem. Her truth track record leaves a lot to be desired. Anything she told us is suspect." I stood up and turned the power off on the radar unit. "Let's get everything gathered up and loaded in the truck."

Trotter headed to a ditch he'd selected as a place to take cover in the event we needed to protect ourselves. He was going there to retrieve a duffel bag with weapons and ammo in it.

The women and I had everything in the truck when Trotter placed the duffel bag in the truck bed. He stopped next to me and asked, "Boss, is this something you want to spend more time on?"

I looked at him several seconds before paraphrasing Edison. "Many people come very close to success and quit at its very doorstep. I succeed because I take the last few steps."

CHAPTER 74

"So that's where we stand, Ellen. I must have the original letter Sally Sumner wrote. There are clues coded into it that I have to have to find your inheritance." I listened for her response. After she remained silent for what I considered too long, I said, "I either have to have it or give up on this whole project."

That jarred her out of her silence. "Mr. Harrell, you have a copy."

"That copy isn't the original. There could be all types of techniques in the original that are the key to using the rest of the letter." I hesitated, then asked, "*Is* the copy we received exactly the same, letter for letter?"

When she hesitated, I knew it wasn't. Ellen's voice was halting, "The only thing different is, when Helen copied the letter, there were misspelled words in it. She corrected the spelling in the copy you have."

"That could be part of the solution. Invisible ink could have been used. A row system to leave a message. There are an endless numbers of possibilities. We'll never know unless we have the original. You either have to trust me with your letter or find someone else to help you." I waited, prepared for either answer.

"Could I send you a picture of it? Maybe I can get a copy from a copy machine?" she asked.

"That won't do . . . the clue could be in the paper itself."

"I'll have trouble getting out."

I purposely sounded disgusted. "I'll drive to where you are to pick it up."

"No. I'll get someone to drive me. Where can I meet you?"

I had arrived at MacDonald's an hour before Ellen O'Neal told me she'd arrive. The extra time had been due to giving her my assurance I would do whatever was required to avoid being followed from the Hays Ranch in Labelle to the Bartow restaurant. No one attempted to follow me. I sat in the corner Ellen said she'd prefer.

I had nothing to do but sip coffee and watch the parking lot. I noticed a brown Honda make three circuits through the uncrowded blacktop. There was only one gray head in the car, so I quickly dismissed it as her possible transportation. It was a little past the ten-thirty meeting time. An uncomfortable feeling had already entered my thinking.

As I watched, Ellen O'Neal appeared outside the restaurant window. She peered in until she saw me and waved. I held up my hand to acknowledge I saw her as she made her way to the door. She leaned heavily on a cane as she walked, profusely thanking a young man who opened the door for her.

It was the first time I'd seen her stand. Ellen was taller than I supposed she was. She clutched the same file folder she'd carried the letter in when she visited my office. I was surprised she was alone.

She smiled as she came close. I started to get up.

"Please, stay seated, Mr. Harrell. The person who brought me can't stay, so I'll just give you the letter and leave. Besides, it is hard for me to get up once I get down." She placed the file folder in front of me. "Would you check to be sure it's there? I'm forgetful at times."

"Sure," I said, though I thought the request was strange. The original was in the folder when I opened it. "It's there. I'll let you know as soon as we decipher it and search."

"Please be careful with it. It has sentimental value to me." She glanced outside and said, "I'm so sorry, but I have to leave. The woman who brought me is afraid. Could you wait here for ten minutes? Just in case you were followed?"

"Sure. I'll stay for fifteen."

"Thank you." She smiled, and as she did, a small crack in her makeup appeared. I wouldn't have noticed. Ellen put her hand up to cover it, and that's what drew my attention. She quickly walked away.

There was a possibility I hadn't thought of before. I called the Foxxes to see if they could do something for me. I wanted to know if they had a way to hack into a system to find the location of a cell phone. If I called Ellen's phone, I could locate where she was living.

Then I called Maureen Diesselli. She knew Ellen O'Neal. My first question was, "Can you describe the Ellen O'Neal you know for me? Height, weight, eye color, those kind of things."

I left MacDonald's with a new sense of urgency. My to-do list now included calls to Clareen, Cindy, and Riaffort. If the real Ellen O'Neal was with an imposter, we had to get her to safety. Those three were the people to do it.

CHAPTER 75

It only took an hour to decipher the additional clues in Sally's letter. I laid the two side-by-side on Dennia's bar. "Okay, I think we'll be successful this time. Come take a look." I motioned for Trotter, Dennia, and Lily to examine what I'd discovered.

I asked, "What do you see that's different?"

All three began reading . . . they stopped to say almost at the same time, "There are words misspelled."

I grinned and said, "You're all right. And . . . that's one of the key things we were missing. Those misspelled words and the clue about the twelve eggs change the instructions of Sally's letter completely. Sally Sumner was one sharp broad." I pointed to the letters. "See if you can figure it out. I've already solved it halfway for you."

They compared the two letters.

The copy of the letter given to me:

> To my Flesh and Soul daughters.
>
> You are as worthy as any. Let it not be a curse to be one that bears children. I wish a wrong to be set right. I start the count.
>
> Unworthy man gains for he is man. Find the one I bore that lies still who earned nothing yet received all. All that was given was

removed. That which was removed will be given.

Let the oldest daughter find what is hers. If she cannot, let
her oldest, then the oldest of each generation look for the way.
Find the long path to recover what is the Sumner women's due.

Daughters, read this! The first day of June go to the place
where we lie, but not I. The one where the cattle pass. Do as these
words here say. Keep the sun in your front. Stand three paces from
the stone of one of the unworthy ones, the grave with the greener
grass. As the clock's arms reach three o'clock, the son above will
point the way to the son below. Beneath the pointed place is the
plate with many strikes. Start as it says and count the strikes. Goins
lies there, beneath a cloud that covers many points. Beware the
cloud but find all that is yours. Remember as I taught you, one of
a dozen eggs may be bad, check for it to the last.

  Mother Sally.

The original letter written by Sally Sumner:

  To my Flesh and Soul daughters.
  You are as worthy as any. Let it not be a curse to be one that
bears children. I wish a wrong to be set right. I start the count.
  Unwirthy man gains for he is man. Find the one I bore thut
lies still who earned nothing yet received all. All that was givin was
removed. That which was removed will be given.
  Let the oldost daughter find what is hers. If she cannot, let
her oldest, thon the oldest of each generation look for the way.
Find the leng path to recover what is the Sumner women's due.
  Daughters, read thus! The first day of June go to the place
where we lii, but not I. The one where the cattle pass. Do as thesa
words here say. Keep the sun in your front. Stand three pacis from
the stone of one of the unworthy ones, the grave weth the greener

> grass. As the clock's arms reach three o'clock, the son above will
> point the way to the son below. Beneath the pointed place is the
> plate with many strikes. Start as it says and count the strikes. Goins
> lies there, beneath a cloud that covers many points. Beware the
> cloud but find all that is yours. Remember as I taught you, one of
> a dozen eggs may be bad, check for it to the last.
>
> Mother Sally.

Lily was the first to capitulate. Dennia shook her head. Finally, Trotter shrugged his shoulders. He said, "Okay, Sherlock, baffle us with your bullshit."

I said, "There's one three-letter word in this letter that is the real key to finding old Sam's money. The trick is finding it. Sally disguised it well. Remember, we couldn't figure out what the egg thing was about? Well, the word egg represents misspelled words. Get it, bad eggs?"

Dennia smiled as I continued.

"She tells us twelve is important. She tells us bad eggs are important. And . . . she tells where to start our count. In the first paragraph, which we thought wasn't important."

Dennia said, "I think I see it!"

I nodded, grinned, and told her, "You may do the honors."

"I'm pretty sure I know. Starting in the next paragraph after she writes 'count,' the first word is misspelled, and every twelfth word afterward for twelve words. Except, the last word isn't misspelled unless it has a different meaning. I think 'son' doesn't refer to one of Sumner's boys; it is a misspelling of sun, that thing that rises and sets every day. She's referring to using the sun as a locator."

"You win the prize," I said. "I'm willing to bet when we shine a light through the hole in the gravestone at a place where the sun would be at around three o'clock. It will point straight at what we're looking for."

Trotter asked. "What do we do, wait for three o'clock tomorrow afternoon? We're only two days away from June first. The location shouldn't vary that much. Even if we're off a little, the GPR should find it for us if we can get the proper line."

"The line and waiting for the sun are not problems. Remember, I took bearings on the graves' orientation. I've sent the information to Russ Foxx. Russ says he can determine where the sun is positioned June 1 and its angle over the horizon, in relation to the grave. He'll send the angle we need to shine the flashlight through the hole in the gravestone. In the next fifteen minutes!" I looked at them and asked, "I'm going to find the indicator tonight, determine where the treasure is from that, and verify it's there. We'll dig it up tomorrow. Who wants to come with me?"

CHAPTER 76

"If there are such things as ghosts, we should see one tonight," Lily said as we got out of the pickup.

Trotter shined his flashlight on his watch. "Not the right time. It isn't midnight yet."

"How long before they come out?" Lily was anxious for the opportunity. I assumed she was jesting.

"It's eleven-seventeen. You have forty-three minutes," Trotter said but didn't move away from the truck. "Sly, you want me to stash the guns in our fallback spot?" He asked.

"Yes."

"I thought we drove around the block twice to be sure they weren't around," Trotter didn't say 'overkill,' but I knew that's what he meant.

"Having safety precautions doesn't work unless you use them," I responded.

"What do we need to get out of the truck?" Dennia asked.

"For tonight, not much. The GPR unit, a shovel, and our flashlights. I have a compass and a protractor in my pockets." As I spoke, Lily dropped the tailgate and was pulling the GPR to its edge, and Trotter shouldered the duffel bag to place it in the ditch.

We unloaded the truck and carried what we needed to the grave with greener grass.

"Move the back a little higher and to the right." Dennia methodically adjusted the flashlight's position so the beam of light would point to the proper location. I directed her by holding the protractor and compass against the gravestone, trying to center the beam along the two angles Russ had calculated.

"A slight bit more right . . . more . . . more. . . . Stop!" I checked the angles of the beam from Trotter's light. "That's damned near perfect. We need to mark the spot," I said.

"With what?" Lily asked. "We didn't bring anything from the truck."

"Please find something. I'm afraid I'll move the light," Dennia sounded stressed.

"Somebody, toss me a flashlight." Lily didn't have one.

"Trotter and your Mom are using theirs, and both my hands are tied up. You'll have to find something else."

"Hurry," Dennia implored.

"Oh, shit." There was the rustling of cloth, and Lily's tee shirt fluttered down on the spot where the beam focused. "One of you go get something to replace my shirt. I don't want the skeeters to eat me alive." She paused for a second and added, "Don't get any ideas about shining your lights on me. If any of you do, I'll make you eat them."

"I'll get something." Trotter was quick to the rescue. He and his flashlight left.

Dennia turned her flashlight off. Within a couple of seconds, light from a nearly full moon illuminated everything, including the bra-clad Lily.

"Mommy! Turn your light back on!"

"Sorry, Lily." Dennia shined her light back toward the truck.

I took the opportunity to see where the light's focus had landed. It was on the second plot over from the grave with greener grass. In that grave, Wilton Sumner was buried! The son below!

"Damned barbed wire," Trotter was returning. "Somebody, come, get this shovel. I'm tangled in the fence."

"Be right there," I said and retrieved the small entrenching tool from him. The moon lighted Lily's figure. I tried not to look. That was difficult. Lining up the shovel handle so that it pointed to the hole in the gravestone, I placed it in the precise spot from which I removed Lily's tee. When I held it behind me, she pulled it from my hand, and I heard the cloth being pulled back in place. "Lights on," I announced.

"I ripped my jeans." Trotter pushed the GPR unit toward me. I flashed my light on him. Blood spattered a four-inch tear in his jeans.

"You okay?" I asked.

"It's just a scratch." He leaned over the unit and turned on the switch. "Where do you want me to put this thing to start?"

"Put it in a straight line with the shovel and the hole in the gravestone. It needs to be close, not exact," I said.

Trotter rolled the unit into position and asked, "You want to push or watch the screen?"

"I'll watch the screen. Push it straight forward after I move the foxhole shovel to one side." I carefully moved the entrenching tool two feet, walked back, and stared down at the screen. I told Trotter, "Okay, straight ahead, *very* slowly."

Trotter crept the unit forward inches at a time, stopping in between movements so that I could scrutinize the whole screen. Dennia and Lily peered at the unit from the other side. Trotter waited for me to say go. We repeated the process until I noticed a straight line that looked like a piece of rod twenty inches long.

"Hold it there!" I said as I marked the location on the ground with the shovel pointing in the direction of its length. The place marked was in the center of where the entrenching tool lay. I thought, *Old Sally knew what she was doing!* "Radar says whatever that is, is down eight inches or so. Roll her straight back, Trotter."

Trotter moved the unit away as I picked up the shovel, keeping the point in the ground to mark the proper location. I handed Lily my flashlight and asked, "Dennia, would you and Lily focus light on where I'll be digging?"

The area where I'd be using the shovel was brightly lighted when I began to unearth what lay beneath. I'd only removed a half-dozen shovelfuls of sand when Dennia pointed, "There is something." She wiggled her flashlight, "See it shine?"

I carefully removed four more shovelfuls, then knelt by the hole and carefully removed the object. It was a brass piece, about two feet long, a couple inches wide, and only a sixteenth of an inch thick. One end was cut into a point. The other had a "V" notch cut into it. It was an arrow pointing the way!

I used my hand and my shirt to remove sand and debris that covered the metal. Deeply engraved were the letters "GR" and five straight lines. I looked at my companions and said, "Sally, old girl, your message is clear as a bell!"

"And that is?" Trotter asked.

"GR means graves, there are five lines or strikes, and the arrow points the direction. We go to the fifth grave in that direction, and we'll find what we're here for." I motioned to Trotter, "Bring the GPR unit."

We walked over Judith Sumner's grave and three vacant lots before I reached the spot indicated to be the treasure trove. It was at the very outside corner of the cemetery and had a very small, unimpressive marker. I read the inscription, "Here Lies G. Oins, Born 1865, Died May 27, 1899." One of the last clues confirmed we were about to see if the treasure was, in fact, buried beneath our feet.

Trotter positioned the GPR unit parallel to the long edge of the grave and eased over it. Lily and Dennia gasped as the unit showed images of what lay buried beneath. Trotter exclaimed, "Holy shit!" I just smiled.

CHAPTER 77

"How are we going to get the backhoe to it?" Trotter was looking at my sketch and visualizing the barbed wire fence we had to decide how to handle.

"Part of the cache is under the fence, Trotter. I don't think we have an alternative. We tear that section of fence down." I took a sip of my bourbon on the rocks. "We need to move that stuff out of the ground as quickly as we can, and that fence will slow us down."

"We have two times, maybe more, dirt to move that we thought we would." Trotter freshened his drink. Our celebration was in full swing . . . and with excellent reason. The treasure was there, and it was many times larger than we had anticipated. "You thought it might occupy a space equal to half a casket." Trotter pulled my sketch in front of him. He read the dimensions from the drawing, "Seven feet by nine and a half feet. We have to get around forty-five inches off the top according to the radar." He scribbled some figures on a napkin. "Plus, or minus, there's around 170 cubic feet of earth to remove from a standard grave." Trotter double-checked his numbers. "Yep, the dirt we'll have to move from over the top works out to around 270 cubic feet. It shouldn't take longer than two hours if we tear down the fence. We got a real break with there not being any adjoining graves. That would have slowed me down."

"How are you going to remove it from the ground?" Dennia asked. "It was probably stored in some form of wooden containers. They have to be rotten."

"I brought a dozen heavy-duty military duffels down. I thought that was way more than I'd need. I don't know now. Dennia, are there any places in LaBelle to buy something like that?"

She shook her head. "You'd have to go to Ft. Myers. But if you can figure a way to pick them up, I have a couple hundred field boxes we use to pick citrus."

"No problem. I can rig a sling and use the backhoe." Trotter pointed to the drawing. "We're going to fill the beds of two or three pickups with that volume of stuff."

"I see that as a good problem to have," I said.

Dennia asked, "What do you think is down there?"

"A lot of coinage, some cloth stuff, swords, a crate of paper . . . maybe money, and stuff that looked like a tea set." I shook my head. "We won't know until we're standing in it."

Lily punctured the balloon we'd been floating on. "What if your friends show up?"

Trotter said, "Bummer."

We sat quietly, trying to reason away a problem that had no intention of going. Trotter's head suddenly jerked up. He said, "Instead of doing it during the day, let's do it at night. There wasn't anyone around. We rent some lights like a road crew uses. If we start around midnight, it takes two hours to get the dirt out, which gives four hours for the two of us to be getting the stuff out and in the trucks."

"The four of us," Dennia corrected, and Lily nodded her agreement.

"There you go, Sly." Trotter was excited. "We can probably have most everything in the pickups by first light. You can drive everything back here while I'm backfilling the hole the best I can. I'll be short dirt."

"We can afford a dump truckload of dirt or two." I smiled. Trotter was correct. The Crisp man and the Kraggens probably wouldn't expect us to excavate at night. At least, I hoped so.

CHAPTER 78

The gas generator chugged and provided power for the lights. Trotter stayed on the backhoe, methodically removing scoop after scoop of sand from on top of what was a true buried treasure. He'd been working for a little longer than an hour, and it looked like seventy-five percent of the covering lay in a swelling pile ten feet from the backhoe.

Though I'd instructed Trotter, Dennia, and Lily to be always on guard against our adversaries' appearance, I firmly believed that we weren't in danger and wouldn't be until *all* the material we were going to extract from the pit was removed. Then the needle of risk would race to the other side of the gauge. It was illogical to consider any other possibility. Crisp and the Kraggens had proven they were smart, in addition to being ruthless. The thought of their trying to take the site by force and then hold it while they removed the treasure was ludicrous. Even if they succeeded in killing us all, the noise, getting away, etc. made considering any such plan limited to those with sub-normal intellect.

The dirt piled higher. Time passed, and at last, Trotter yelled, "My bucket hit something solid! Take a look, Sly."

I rushed to the pit's edge and peered down at the backhoe's bucket. The steel on one corner had pried part of a disintegrating wooden plank into the bucket. Trotter removed the earth in layers. Layers one and two were each a foot in depth. The next two were half the first two. He was working on his fifth layer, and the upper end of the treasure was precisely the depth the radar predicted. Lily stood next to me, camera in hand, and asked, "Do you want any special shots of this?"

"No, just what you've been doing right along. Lily, in a few minutes, you, your mother, and I stop being spectators and become the hired help. How good of a mechanic are you?"

"Damned good. I have a dune buggy I built. I help with the maintenance if our hands are swamped."

"We'll start loading the pickups soon. They'll be backed up to the edge of the pit one at a time. You'll be in the beds, unloading the bags and boxes of material Trotter lifts with the backhoe. I want you to be in charge of moving the pickups. When one gets full," I leaned forward to emphasize my next words, "park it over there." I pointed to a spot that was illuminated by the lights fifty feet from the pit. "And—this is important—after you park it, *disconnect the battery cables*. Put the hoods down, *but don't latch them*."

Lily's face told me she thought I was crazy, but she answered with, "Sure."

"What do want me to do?" Trotter was getting impatient.

"How good are you with that thing?" I asked.

"Pretty good. What do you want done, Sly?"

"I'd like to skin as much dirt as possible off the wood. Can you, like, feel your way on top of the ceiling or whatever, remove the sand you can, and peel the wood away? It will speed up the loading process if we aren't working in six inches of sand."

"I probably can. Depends what kind of carpenters built it." He raised the bucket enough to allow the dislodged plank to settle back in place. Then he scraped the bucket, slowly taking a thin layer of sand off the wooden surface. In a few places, the bucket nicked and partly lifted boards. At the completion of his sweep, he held his thumb up. As he dumped the bucket of dirt on the pile, I told him, "Great, I'll get us ready to load."

Trotter removed the last of the plank and post structure that covered the items the four of us were gazing at in awe and disbelief. In the pit was every type of device used to contain and store material in the time period when they were hidden. The containers were stacked and wedged into the big hole. Steamer trunks . . . sacks of all sizes, composition, and shapes . . . carpet bags . . . wooden crates . . . suitcases . . . kettles . . . tubs. They represented anything that could be quickly found and used to move a deceased man's wealth from his home. Many of the sacks were split as the material rotted and exposed their contents: gold coins. Judging from the number of containers that were full to bursting with coins, I guessed their face value was over $185,000. I knew that most of the coins were probably Liberty Dollars, which has a value today of $80. Plus. That translated into a current amount of $14,800,000! In addition, the potential for millions in Civil War artifacts and other historical items would swell the total value significantly.

The rest of Sally Sumner's clues and warnings were clear when Trotter stripped away the 'cloud.' That was the wooden structure of planks that created a ceiling to preserve what lay under it. The points were swords place hilt down with their blades pointing upward. They would have presented a real danger to a person trying to reclaim the gold before the 1940s. The advent of power equipment made the booby traps toothless. In two small places, the earth's weight broke through the 'ceiling,' and we were faced with handling it.

Trotter asked, "What do you think is in all those boxes and luggage?"

"I have no idea, Trotter. We can find out after we haul all this stuff back to Dennia's. Right now, it's load time!"

Dennia asked, "What do you want us to do?"

"Trotter will operate the backhoe and move stuff from the pit to the truck bed. Lily said she'd arrange stuff in the beds. You and I will go into the pit and load stuff in the backhoe's bucket. If you're willing."

Dennia was already moving to one of our three pickups. As she walked, she said, "I'll get the ladder and the duffel bags."

I had a nagging feeling I was neglecting something. . . . I hadn't kept the threat of violent confrontation at the very front of my thinking.

CHAPTER 79

It was still an hour before light, and we were close to removing the last treasure from its hiding place. Even though our arms and backs ached, the smiles on all our faces reflected how well things had gone. We were fortunate that most of the containers held together long enough to pull and push into the backhoe bucket. Except for one mishap, they made the trip to the pickup truck beds, and Lily unloaded and stored them with occasional help from Trotter on heavier and large, awkward items.

"How much more do you have down there?" Lily yelled. "I've just about filled the last bed."

"Two duffel bags filled with coins and a box that's about two feet long, foot-and-a-half wide, and a foot deep. Give or take a little," I answered.

"That will just about fill it up. Send the box up first. I can put the bags on top if I have to."

Dennia and I struggled with the iron-bound box, pulling, pushing, and heaving the chest into the bucket. I yelled, "Ready," and the backhoe's engine growled as Trotter lifted the load and placed it in a position that Lily and gravity could unload the bucket.

By the time Trotter positioned the backhoe for us to load, Dennia and I had one of the duffel bags ready to lift and place in the bucket.

We watched the load disappear as it reached the truck bed.

"This is the last one." Dennia was excited. "I can't wait to get these boxes back to the ranch! I want to see what's inside."

"It will be fascinating to see what's in some of them."

The bucket reappeared above the pit, and Trotter slowly and skillfully positioned it on the ground. In thirty seconds, the last load was on its way to completely filling the third pickup's bed.

I felt Dennia in front of me. She leaned toward me, raised up, and kissed me with a light brushing movement. Before I could react, she'd climbed halfway up the ladder.

I heard the backhoe shut down and the pickup engine start as I climbed out. For the first time since we'd arrived, I gave thought to our adversaries. We were in the highest risk period for Crisp and the Kraggens to take some action; that hit me full force.

I stepped around the backhoe and looked down the road in both directions. It was five-fifty. There were the first vestiges of morning travel—traffic is not an applicable term—down the road four-tenths of a mile distant. The first glimmer of predawn was in the eastern sky. Lily appeared from around the front of the pickup that she'd just moved and parked. Trotter waited for her halfway between us.

Dennia shook her head and said, "I cannot believe what we've seen and done over the last six hours."

"When I took on this project, I had the belief there was a good chance we'd recover something; I wasn't sure what." I took a breath and stretched my arms over my head. "In a million years, I'd never have dreamed anything like this."

Trotter's broad smile made a lot of words unnecessary. "Sly, we did it!"

"We sure did."

Lily asked, "What's sitting in those trucks represents a huge, huge amount of money. What are you going to do with it?"

"Only a quarter of that is mine. The weirdest part of this is the other three-quarters of that goes to a woman I've never meet who may not even be alive. And the woman who solicited me to take on this project was an imposter and is sitting in a South Carolina jail charged with murder."

We stood in a tight circle. Lily stood with her back to the pit. I watched her as she looked past me into the pasture and darkness. I turned to see on what her eyes focused. I saw nothing. I asked, "Lily, did you see something?"

She hesitated for a second, then said, "I thought I saw something, maybe a flashlight, way out in the pasture."

I didn't have to think about what to do! "Dennia, you and Lily, get in the first truck we loaded. Lily, hook up the battery and get out of here as fast as you can. Don't stop for anybody. Run over them if you have to. Dennia, call the sheriff and tell him that there is likely going to be shooting out here. Go!"

Trotter said, "Just a second." He reached behind his back, removed his Colt .45, and handed it to Dennia. "Two in the chest . . . it kicks."

Dennia started to say, "I want to—"

"No! Go! Don't run! Walk fast!" I nodded to the truck. Lily was already moving to it.

"Be careful! Sly. . . ." She never finished. She turned and trotted after her daughter.

The people stalking us had to see what we were doing. They would react in some way. I reasoned that as long as Trotter and I didn't head for the trucks, they wouldn't start shooting. Their primary concern was to seize part of the treasure. My primary concern was to be sure Dennia and Lily could leave without driving through a hail of bullets.

I stepped toward the pasture and signaled for the women in the pickup to pass behind me and exit through the section of torn-down fence. When they reached the road, I said, "Trotter, get to the ditch, fast!" I sprinted to our 'fall back' position as fast as I could. I'd covered two-thirds of the distance when the zing of bullets overhead and the familiar staccato chatter of an AK-47 crashed through the pre-dawn air. The firing stopped. Trotter dove into the ditch; I was three steps behind. He had the bag containing the guns opened by the time I came to a stop.

"What do you want?" he asked.

"My Hellcat and an AR-15."

"You can't shoot them both at the same time."

"Shit, Trotter, just give me something!"

Trotter handed me the rifle then the 9 mm automatic. He asked, "Why'd they stop shooting?"

"They aren't interested in killing us. They want what's in the trucks and know they only have a few minutes to do it. We need to see what's going on. Can you shoot our spotlights out?"

A short burst from Trotter's MAC 10 turned them off.

We heard someone shout, "They've got guns!"

"They're going to try getting into the trucks and just drive off. They won't be able to. If we fire a few rounds high, they might run." I chambered a round in the AR.

"What if they don't?" Trotter asked.

My silence told him.

"Disable first?"

"Yes, sure, but don't expose yourself to getting shot to do it." I slipped my automatic in my belt behind my back. "I'll crawl down the ditch some so I can get a better look at the front of the trucks. They'll have to end up going there if they want to get them started. When I get into position, I'll fire a couple shots in the air . . . you follow suit."

Trotter grabbed my arm. "Think they'll hightail when the trucks won't start?"

"I don't know." I paused and added, "Probably not." Pulling my arm away, I began a fast crawl. I'd covered seventy percent of the ground to be able to watch the hood area of the trucks when cursing and inaudible talking came from the pickups. *They found they won't start*, I thought. It was the right psychological time to scare them off. I sat up and fired three rounds into the air, and immediately, Trotter fired a short burst.

Concurrent with our gunfire, the wails of distant sirens became audible. I heard a voice say, "This is horse shit." Another voice said, "Coward!" The AK-47 barked, and there was a scream. Within a few more seconds, a woman yelled, "Harn, you bastard!"

I got up and ran to a point where I was straight in front of the trucks. Kneeling, I assumed a stable firing stance and covered the area around the hoods. Within seconds, a man's silhouette presented a ghostly target between the two vehicles. The question, if I should announce, didn't enter my mind. I was dealing with someone who was ruthless, desperate, and homicidal. I aimed and rapidly fired six rounds at the man's thighs. Screams followed immediately. Another silhouette sprinted away from the trucks into the pasture. The screams continued. I cautiously approached. Trotter was at my side in seconds with a flashlight. He kicked the AK-47 out of reach as we looked down on the man. His face contorted with pain.

"Harn Crisp, I presume."

He glared at me and my words. Harn's eyes searched for his weapon.

I leaned over and placed the muzzle of my AR a few inches from the bridge of his nose. He became motionless. I told him, "Good. Don't move at all, because if you do, I don't have a problem saving the state of South Carolina the cost of a murder trial."

Within minutes, the first sheriff's cruisers arrived. Trotter found Edward Kraggen seriously wounded but not dead. Ambulance sirens added to the cacophony of sound. Daylight was creating a brighter scene. As the sheriff's deputies walked up to me, I placed my weapons on the ground. I was now entering the next phase of my ordeal . . . and triumph.

EPILOGUE

"May I record this?" Norma Reeves laid a recorder on the bar in the Hays' ranch house.

I nodded and said, "With one condition, that being, I get to make a copy of it before you leave. I don't mind being responsible for what I say, but not for what I don't."

She frowned but said, "Sure."

"Where do you want to start?"

"How about answering this question? When I first spoke to you, you told me that you were here on a historical project, and it was not connected to your other business. I believe it's called *The Finder*. I understand you locate items for people and, shall we say, obtain what they're looking for. Did you tell me the truth your Finder business wasn't involved?"

"Not entirely. And your question is not entirely correct. I told you I was looking for information on pioneer family gravesites. That's true. I told you it wasn't connected to the Finder. That's false. I have contracts and a responsibility to execute them to my client's best interest while causing as few collateral problems as possible. Publicity is a problem. Your article in your paper caused severe injury to people that probably would not have occurred. The fact that they are criminals doesn't change that. I hope you'll see fit to print that in your article."

The expression on Norma Reeves' face told me my answer had shortened the length and changed the tone of the interview.

"Can you tell me what you were chartered to do?" she asked. Her tone became more civil. So did my answer.

"I was approached by a woman at one of my historical presentations to assist in finding and recovering an inheritance for another woman who she claimed was her relative. Later, she presented evidence that led me to believe that the existence of the inheritance was real. I accepted her invitation."

"Did you know what you were looking for?"

"The woman told me it consisted of gold coins, antiques, and heirlooms. She didn't know the size but represented it as much smaller than it actually was."

"It's been reported that the woman who contracted with you was not the true owner. Is that true, and if so, what effort did you make to verify her identity?"

I grinned. I thought I saw where the questioning was going. "I used the same due diligence that an election board uses to allow you to vote. The woman who claimed to be the representative of the recipients of the inheritance presented IDs, including a current driver's license. Subsequently, I insisted on a meeting with the primary inheritor to substantiate her existence and her claim. Both used fraudulent documents. I later found that the legitimate heir was being held in forced confinement. The people responsible for the fraud and confinement have been incarcerated by the authorities. That portion of the treasure that was to be recovered for the legitimate heir is currently in trust for her."

Norma turned the page on the notes she was taking. She asked the next questions, expecting the answers she got. "Mr. Harrell, can you estimate the value of what you recovered?"

"No, for two reasons. First, the total isn't known, and won't be, until valuable items are sold at auction. The many Civil War artifacts and other antiques could have significant value. Second, by contract, the information is confidential."

"Can you tell us how you'll be compensated?"

"That is confidential." I shook my head. "Ms. Reeves, any information regarding questions about the trust, the heir, or related subjects, you'll have to contact her lawyer, Riaffort O. Richards." I thought, but didn't say, *good luck*!

"Is it true that your investigation had something to do with solving multiple murders? One in Beaufort, South Carolina and two committed here 125 years ago?"

"Yes. The people involved with the shooting incident here were involved in multiple murders in South Carolina. I'll refer you to Detective Nina Dupree of the Beaufort Police's Homicide Department for that information. The historical murders we appear to have solved are that of Samuel Sumner, Jr. and his female companion. The story of those two individuals is a rural legend. We won't know for certain until DNA is extracted from the skeletons. I'd suggest you contact one of the local historical societies for details."

"Does the fact that the treasure you recovered was stolen, and the rightful owner might seek recovery, worry you?" Norma looked happy.

"No. My lawyer assures me as the contracted agent, my right to my fee is protected. I recovered something that was only speculation prior to my finding it. As far as who the legal owners are, that's for Florida Courts to determine." Norma looked sad.

"A bystander described the event in the graveyard as a war. Can you comment?"

"Really? I'd check my source. I didn't see anyone anywhere near the scene until after the first deputies arrived. However, I can confirm there were a large number of shots fired. The people who assaulted us, they did fire first, were firing an AK-47 and a Smith and Weston .32. I don't know the exact number of shots. You'd have to get that from the sheriff. My best guess would be eighteen from the AK and five from the revolver. I can tell you exactly what we shot. Nine from my rifle, and my associate used twelve shells. That's not the Battle of the Bulge, but it is more ordnance than a normal shooting, I suppose." I hesitated but added before the reporter could ask, "All my weapons are federally licensed. We responded in defense only, and one of the two men injured was shot by his . . . friend? There was a third individual, a woman, who was picked up by one of the deputies. She and her two associates are all extradited to South Carolina. Again, I refer you to Detective Dupree in Beaufort." I hesitated, then asked, "Is that all?" The intent of my question was clear.

"One last question?"

"One," I agreed.

"Now that everything is over and you have had a once in a lifetime experience, how do you feel?"

I took a deep breath. And thought. The thing I was uncertain about was the welfare of Ellen O'Neal, the real one. Cindy and Clareen drove over to rescue her from the imposter Thelma Crisp. Riaffort took over her legal affairs. . . . she was one of the suddenly rich. My concern was for her well-being. To my surprise, the line of relatives oozing love and concern stretched 'round the theater.' She was safe; Riaffort would see to that. Thelma Crisp was last seen trying to talk her way out of a Polk County Sheriff's Cruiser. She was destined to join her husband in the Beaufort jail. She fled Harn's company in terror after he tortured, raped, and murdered the Sumner couple. Nina Dupree assured me that five of the six would spend significant time in jail and that Harn Crisp would probably receive a vein cocktail. Various charges waited in Florida for an assortment of crimes, including the murder of Mr. Burrows. Those were probabilities, not certainties.

The thing that *was* certain, the relationship . . . wrong word, fire. . . . I wished to kindle with Dennia burned brightly. My possible future was in sight. An exciting, sensuous one. I looked at the lady, my lady, sitting at the edge of the pool with her feet dangling in the water. I saw sharing exciting adventures, the warmth of a special relationship, and other things with her in the future.

"Norma, it was one of the most gratifying experiences of my life. Whenever I'm faced with a great challenge and overcome it, I experience a tremendous feeling of exhilaration. One part of your question I don't believe is valid. I don't believe this an end of a one-time experience. . . . It's just the beginning."

Acknowledgements

For years I read acknowledgements in books with little or no appreciation of what they represented. After over twenty years of writing I read them with understanding and reverence. Anyone who writes has had others make contributions to their successes and mitigate their failures. I've benefitted greatly from many peoples' assistance in many different ways.

The untiring efforts of the Seymour Literary Agency, and my superb agents Nicole Resciniti and Julie Gwinn and their belief in my work is what allowed this book to be published. My sincerest thanks go to them. They forged a relationship with TouchPoint which I am looking forward to with great anticipation. A special thank you goes to Kathleen McIntosh, this book's editor, who was a dream to work with and made the book better.

I owe a continuing debt of gratitude to my mentor/editors, Robert Fulton, PhD. who forged some raw material into a writer, and Babs Brown. who has been my writings watch dog. Authors Bev Browning and Robert B. Parker, agents Mary Sue Seymour and Anne Hawkins provided me with encouragement when my confidence waned and kept me at the keyboard.

I owe special thanks to Taylor & Seale Editor-in-chief, Mary Custureri, PhD. Mary's stellar resume in support of the written word is unparalleled. Her belief in my work and encouragement is supremely appreciated. I'd like to express my thanks to Rebecca Melvin my editor for previous publications who staunchly supported my writing.

I've been blessed with many excellent "test pilot readers" during my career. The list has grown too long to mention them all, but there are several that have been with me for a long time. Chet Collins, Linda Kay Solinger, Tammy Dahl, Paul Owens, Carol Robb, Nancy Rogge, Gloria Andrews, Linda Hilliard, and Pat Cole don't spare criticism or praise . . . if it's earned.

Finally, I reserve my largest, most heart-felt thank you for my loving wife, partner and do all assistant—Jeanelle. Without her support, encouragement, understanding and tolerance I'd have abandoned writing long ago.

9 781946 920959